Sabine Baring-Gould

Margery of Quether

And other stories

MARGERY OF QUETHER

And other Stories

BY

S. BARING GOULD

AUTHOR OF "MEHALAH," "OLD COUNTRY LIFE," ETC.

Methuen & Co.
18, BURY STREET, LONDON, W.C.
1891

CONTENTS.

MARGERY OF QUETHER.

CHAPTER I.

THIS is written by my own hand, entirely unassisted. I am George Rosedhu, of Foggaton, in the parish of Lamerton, and in the county of Devon—whether to write myself Mister or Esquire, I do not know. My father was a yeoman, so was my grandfather, item my great-grandfather. But I notice that when anyone asks of me a favour, or writes me a begging letter, he addresses me as Esquire, whereas he who has no expectation of getting anything out of me invariably styles me Mister. I have held my acres for five hundred years—that is, my family the Rosedhus have, in direct lineal descent, always in the male line, and I intend, in like manner, to hand it on, neither impaired nor enlarged, to my own son, when I get one, which I am sure of, as the Rosedhus always have had male issue. But what with Nihilism, and Communism, and Tenant-right, and Agricultural Holdings legislation, threatened by Radicals and Socialists, there is no knowing where a man with ancestral acres stands, and, in the general topsy-turvyism into which we are plunging—God bless me!—I may be driven, heaven preserve me, to have only female issue. There is no knowing to what we landed proprietors are coming.

Before I proceed with my story, I must apologise for anything that smacks of rudeness in my style. I do not mean to say that there is anything intrinsically rude in my literary productions, but that the present taste is so vitiated by slipshod English and effeminacy of writing, that the modern reader of periodicals may not appreciate my composition as it deserves. Roast beef does not taste its best after Indian curry.

My education has been thorough, not superficial. I was reared in none of your "Academies for Young Gentlemen," but brought up on the Eton Latin Grammar and cane at the Tavistock Free Grammar School. The consequence is that what I pretend to know, I know. I am a practical man with a place in the world, and when I leave it, there will be a hole which will be felt, just as when a molar is removed from the jaw.

There is no exaggeration in saying that my family is as old as the hills, for a part of my estate covers a side of that great hog's-back now called Black Down, which lies right before my window; and anyone who knows anything about the old British tongue will tell you that Rosedhu is the Cornish for Black Down. Well, that proves that we held land here before ever the Saxons came and drove the British language across the Tamar. My title-deeds don't go back so far as that, but there are some of them which, though they be in Latin, I cannot decipher. The hills may change their names, but the Rosedhus never. My house is nothing to boast of. We have been yeomen, not squires, and we have never aimed at living like gentry. Perhaps that is why the Rosedhus are here still, and the other yoemen families round have gone scatt (I mean, gone to pieces). If the sons won't look to the farm and the girls mind the dairy, the family cannot thrive.

Foggaton is an ordinary farmhouse substantially built of volcanic stone, black, partly with age, and partly because of the burnt nature of the stone. The windows are wide, of wood, and always kept painted white. The roof is of slate, and grows some clumps of stone-crop, yellow as gold.

Foggaton lies in a combe, that is, a hollow lap, in Yaffell—or as the maps call it, Heathfield. Yaffell is a huge elevated bank of moor to the north-west and west, and what is very singular about it is, that at the very highest point of the moor an extinct volcanic cone protrudes, and rises to the height of about twelve hundred feet. This is called Brentor, and it is crowned with a church, the very tiniest in the world I should suppose, but tiny as it is, it has chancel, nave, porch, and west tower like any Christian parish church. There is also a graveyard round the church. This occupies a little platform on the top of the mountain, and there is absolutely no room there for anything else. To the west, the rocks are quite precipitous, but the peak can be ascended from the east up a steep grass slope strewn with pumice. The church is dedicated to St. Michael, and the story goes that, whilst it was being built, every night the devil removed as many stones as had been set on the foundations during the day. But the archangel was too much for him. He waited behind Cox Tor, and one night threw a great rock across and hit the Evil One between the horns, and gave him such a head-ache that he desisted from interference thenceforth. The rock is there, and the marks of the horns are distinctly traceable on it. I have seen them scores of times myself. I do not say that the story is true; but I do say that the marks of the horns are on the stone. It is said also that there is a depression caused by the thumb of St. Michael. I have looked at it carefully, but I express no opinion thereon—that may have been caused by the weather.

Looking up Foggaton Coombe, clothed in oak coppice and with a brawling stream dancing down its furrow, Brentor has a striking effect, soaring above it high into the blue air, with its little church and tower topping the peak.

I am many miles from Lamerton, which is my parish church, and all Heathfield lies between, so, as divine service is performed every Sunday in the church of St. Michael de Rupe, I ascend the rocky pinnacle to worship there.

You must understand that there is no road, not even a path to the top; one scrambles up over the turf, in windy weather clinging to the heather bushes. It is a famous place for courting, that is why the lads and lasses are such church-going folk hereabout. The boys help the girls up, and after service hold their hands to help them down. Then, sometimes a

maiden lays hold of a gorse bush in mistake for a
bunch of heath, and gets her pretty hand full of
prickles. When that happens, her young man makes
her sit down beside him under a rock away from the
wind, that is, from the descending congregation, and
he picks the prickles out of her rosy palm with a pin.
As there are thousands of prickles on a gorse bush,
this sometimes takes a long time, and as the pin
sometimes hurts, and the maid winces, the lad has to
squeeze her hand very tight to hold it steady. I've
known thorns drawn out with kisses.

I always do say that parsons make a mistake when
they build churches in the midst of the population.
Dear, simple, conceited souls, do they really suppose
that folks go to church to hear them preach? No
such thing—that is the excuse ; they go for a romp.
Parsons should think of that, and make provision
accordingly, and set the sacred edifice on the top of
moor or down, or in shady corners where there are
long lanes well wooded. Church paths are always
lovers' lanes.

When a woman gets too old for sweethearting—if
that time ever arrives, in her own opinion—she goes
to church for scandalmongery, and, of course, the
farther she has to go, the more time she has for talk
and the outpour of gossip. I know the butcher at
Lydford kills once a week. Sunday is the character-
killing day with us, and all our womenkind are the
butchers.

Well !—this is all neither here nor there. I was
writing about my house, and I have been led into a
digression on church-going. However, it is not a

digression either ; it may seem so to my readers, but I know what I am about, and as my troubles came of church-going, what I have said is not so much out of the way as some superficial and inconsiderate readers may have supposed. I return, for a bit, to the description of my farmhouse. As I have said once, and I insist on it again, Foggaton makes no pretensions to be other than a substantial yeoman's residence. You can smell the pigs' houses as you come near, and I don't pretend that the scent arises from clematis or wisteria. The cowyard is at the back, and there is plenty of mud in the lane, and streams of water running down the cart ruts, and skeins of oats and barley straw hanging to the hollies in the hedge. There is no gravel drive up to the front door, but there is a little patch of turf before it walled off from the lane, with crystals of white spar ornamenting the top of the wall. In the wall is a gate, and an ascent by four granite steps to a path sanded with mundic gravel that leads just twelve feet six inches across the grass plot to the front door. This door is bolted above and below, and chained and doubled-locked, but the back door that leads from the yard into the kitchen is always open, and I go in and out by that. The front door is for ornament, not use, except on grand occasions.

The rooms of Foggaton are low, and I can touch the ceiling easily in each with my hand; I can touch that in the bedrooms with my head. Low rooms are warmer and more homelike than the tall rooms of Queen Ann's and King George's reigns.

On the other side of Heathfield is Quether, a farm

that has belonged to the Palmers pretty nigh as long
as Foggaton has belonged to the Rosedhus. Farmer
John Palmer is a man of some substance, one of the
old sort of yeomen, fresh in colour, with light blue eyes
and fair hair; he is big-made and stout. He is a man
who knows the world and can make money. He has
a lime-kiln as well as a farm, but the lime-kiln is not
his own; he rents it. His daughter Margaret is a very
pretty girl. He has several sons, and a swarm of
small children of no particular sex. They are all in
petticoats. So Margaret can't take much with her
when she marries. Margaret used to go to chapel,
but her religious views underwent a change since one
Sunday afternoon she visited Brentor church. This
change in her was not produced by anything in the
parson's sermon, but by the fact that I was there,
aged three-and-twenty, was good-looking, and the sole
owner of Foggaton. I accompanied her back to
Quether. Since that Sunday she has been very
regular in her devotions at St. Michael de Rupe;
she has, I understand, returned her missionary box to
the minister of the chapel, and no longer collects for
the conversion of the heathen. As for me, I became a much more regular attendant at church
after that Sunday afternoon than I had been before.
When the day was windy, I helped Margaret up the
rock, and held her hand very tightly in mine, for
had she missed her footing she might have perished.
When the day was rainy, we shared one gig umbrella.
When the day was windy *and* rainy, it was better
still; for the gig umbrella could not be unfurled, so 1
folded my wide waterproof over us both When the

day was foggy, that was best of all, for then we lost our way in the fog, and could not find the church door till service was ended. On sunshiny days we were merry; in rain and fog, sentimental.

One Sunday she and I had gone round to the west end of the church after service. I told her that I wanted to show her Kit Hill, where the Britons made their last stand against King Athelstan and the Saxons; the real reason was that there is only a narrow ledge between the tower and the precipice, on which two cannot walk abreast, but on which two can stand very well with their backs to the wall, and no one else can come within eye and ear-shot of them. Whilst we stood there, a sudden cloud rolled by beneath our feet, completely obliterating the landscape, but we were left above the vapour, in sunlight, looking down, as it were, on a rushing, eddying sea of white foam. The effect was strange; it was as though we were insulated on a little rock in a vast ocean that had no bounds. Margaret pressed my arm and said, "We two seem to be alone in a little world to ourselves."

I answered, looking at the fog, "And a preciously dull world and dreary outlook."

I have not much imagination, and I did not at the moment take her words as an appeal for a pretty and lover-like reply. I missed the opportunity and it was gone past recall. She let go of my arm in dudgeon, and when I turned my head Margaret had disappeared. With a step she had left the ledge, and a few paces had taken her to her father. The fog at the same time rose and enveloped the top of the Tor and the

church, so that I could no longer see Margaret, and
the possibility of overtaking her and apologising was
lost.

Next Sunday she did not come to church. This
made me very uncomfortable. I like to have the even
tenor of neither my agricultural nor my matrimonial
pursuits disturbed. I had been keeping company
with Margaret Palmer for seven or eight months, and
I had begun to hope that in the course of a twelvemonth, if things progressed, I might make a declaration of my sentiments, and that after the lapse of
some three or four years more we might begin to
think of getting married. This little outburst of
temper was distasteful to me; I knew exactly what it
meant. It showed an undue precipitancy, an eagerness to drive matters to a conclusion, which repelled
me. My sentiments are my own, drawn from my own
heart, as my cider is from my own apples. I will not
allow anyone to go to the tap of the latter and draw
off what he likes; and I will not allow anyone to turn
the key of my bosom and draw off the sentiments
that are therein. On the third Sunday, I did not go
to church, but I sent my hind, and he reported to me
that Margaret Palmer had been there. I knew she
would be there, expecting to find me ripe and soft to
the pitch of a declaration. By my absence I showed
her that I could be offended as well as she. That
next week there came a revivalist preacher to the
chapel; he was a black man, and went by the name
of "Go-on-all-fours-to-glory Jumbo." I heard that
Margaret Palmer had been converted by him. The week
after there came a quack female dentist to Tavistock,

and I went to her and had one of my back teeth out.
Margaret Palmer learned a lesson by that. I let her
understand that if she chose to be revived by
Methodics, I'd have my teeth drawn by quacks. I'd
stand none of her nonsense. My plan answered.
Margaret Palmer came round, and was as meek as a
sheep, and as mild as buttermilk after that. Next
Sunday I went as near a declaration as ever a man
did without actually falling over the edge into matri-
mony. Foggaton is a property of 356 acres 2 roods
3 poles, and it won't allow a proprietor to marry much
under fifty; my father did not marry till he was fifty-
three, and my grandfather not till he was sixty.
Young wives are expensive luxuries, and long families
ruin a small property. One son to inherit the estate,
and a daughter to keep house for him till he marries,
then to be pensioned off on £80 a year, that is the
Rosedhu system. Now you can understand why I
object to being hurried. Foggaton will not allow
me to marry for twenty-seven years to come. But
women are impatient cattle. They are like Dartmoor
sheep; where you don't want them to go, there they
go; and when you set up hurdles to keep them in,
they take them at a leap. I've known these Dart-
moors climb a pile of rocks on the top of which is
nothing to be got, and from which it is impossible to
descend, just because the Almighty set up those rocks
for the sheep *not* to climb. To my mind, courting is
the happiest time of life, for then the maiden is on her
best behaviour. She knows that there is many a slip
between the cup and the lip, and she regulates her
conduct accordingly. I've heard that in Turkey

females are real angels; they never nag, they never
peck, they never give themselves airs. And the
reason is that a Turkish husband can always turn his
wife out of the house and sell her in the slave market.
With us it is otherwise; when a woman is a wife she
has her husband at her feet in chains to trample on as
she pleases. He cannot break away. He cannot send
her off. She knows that, and it is more than a woman
can bear to be placed in a position of unassailable
security. As long as a man is courting, he holds the
rod, and the woman is the fish hooked at the end;
but when they are married the positions are re-
versed.

Well, to turn to my story. We made up our
quarrel and were like two doves. Then came the
event I am about to relate, which disturbed our
relations.

It had been the custom on Christmas Eve from
time immemorial for the sexton and two others to
climb Brentor, and ring a peal on the three bells in
the church tower at midnight. On a still Christmas
night the sound of these bells is carried to a great
distance over the moors. I dare say in ancient times
there may have been service in the church at midnight, but there has been none for time out of mind,
and the custom being unmeaning would have fallen
into disuse were it not that a benefaction is connected
with it—a field is held by feoffees in trust to pay the
rent to the sexton and the ringers, on condition that
the bells are rung at midnight on Christmas Eve. Of
late years there has been some difficulty in getting
men together for the job. Wages are so high that

labouring men will not turn out of a winter's night to climb a tor to earn a few shillings. Besides, the sexton has been accused of disseminating a preposterous, idle tale of hobgoblins and bogies to frighten others from assisting him, so that he may pocket the entire sum himself.

Be this as it may, it is certain that on the Christmas Eve that followed the quarrel I have spoken of, no additional ringers were forthcoming. The sexton, who was also clerk, Solomon Davy, worked for me and occupied one of my cottages. I beg, parenthetically, to observe that the cottages that belonged to me would do credit to any owner. My maxim is, look to your men and horses and cows that they be well fed and well housed, and they are worth the money. Solomon Davy was an old man. His work was not worth his wages, but I kept him on because he had been on the farm all his life, and had married late in life. During the afternoon of Christmas Eve, Solomon Davy sent for me. He was taken ill with rheumatism and could not leave his cottage.

" I've ventured on the liberty of asking you to step in, sir," said he, when I entered his door, " because I've been took across the back cruel bad, and I can't crawl across the room."

" Sorry to hear it, Solomon. Who will do the clerking for you to-morrow ? "

" I'm not troubled about that, master, as Farmer Palmer do the responses in a big voice. That which vexes me is about the ringing the bells this night."

" It can't be done," said I.

" But, sir, meaning no offence, it must be done, or I

don't get the money. The feoffees won't pay a farthing unless Christmas be rung in."

"You must send somebody else to do it."

Solomon shook his head. "Then that person pockets the money, and I get naught." He remained silent awhile, and then added, " Besides, who'd go?"

"Make it worth a man's while, and he'll do anything," said I.

Again he shook his head, and this time he said, "There's Margery of Quether."

"What do you mean?" I asked, flushing. "What has Miss Palmer to do with the bells? Oh, I understand; she likes to hear the peal, and you would not disappoint her."

Solomon looked up at me slyly. "I didn't mean she."

"Then who the deuce do you mean?"

"Her as never dies."

"Solomon, the lumbago has got into your brains. I'll tell you what I'll do. I will ring the bells for you, and you shall draw the fee for having done it. That, I hope, will content you, my good man."

"Now that be like you, master, the best and kindest of your good old stock," exclaimed Solomon. "I never heard of a master as was of such right good stuff as you. You don't turn off an old man because he is past work, nor grudge him a bit of best garden ground, took out of one of your fields, nor deny him skimmed milk because you want it for the pigs and calves, nor refuse him turnips and pertatees out of the fields as many as he can eat." So he went on. I do not hesitate to repeat what he said, because he confined himself strictly within the bounds of truth. I flatter myself I always have been a good master, and just, even generous, to my men. I have been more, I have been considerate and kind. Lights were not made to be put under bushels, and I am not one of those who would distort or suppress the truth, even when it concerns myself. I know my own merits, and as for my faults, if I light on any at any time, I shall not scruple to publish them.

The old sexton jumped at my offer—I mean metaphorically, for his lumbago would not allow him to jump literally. I had made the offer out of consideration for him, but without considering myself, and I repented having made it almost as soon as the words had left my lips. However, I am a man of my word, and when I say a thing I stick to it.

"Where is the key?" I asked.

"Her be hanging up on thicky (that) nail behind the door," answered the old man.

As I took down the great church key, Solomon said, in a hesitating, timid voice, "If you should chance to meet wi' Margery o' Quether, you won't mind."

"I do not in the least expect to see her," I said, getting red, and hot, and annoyed.

"No—meb-be not, but her has been seen afore on Christmas Eve."

"Margaret on the tor at midnight!" I exclaimed; then, highly incensed at the idea of the old man poking fun at me, and even alluding to my weakness for Margaret Palmer—love is a weakness—I said testily, as I walked out swinging the key on my fore-

finger, " Solomon, I object to Miss Palmer's name
being brought in in this flippant and impertinent
manner. What with the Gladstone-Chamberlain
general-topsy-turvyism of the Government, the working classes are forgetting the respect due to their
superiors, and allow themselves liberties of speech
which their forefathers would have turned green to
think of."

If I was regular in my devotions every Lord's Day,
a labouring man in one's employ earning thirteen
shillings a week had no right to suppose that I did
not ascend Brentor from the purest motives of personal piety. It is the duty of one in his position to
think so. His insolence jarred my feelings, and I
already regretted the offer I had made. It is a mistake to be good-natured. It is lowering in the eyes
of inferiors ; it is taken for weakness. The man who
is universally respected, and obtains ready attention
and exact obedience, is he who cares for nobody but
himself; is loud, exacting, and self-asserting. To be
good-natured involves a man in endless troubles. I
had undertaken to ring the bells at midnight in mid-
winter in the windiest, most elevated steeple in England ; I had to ascend a giddy peak on which one
false step would precipitate me over the rocks, and
dash every bone in my body to pieces. I am not one
to shrink from danger, or to shirk a responsibility,
freely, if inconsiderately undertaken. I have already
said that I would frankly admit my faults when I
noticed them ; and now the opportunity arises. I
admit without scruple that I am too prone to do kind
acts. This is a fault. A man ought to consider him-

self. Charity begins at home. In this instance I did not think of myself, of the discomfort and danger involved in ascending Brentor at midnight.

I took a stiff glass of hot rum and water about half-past ten or a quarter to eleven, and then turned out.

There was no snow on the ground ; we are not likely to have seasonable weather so long as this Gladstone-Chamberlain-Radical topsy-turvy Government remain in power. Our sheep get cawed with the wet, the potatoes get the disease, the bullocks get foot-and-mouth complaint, and the rain won't let us farmers get in our harvest. If only we had Beaconsfield back ! But there, politics have nothing to do with my story.

The evening was not cold, it was raw, and the night was black as pitch. I had a lanthorn with me (I spell the substantive advisedly in the old way, *lanthorn* and not *lantern*, for mine had horn, not glass, sides). I knew my road perfectly. The lane is stony, wet, and overhung. Stony it must be, for it is worn down to the rock, and the rock breaks up as it likes and stones itself, just as the coats of the stomach renew themselves. Wet it is, because it serves as main drain to the fields on either side. Overhung it is, because trees grow on either side. If the trees were not there, it would not be overhung. You understand me. I like to be explicit. Some intelligences are not satisfied with a hint, everything must be described and explained to them to the minutest particular.

By the lanthorn light I could see the beautiful ferns and mosses in the hedge, and the water oozing out of

the sides, and the dribble that ran down the centre of
the lane and then spread all over it, then accumulated
on one side, and then took a fancy to run over to the
other side. I notice that a stream in going down a
hill zigzags just as a horse does in ascending a hill,
and as a woman does in aiming at anything. The
road rises steeply from my backyard gate to the
church porch. When I say road, I mean way. For
after one comes out on the moor, there is not even a
track.

I knew my direction well enough, so I went straight
over the heath to the old volcano, and as I ascended
the peak I thought to myself, if any traveller were on
Heathfield to-night, what a tale he would make up of
the Jack-o'-lanthorn seen dancing in and out among
the rocks, and winding its way up the height, till at
last it hopped in at the church door of St. Michael on
the Rock, and then a faint glimmer was visible issuing
from all its windows. Probably he would suspect
some witches' frolic was going on there such as Tam
o' Shanter saw on All Hallowe'en, when—

"Kirk Alloway seem'd in a bleeze,"

though the "bleeze" could not be bright that issued
from my tallow candle in a lanthorn.

The sky was overcast. Not a star was visible; only
in the S.W. was a little faint light, and a thread of it
ran round the horizon. The simile is not poetical,
but it is to the purpose, when I say that the earth
seemed under a dish-cover which didn't quite fit.

I reached the church in safety, dark as the night

was ; the few gravestones lit up with a ghastly smile as the lanthorn and I went by them in the little yard. I set down the clickering article on the stone seat in the porch, turned the key, resumed my lanthorn and went into the tower.

The church was not in first-rate repair. I believe the Duke of Bedford, who owns all Heathfield, did intend to do something to the church. He brought an rchitect there, and the architect said he must pull down the old church that dates from the thirteenth century, and build a sort of Norman Gothic cathedral in its place. You see the architect thought only of the duke's pocket 'from which to draw ; he gets five per cent. on the outlay. But when the parson heard that, and I too, being churchwarden, we put our foot down and said, No ! We loved the little old church ; it was seen by Drake and Raleigh as they sailed into Plymouth Sound, just the same as we see it to-day, and we would not have a stone changed of the carcase. They might do what they liked with the vitals inside, that we conceded. Since that day we have heard nothing more of the restoration of Brentor church. Consequently, the sacred edifice has been getting more and more out of repair.

The rain had driven for centuries through the joints of the masonry, even through the stone itself, and had streamed down inside, rotting the joists of the bell-chamber where they rested in the wall. I don't blame the builders, they did their best. The walls are thick, but there is no stone in the country that is impervious to a south-western wind charged with rain. Granite is worst of all. You might as well build of sponge. Brentor church is built of the stone of the hill on which it stands, a sort of pumice, full of holes, and therefore by nature spongy. It holds the wet, and weeps it out at every change of weather. Now the belfry joists had given way, rotted right off, and had brought the planking down with them, and lay a wreck at the bottom of the tower. By day, I have no doubt, anyone looking up would see the three bells, and the holes in the lead roof above them. It was difficult for me to get at the ropes, so encumbered was the floor with fallen beams and boards that smelt of mildew and death. I fancy the floor had given way since last Sunday, and that was why the litter lay there. Some of the sexton's tools had been knocked over by the falling beams. He wants strong tools, for the graves have to be hewn in the rock.

After I had removed some of the rotten timber, I made myself space, and stood in a pool of coffee-coloured water that had leaked from the roof, and drained from the sodden joists, and then I began to ring the bells. As I rang I looked round now and then. It was, of course, possible, though hardly probable, that the blacksmith or Luke Petherick might come up and take a turn at the ropes. I did not *expect* anyone, but I thought one *might* come; and I almost wished I had knocked the blacksmith up on my way, and asked him as a personal favour to join me. He couldn't have refused, for he does all my blacksmithing *for* me. But it might have seemed as if I were afraid to go alone, and it would have deprived Solomon of half the ringer's fee. Looked at in another light, it would not have done, for one in

my position is hardly the person to be seen ringing a
church bell, and to be known to have done it out of
good-nature.

I soon found that, for one unaccustomed to bell-
ringing, the exertion was great ; it brought into play
muscles not usually exercised, and I began to feel the
strain.   I paused and wiped my forehead.   My hands
were getting galled.   I did not moisten them in the
customary way, which is vulgar ; but I dipped my
palms in the coffee-coloured solution on the pavement
at my feet.   I had hitherto rung the " cock," as Solomon designates one old heavy bell that has a curious
Latin inscription on it, which begins, " *Gallus vocor.*"
Now, as I rose from moistening my palms, I looked
at the rope of the tenor bell, intending to pull that
next.   As I did so, I noticed something dark, like a
ball of dirty cobwebs, hanging to the cord, rather
high up.   I elevated my lanthorn to see what it was,
but the light afforded by the tallow dip was not sufficient to enable me to distinguish the outline of the
object.   I supposed it might be a great mass of filthy
cobweb, or perhaps a piece of broken flooring which
had remained attached to the rope, caught when the
rest fell away.   I considered that if I pulled the rope,
I should probably bring the thing—whatever it was—
down on my head.   You will understand that my
desisting from touching that cord was prompted by
the wisest discretion, not by inane fear.   So I rang
the treble bell, and ever and anon cast up my eye at
the remarkable mass above.

Presently, I desisted from ringing altogether.   I
thought that the object was descending the rope

slowly. I say I *thought* so, I did think so at first, but very soon I was certain of it. So certain was I, that I stepped back, and in so doing fell over a balk. When I had picked myself up the thing had reached the bottom. I should have liked to leave the church, but to do this I must step past this creature ; I must do more ; it was in the only clear space between me and the tower arch, so that to get out I must lift it from its place to make a passage for myself, and this I did not feel inclined to do. I never have believed in the supernatural. I do not believe in it now. Ghosts, goblins, and pixies are the creations of fevered imaginations and illiterate ignorance. .It puts me out of patience to hear people, who ought to know better, speak of such things. I did not for a moment, therefore, suppose that the object before me was a denizen of another world. As far as I can recollect and analyse my sensations at the time, I should say that blank amazement prevailed, attended by a dominating desire to be outside the church and careering down the flank of the hill in the direction of Foggaton. I had no theory as to what the thing was ; indeed the inclination to theorise was far from me. The creature I could now see had a human form. It was of the size of a three months' old baby. I have had no experience in babies myself, and am no judge of ages, so that when I say three months I do not wish to be tied down to that period exactly. In colour the object was brown, as if it had been steeped in peat water for a century, and in texture leathery. It scrambled, much as I have seen a bat scramble, out of the puddle on the pavement to the heap of broken

timber, and worked its way with its little brown hands
and long claws up a rafter, and seated itself thereon,
holding fast by a hand on each side of what I suppose
was the body, and then blinked, much in the same
way as a monkey blinks, drawing a skin over the eyes
different in colour from the skin of the face.

"I be Margery Palmer of Quether," it said in
strange, far-off, mumbling words. "I couldn't bide up
yonder no longer ; the wood be that rotten, it is all
giving way, and I be afeard I may fall and break my
bones. That 'ud be a gashly state o' things, my dear,
to hev' to bide up there year after year with a body
o' bones all scatted abroad (broken to pieces), and
never no chance of the bones healing."

"Who are you?" I asked, perhaps not as loudly or
with as firm a voice as that in which I usually accost
a stranger. The creature did not hear me. It went
on, however, in its mumbling voice, and with a queru-
lous intonation, "I be Margery Palmer of Quether.
I reckon there be some one before me, but, my dear, I
cannot see you, and if you speak I cannot hear you.
I be deaf as a post, and I've the eyes white wi'
caterick."

"Are you a spirit?" I inquired. She did not hear
me ; so, waxing bolder, I put my hands to my mouth
and shouted, as through a speaking trumpet, "Are you
a spirit?"

"Spirit—spirit!" she echoed. "Lauk a mussy!
I wish I was ! Spirit! No such luck comed to me
yet. If I was I'd be thankful ! Ah ! Wishes don't
fulfil themselves like as prayers do."

"How came you here?" I called.

"Hear!" she repeated. "I can't hear. I be got too old for that, I reckon I be Margery Palmer o' Quether."

"Impossible," I said. Were my senses taking leave of me? "This is a sheer impossibility." She did not hear my protest, but went mumbling on. "I lives up yonder among the bells. I've lived there these hundreds of years. I reckoned it were the safest place I could be in. I'd not ha' come down now, but that I were fear'd the bells would give way and all fall together, and my bones would ha' broke. It 'ud be a gashly thing to live on for hundreds o' years wi' broked arms and legs, and mebbe also a broked neck, so that the head hung down behind, and with no power to move it, not a bit and crumb. There ain't no healing power in my old bones now; they be as ancient as they in the graves, and no more power of joining in them, than the dead and mouldering bones hev."

I held up the lanthorn to inspect this curious creature squatted before me on a beam. It was, as I said, of the size of a baby; but otherwise it was a grown woman very aged and withered. The face was not merely wizen, it was dried up to leather, quite tanned brown, the colour of the oak beams; the hands and arms were shrivelled and like those of a bat. There was actually no flesh on them, they were simply dry, tanned skin about bone. The garments seemed to have been tanned like the hide by the liquor distilling from the oak. The eyes were blear.

"I can't see, and I can't hear," she went on, "except just a little scrap o' light which I take to be a link. I gets blinder and ever blinder, till in time I shall look into the sun and see only blackness and darkness for ever. I gets deafer and deafer, but I can hear the bells still. I can also feel a little with my skin, but not much. I've one tooth remains in my head, and I hang on by that. I drive it into the oak beam, and cling round the beam wi' my arms, and strike my nails in too, and so I hold fast. But I knowed very well that the wood were rotten; I knowed it by a sort of instink, and so I've a-comed down to-day. I reckon my hair be all falled off now; I can't tell by the feel, my hands be that numb wi' clinging, that the feeling be most gone from them. But you can see for yourself." She put her hand to her head and thrust back a leathery hood that had covered it. The little skull was bald. I opened the door of my lanthorn and took out the candle to in- spect her better. The head was as if cut out of a thornstick. Only at the back at the junction with the neck was a little frizzle of ragged white hair. I observed as she moved that her neck creased like old hide that threatened to crack at the creases. The flexibility was gone from it. "Hold the candle before my eyes," she said; "I like the light. I can feel it shining through my dull eyes down into my stomick. What be your name, now?"

"George Rosedhu." I yelled my name into her ear.

"Ah, George! George!" exclaimed old Margery, "you put off and off too long. You should have married when the fancy first took you. Now it be too late; we be shrumped up (dried up) like old apples."

What could this extraordinary creature mean?

"Ah, George! George!" she went on, "that were a cruel, unkind act of yours, keeping company with me so long, and then giving me the slip after all. Do you mind how we used to meet here of Sundays, and how on the windy days you helped me up the rock, and on windy and rainy days you wrapped your cloak round the both of us, and how, when the days were foggy, we used to lose our way in the mist, and never were able to find the church door till the service were over? And do you recall how one day you took me round to the west end of the church, after service, where we could stand at the edge of the rock, wi' our backs to the tower, and you said you wanted to point out Kit Hill to me—"

I sprang forward and put my hand over her mouth.

"Good heavens!" I exclaimed. "Will you drive me mad? What do you mean? Who are you?"

She went on, when I withdrew my hand, "Ah, George, George, you knew there was not much to be got with me. There were my brothers and a swarm of little ones coming on, and so you left me out in the cold, and took up with Mary Cake, of Wring-worthy, who was twenty years older than me. You said I were too young; and now Mary Cake that became Mary Rosedhu be dead and mouldered these hundreds of years, and I—I be alive and old enough even for a Rosedhu."

Then the old creature began to laugh, but stopped with a short scream. "I must not do it. I dare not laugh. I be too old, and I shall crack my sides and

tear my skin. Then what is cracked bides cracked,
and what is tore bides tore."

What did the creature mean by her allusion to
Mary Cake? That was my great, great—I am afraid
to say how many times removed—grandmother. She
died about two hundred years ago. She brought an
addition to the property of fifty-three acres, which I
now possess. I have the marriage settlements in the
iron deeds-chest under my bed, the date 1605.

"Well, well," the little old woman went on, "we all
make mistakes. Life is but a string of them. Coming into the world is the first; courting, marrying,
everything in succession is a mistake. You, George,
made a mistake in taking Mary Cake instead of me.
Her led you a cruel, sour life to my thinking. Her
had a vixenish temper as would worry any man out
of conceit with life. I, on the other hand, was all
lightsomeness and fun. You knew that; but what
cared you for a pretty face and a sunny temper
alongside of a few acres of moorland? You Rosedhus
are a calkelating family, and you reckon up everything wi' a bit o' chalk on the table. I hadn't the
land that Mary brought, but I'd youth and energy
and a cheerful disposition. But, Rosedhus, you are
all afraid of long families, and are a grasping and a
keeping set. You always marry late in life, and
oldish women, lest a lot of children should eat the
property as mice eat cheese. It be a mistake, a
gashly error. But there, now, I won't aggravate you.
Now tell me this : How come you alive at this
time? I thought you'd been dead these two hundred and fifty years. Can't you find your rest no

more nor I ?   Did you also pray that you might never die ? "

I could not answer. I have no imagination, and I was unable to follow her, mixing up the past and the present in such an unaccountable manner. As far as I could understand, she confused me with a remote ancestor of the same name who died in 1623. That was the George Rosedhu who married Mary Cake, of Wringworthy, in 1605.

" I made my mistake when I prayed for life," said the old woman. " I was so joyous and fond of life and full of giddiness that I used to pray every Sunday when I came to church, and every evening when I said my Matthew, Mark, Luke, and John, that I might never die. I were also mortal afraid of death. The graves here be digged out of the living stone, and be full of water afore the coffins be splashed into them, and the corpses don't moulder ; they sop away and go off the bones just as if they was boiled to rags. That terrified me, so I always prayed for one only thing, that I might never die, and my prayer hev been heard and answered. I cannot die, but I can grow older and more decrepit and dried, for I never considered to pray that I might always bide young. So you see, even when we pray, we make mistakes. Now I cannot die. I get older and older, and shrump (wither) up more and more, and get drier, and blinder, and deafer. I can no longer taste, and I cannot smell, and I can hardly feel. I have no pleasure in life at all now, and the only feeling in me is fear—fear lest I should get broke or tore, for I be past mending; if I be broke or tore I must so bide to

the end of time. On a very hot day, when the sun
shines, I seem to have a sort o' a sense of warmth,
and the frost must cake me up in ice before I knows
I'm cold. I reckon in another hundred years my
tongue will have dried up, and then I sha'n't be able
to talk no more; but that is the last organ to go in a
woman, as her temper is the first; her mind may go,
her teeth may go, her sight may go, her hearing may
go—but her tongue dies hard. In another hundred
years I shall not be able to feel the streak of mid-
summer sun that falls on my back, nor the winter
icicle that hangs from my nose. I sit bunched up on
a beam above the bells, and hold on with a tooth
drove fast into the wood right home to the gum, and
my nails hev grown till they go round the beam I
clutch. The dry rot has got into the wood, and it be
turned to powder, so that the crust has given way
and I've sunk into the dust and mildew. You must
put me away where I can be safe for another two or
three hundred years out o' the way of dogs, and rats,
and boys. Dogs would tear my skin, and rats gnaw
holes in me, and boys pelt me wi' stones and break
my bones. What is broke is broke, and what is tore
is tore—I be past all healing. I were put up in the
belfry above the bells as the place where I might be
safest, but now that the rafters and joists be rotten
and falling about me, it b'aint safe no more."

She ceased, and sat blinking at me. The skin of
her eyelids was the only part of her that retained any
flexibility, and any likeness to human skin in colour
and texture. The eyelashes were white like frost
needles. I was touched with compassion. As I have

already said, I have no intention of disguising or hiding my faults, and I frankly confess that a too great readiness to be moved by a tale or stirred by a spectacle appealing to human sympathy is one of my worst faults. I fear it is ineradicably ingrained in my constitution; I was born with this just as some unfortunates come into the world with the germs of scrofula in their blood and tubercles in their lungs. I remembered now to have heard, when a boy, of a certain girl who was said to have been so much in love with life that she had prayed she might never die, and who, accordingly, was doomed to live for ever; but I thought that she raced on stormy nights with a white owl hooting before her over the moors in the train of the Black Hunter and the Wisht Hounds. I know my old nurse had told me some such a tale to draw a moral from it of content with what Providence disposes; but it was news to me that this Undying One had been put away to wither up among the bells of Brentor Church. What a wretched existence this poor creature had dragged on! My ancestor, who had flirted with her, and then jilted her, had lived over two hundred years ago, and she would be alive, drier and more wretched two hundred years hence, when Margaret and I are fallen to dust, and our lineal descendant in the male line is reigning at Foggaton. My kindly disposition was touched—my heart softened. In a sudden access of pity, I put my arms round the poor old creature, she was as light as a doll, and crooking my finger through the ring of the lanthorn, I said, " I will carry you home, old Margery ! You shall feel a Christmas fire, and taste Christmas beef and plum-pudding."

She did not understand. I do not think she heard
me, but she laid hold of me tenaciously, as she had
laid hold of the beam on which she had crouched for
two centuries ; she drove her single tooth through my
coat and waistcoat, even cutting my skin, and her bat-
like hands and claws clutched me, the nails going into
me like knife-blades. I left the church with her, and
carried her home ; that is to say, she adhered to me
so tenaciously—I might say voraciously—that I had
no occasion to use my arms for her support ; she was
like a knapsack slung on the wrong way, and quite as
securely fastened—faster, for a knapsack will oscillate,
but old Margery stuck to me as tight as a tick on a
dog.

When I got home I said, "Now, old Margery, shake
yourself off and sit by the brave big fire, and I'll give
you something warm to drink that will cheer the
cockles of your leathery heart." But not a bit would
she budge. I shouted into her ear, but she could or
would not hear. Her tooth, which was driven into
my chest like the proboscis of a mosquito, held her
fast, and her hands were no more to be unlocked from
my arms than the laces of old ivy from an oak. There
was nothing for it but for me to sit down in my arm-
chair nursing her. The situation was almost grotesque;
it was altogether undignified. So I sat on, occasionally expostulating, and always in vain ; and I thought
I should have next morning to get a man with a knife
to slit up my coat and waistcoat behind so as to let
the old creature slip off with the garments. But I
was saved this annoyance by her tooth gradually
being withdrawn, and her fingers relaxing. She fell

off, and dropped on my knees, and lay there like a sleeping infant after its meal.

I threw a bunch of gorse on the fire, and it roared up the chimney in a sheet of golden flame, filling the little parlour with light. I was able now to study the face of the little creature on my lap, entirely at my ease. It struck me now that old Margery looked younger than I had taken her to be when I saw her in the belfry. She was a very old woman, indeed, still, but there was a human-like moisture on the leathery skin, which also looked less liable to part at the folds, and there was even a rosy tinge on the lips. I suppose that from holding her so long I was somewhat more able to appreciate her weight. It was not that of a doll stuffed with bran, but of a baby with milk and flesh and blood in it adapted to its age. I thought her also rather larger than I had at first supposed, but that may be because she was now asleep on my knees, and there is a gain of an inch or two in repose, owing to muscular relaxation.

I put her down very gently on my sofa, and set a chair against the side, lest she should roll off on the floor; then I went in quest of a clothes basket, which I filled with soft pillows. This I set in the ingle nook, and laid old Margery in the maund. I covered her over with an eider-down quilt taken from my own bed, and she seemed very cozy in the extemporised cradle. I did more. I got a Florence flask that had contained sweet oil, and rinsed it well out with a strong solution of soda. When it was quite clean, I filled it with hot strong rum and sugar and water. I wished I could find a flexible india-rubber tube, but I was unprovided with such things. There had been no call for them hitherto, in my house—Hold! there, was though! I recollected that one of the cows after calving had died of milk-fever, and the calf had been brought up by hand. I remembered a vulcanised india-rubber contrivance that had been tried but had not answered, as the calf disliked the taste of the sulphur I now found this, and with some little ingenuity adapted it to the Florence flask, and then put it into the basket beside Margery. I put my finger into her mouth first to encourage her, but she only played with it, and then I inserted between her almost toothless gums the vulcanised india-rubber contrivance—I forget its proper name. I thought it would keep her quiet, but she dragged so hard at it that the tube came out, and all the rum and water ran among the pillows. So I had to take her out again, and dry the cushions before the fire, and make up the bassinet with fresh pillows. Poor little thing, she slept through it all, like an angel.

All this took me a long time, and gave me great exertion; it called into requisition faculties of the mind and heart that had not been previously exercised. I was very tired; I sat back in my chair and fell asleep. I did not dare to go to bed lest old Margery should wake and want me. When I opened my eyes it was Christmas Day. The clerk was ill, I was church-warden, and must be at St. Michael de Rupe on that sacred festival to give the good day and the best wishes of the season to all my neighbours—sweet, blooming Margaret Palmer of Quether included. I went up-stairs and dressed myself in my Sunday suit, and a

blue neckcloth, and I put on my cairngorm pin with a
terrier's head in it, put some pomatum on my hair—
that I always do on Sunday the last thing before
going to church—and before I left I drew down the
coverlet and looked at old Margery.

She was sleeping still—bless her!—with her old
brown thumb in her mouth. I was uneasy because
the nail was so long, I thought it might scratch her
palate or irritate the uvula, so I got a pair of scissors
and cut it. I felt strangely moved with pity, and
with that pity there awoke in me a sort of sense of
personal property in old Margery. Also, I presume,
because of that, I was aware of some pride in her. I
knew that she was wizen and old and hideous, and I
knew also, that if any woman had come into my house
with her baby in her arms and had asked me to admire
it, and then had looked disparagingly at Margery, I
should have hated that woman ever after. As it was,
that day a child was christened in the church. I
looked at its soft pink skin, and went away from the
sacred edifice with envy and anger rankling in my
heart.

CHAPTER II.

I LEFT Foggaton that morning with great reluctance, and all the time of divine service I was thinking far more of old Margery than of young Margaret, as I ought—and I do not mind confessing my fault openly. My seat is a little forward of the Quether pew on the other side. Usually, when standing for the psalms and hymns, I stand sideways, that the light may fall on my book, and I may look over the top at Margaret, who does the same; but as she is on the other side and the window opposite mine, she turns towards me that she may get the light on her print, and so our eyes are always meeting. When the parson is praying to us, I lean forward with my head on the book board, and let my eyes go diagonally backward; Margaret leans her head in an opposite fashion, and so her eyes go diagonally forward, and our eyes are always meeting in the prayers, as in the psalms. During the sermon I am obliged to turn round on my seat, as I am hard of hearing in my right ear, owing to a cricket ball having hit it when I was at the Tavistock Grammar School. Margaret always somehow has her bonnet string over her left ear, so she is forced to sit roundabout on her seat and expose the hearing ear to the preacher, and so it always comes about that during the sermon our eyes are meeting. This Christmas Day it was other with me; I could think of nothing but my poor little old Margery in her bassinet by the fire, and I kept on wondering whether she would wake up in my absence and fret for want of me. Then I had all through the sermon a pricking feeling in my chest—I suppose where her teeth and nails had held so tight—and I was restless and uncomfortable to be back at Foggaton.

After service, as I was shaking hands all round, feeling eager to get it over and be off, Farmer Palmer said to me, "Come home to Quether with us, Rosedhu, and eat your Christmas dinner there. We are old friends and hope to be closer friends in time than we are now. I don't like, nor does Margaret here, to think of you sitting lonely down to your meal on Christmas Day. There is a knife and fork laid ready for you, and I will take no refusal."

I made a lame sort of excuse. I said I was unwell.

"That is true enough," said Palmer; "you don't look yourself at all to-day, and Margaret is uneasy about you. Your face is white, your hand shakes, and you look older by some years than when I last saw you. When was that?"

"Sunday, father," said Margaret with a sigh.

I assured them that I was too indisposed to accept their kind invitation, and I saw that they believed me. Margaret's brown eyes were fixed anxiously and intently on me. I had been up all night, and much worried, that was why I looked older and unwell, but I only said by way of explanation to Palmer, that I had something "on the nerve," which covers all . kinds of ailments.

As I walked home every person I passed and spoke

to said, "How oldened you are!" or "How ill you look!" or "Why, surely that baint you, Mr. George, looking nigher forty than twenty."

I wish Mr. Palmer would not try to thrust Margaret on me. Margaret invites me to dinner. Margaret is concerned at my looks. Margaret remembers when last we met. That is all hyperbole and figure and flower of speech, and means in plain English, I want you to take my eldest daughter off my hands, but I am not going to give more than a trifle with her.

I never was more pleased than on this occasion when I got home again. I unlocked my parlour door, and ran in and up to the clothes' basket, and cried in a sort of fond foolish rapture, "Bless it! bless it! O my Beauty!"

The little old woman opened her eyes—they were not clouded with cataract; that must have been a fancy of mine before; she saw me and smiled, and made a sort of crowing noise in her throat. I stooped over to kiss her, when—click! in an instant she had fastened herself on me, and driven her tooth into my chest, and grabbed me with her hands, so that I was held as in a vice. To wrench her off would have been impossible. I believe if torn away the hands would have held to me still, and the arms come off at the wrists. I know that when a ferret fastens on a rabbit you may kill the beast before he will let go, unless you nip his hind foot; then he opens his mouth to squeal, and loosens his grip to defend himself. I did not think of this at the time, or I might have called in some-one to pinch Margery's foot; but I doubt, even if I had remembered this, whether I should have had recourse

to this expedient. I did not care to have my situation
discussed ; moreover, I was conscious of a soothing
sensation all the time Margery was fast. Besides, I
knew by this time that when the little old woman had
had enough she would drop off, just as a leech does
when full. I would not have you suppose that
Margery was sucking my blood. Nothing of the sort ;
that is, not grossly in the manner of a leech. But she
really did, in some marvellous manner, to me quite
inexplicable, extract life and health, the blood from
my veins and the marrow from my bones, and assimi-
late them herself.

Presently she fell off, as I knew she would when
satisfied, and lay in my lap, across my knees. She
looked up at me with a smile that had something
really pleasant in it. She was positively taller, her
skin fresher, her eye clearer than before ; her eyelashes
were grey, not snowy ; and there was actually a down
of grey hairs covering her poll, like the feathers on a
cockatoo. I wrapped a blanket round her, and was
about to replace her in the basket, when I found, to my
surprise, that it would cramp her limbs ; she could not
kick out in it. So I got a drawer out of my bureau,
fitted it up with pillows, and laid her in that.

I really do think there is something taking about
her expression. When you consider her age, she gave
wonderfully little trouble. At first it was strange to
me to have to do with this sort of little creature—it
was my first and only—but I saw that I should soon
get used to it. In the afternoon I employed myself
in making a pair of rockers, which I adjusted to the
drawer, and by this means converted it into a very

tolerable cradle.　　I am handy at carpentering. Indeed there are not many things which I cannot do when put to it.　When the emergency arose, as the reader will see, I became really a superior nurse, without any training or experience.　Indeed, I feel confident that in the event of this Radical Gladstone-Chamberlain Government altering the land laws, and robbing me of Foggaton, I could always earn my living as a nurse; I could take a baby from the month, if not earlier, or a person of advanced age lapsed into second childhood.　Never before have I taken in hand the tools of literature, and yet, I venture to say that—well! there are idiots in the world who don't know the qualities of a cow, and to whom a sample of wheat is submitted in vain.　Such persons are welcome to form what opinion they like of my literary style.　Their opinion is of no value whatever to me.　There is no veneer in my work, it is sterling. There is no padding, as it is called; my literary execution is substantial and thorough as were the rockers I put on thicky (I mean, that there) cradle. The rockers were not put on many days before they were needed.　Old Margery became very restless at night, and she would not let me be long out of the house by day.　She was cutting her teeth.　The back teeth are terribly trying to babies—they have fits sometimes and big heads and water on the brain, all through the molars.　If it be so with an infant of a few months, just consider what it must be with an old woman in her three-hundredth year, or thereabouts!　I bore with her very patiently, but broken rest is trying to a man. Besides, about the same time I suffered badly in my jaws,

for my teeth, which were formerly perfectly sound,
began to decay, break off, and fall out. I may say,
approximately, that as Margery cut a tooth I lost one;
also that, as her hair grew and darkened, mine came
out or turned grey. Moreover, as her eye cleared,
mine became dim, and as her spirits rose, mine became
despondent.

In this way, weeks, and even months passed. It
really was a pretty sight to see the havoc of ages
repaired in the person of Margery; the sight would
have been one of unalloyed delight, had not the
recovery been effected at my expense. The colour
came back into her cheek as it left my once so florid
complexion ; she filled out as I shrivelled up, she
grew tall as I collapsed ; the drawer would now no
longer contain her, and a bed was made for her by the
fire in the parlour. I noticed a gradual change in the
tenor of her talk, as she grew younger. At first she
could think and speak of nothing but her ailings, but
after, she took to talking scandal, bitter and venomous,
of neighbours, that is, of neighbours dead and dropped
to dust, whose very tombstones are weathered so as to
be illegible. Little by little her talk became less virulent,
and softened into harmless prattle, and was all about
the things of the farm and house. She was a first-
rate worker. I was glad she took such an interest in
the farm ; she brisked about and saw to everything.
I was not able now to get about as much as I might have
liked, as I suffered much from rheumatism and
bronchitis. Neighbours came to see me, and all were
in the same tale, that I was becoming an old man
before my time, that the change in me was something

unprecedented and unaccountable. I could not walk without a stick. I stooped. My hair was thin and grey, my limbs so shrunken that my clothes hung on me as on a scarecrow. I was advised to see a doctor; that is—everyone had a special doctor who was sure to cure me; one said I must go to Dr. Budd at North Tawton, and another to Dr. Hingston at Plymouth, and one to this and one to that; they would have sent me flying over the county consulting doctors, and varying them every week. Some said—and I soon found that was the prevailing opinion—that I was bewitched, and advised me strongly to consult the white witch either in Exeter or Plymouth. I turned a deaf ear to them all. I wanted no doctors. I needed no white witch. I knew well enough what ailed me. I never now went up Brentor to church. Dear life! I could not have climbed such a height if I had wished it! My poor old bones ached at the very thought, and my back was nigh broken when I walked through the shippen one day to the linney (cattle shed). Besides, I had grown terribly short of wind, and I had such a rattling in my chest. I almost choked of a night. That was the bronchitis, and when I coughed it shook me pretty well to pieces.

So time passed, and I knew that I was sinking slowly and surely into my grave; there was no real complaint on me to kill me. I was breaking up of old age, and yet was no more than three and twenty. Everyone said I looked as if I was over ninety years. If I could see the hundred, it would be something to be proud of before I was four and twenty. One thought troubled me sorely. Whatever would become

of Foggaton without a Rosedhu in it?   I should
die without leaving a lineal descendant in the male
line.   It would go out of the family.   I had not a
relation in the world.   We Rosedhus always marry
late in life, and never have large families.   I was the
single thread on which the possible Rosedhu posterity
depended.   I believe that an aunt had once married,
and had a lot of children, but she was never named in
the family.   It was tantamount to a loss of character
in Rosedhu eyes.   I did not even know her married
name.   She was dead ; but her issue no doubt remained, though I knew nothing of them.   They, I
suppose, would inherit.   I found as I grew older that
this fretted me more and more.   I would soon pass
beyond the grave into the world of spirits, and I
knew, the moment I turned up there, that all the
Rosedhus would be down on me for not having left
male issue to inherit Foggaton, each, with intolerable
self-assurance, setting himself up before me as an
example I ought to have copied.   As if, under my
peculiar circumstances, I could help myself.   The
only one of my ancestors with whom I would be able
to exchange words would be the George Rosedhu who
had married Mary Cake.   I could cast it in his teeth
that had he been faithful to his first love, this
disastrous contingency would not have occurred.

"Ah !" said I, in a fit of spleen, "it is all very well
of you, Margery, to go about the house singing.
What is to become of the Rosedhus?   To whom will
Foggaton fall?   You have drawn all the flush and
health out of me and made yourself young at my
charge—but I get nothing thereby."

"I will nurse you in your decrepitude, dearest George," she answered, and a dimple came in her rosy cheek, the prettiest twinkle in her laughing, blue eye. Upon my word she was a bonny buxom wench, and it would have been a delight to be in the house with her, had I been younger. Now I could only gaze on her charms despairingly from afar off, as Moses looked on the Promised Land from Pisgah. What a worker she was, moreover! What a manager! What an organiser! What a housekeeper, cook, dairy-woman, rolled into one! Never was the house so neat, the linen so cared for, the brass pans so scoured, the butter so sweet, the dairy so clean. She had been brought up in the old-fashioned, hard-working, sensible ways of a farm in the reign of Good Queen Bess. In our days, the women are all infected with your Gladstone-Chamberlain topsy-turveyism, and farmers' daughters play the piano and murder French, and farmers' wives read Miss Braddon and Ouida and neglect the cows. Her ways were a surprise to all on the estate. The men and the maids had never seen anything like it. Folks could not make Margery out, who she was, and where I had picked her up. No-body seemed to belong to her; she had never been seen before, and yet she knew the names of every tor, and hamlet, and coombe, and moor, as if she had been reared there. But though she knew the places, she did not know the people. She spoke of the Tremaines of Cullacombe, whereas the family had left that house two hundred years ago, and were settled at Sydenham. She talked of the Doidges of Hurlditch, a family that had been gone at least a hundred years. Kilworthy, she supposed, was still tenanted by the Glanvilles, whereas that race is extinct, and the place belongs to the Duke of Bedford, who has turned it into a farm. On the other hand, what was curious was, that Margery hit right now and then on the names of some of the labouring poor; she would salute a man by his right Christian and surname, because he was exactly like an ancestor some two hundred and fifty years ago. Though the great families have migrated or disappeared, the poor have stuck to their native villages, and reproduce from century to century the same faces, the same prejudices, the same characteristics. They are almost as unchangeable as the hills.

As I have said, Margery was a puzzle to everyone, and because a puzzle, the workmen and girls looked on her with suspicion. They resented the close way in which they were kept to their work and the rigid supervision exercised over them. Solomon Davy, the clerk, alone suspected who she was. He called several times to see me, and looked hard at me, with an uneasy manner, and seemed as though he wanted to ask me something, but lacked the courage to do so. Margery is always pleasant to Solomon, she knew the Davys that went before him, but he gives her a wide berth; he never lets her come within arm's reach of him. She feels it, I am sure, by her manner; but she is too good-hearted to remark on it.

I cannot deny that she was goodness and attention itself to me, and that I was fond of her. Just as a mother idolises her baby that draws all its life and growth from her, so was it with me. I begrudged her none of her youth and beauty; I took a sort of motherly pride in her growth and the development of her charms, and for precisely the same reasons—they were all drawn out of me.

One day Margery announced that she intended to marry me, and told me I must be prepared to stir my old stumps and go to church with her. She explained her reason candidly to me. She knew that I had a clear business head, and so she consulted me on the subject, which was flattering, and I should have felt more grateful had I not almost reached a condition past acute feeling. She told me that she would nurse me till I expired in her arms, and then, as my widow, would have Foggaton. This would secure her future, for with her renewed youth and with her handsome estate she could always command suitors and secure a second husband, from whom she could extract sufficient life and health to maintain her in the bloom of youth. When he was exhausted and withered up and dead, she could obtain a third, and so on *ad infinitum*. She objected to being again consigned to mummification in the tower of Brentor Church, and this was the simplest and most straightforward solution to her peculiar difficulties. The plan suggested was feasible, and, from her point of view, admirable. I was now so shattered mentally and physically that I was in no condition to raise an objection. Indeed, I had no objection to raise. I freely, willingly submitted to her proposal. She exercised no undue compulsion on me; she appealed to my reason, and my reason, as far as it remained, told me that her plan was sensible, and in every way worthy of her. She was a handsome woman, with a fine head of brown hair, and the brightest, wickedest, merriest pair of blue eyes. As for her cheeks— quarantines were nothing to them. A man in the prime of life would be proud to have such a woman as his wife, and her selection of me was, in its way, complimentary, even though I knew that I was taken for the sake of Foggaton.

So I consented, and she herself took the banns to the clerk. Solomon opened his eyes when she told him her purpose, moved uneasily on his seat, and scratched his head. He hardly knew what to make of it. He came to see me, and looked inquiringly at me, but I had one of my fits of coughing on me. When I was sufficiently recovered to speak, I told Solomon how impatient I was for my wedding day to arrive, and how kind and excellent a nurse Margery was to me. He went away puzzled, and rubbing his forehead. I made but one stipulation with respect to my wedding, that was, that I should be conveyed to the foot of Brentor in a spring-cart, laid on straw, and thence be conveyed up the hill to the altar by four strong men, in a litter, laid upon a feather-bed, and with hot bottles at my feet and sides. I was entirely incapable of walking.

This was at the beginning of November. Consequently ten months had elapsed since that fatal Christmas Eve on which I had made the acquaintance of Margery of Quether. So the banns were read on the first Sunday in the month at the afternoon service, there being no service that day in the morning in the little church. The banns were published between George Rosedhu, of Foggaton,

bachelor, and Margaret Palmer, of Quether, spinster.
If anyone knew any just cause or impediment why
these two should not be joined together in holy matri-
mony, they were now to declare it.   That was the
first time of asking.

A pretty sensation the reading of these banns
caused.   Farmer Palmer's face turned as mottled as
brawn, and Miss Palmer blushed as red as a rose and
buried her face in her hymn-book.   My old Margery
had overshot her mark, as the sequel proved.   She
had not reckoned with young Margaret, her great,
great, great, great grand-niece.

When public worship was concluded, Mr. Palmer
and his daughter, instead of directing their steps
homeward towards Quether, where tea was awaiting
them, walked in the opposite direction, and descended
on Foggaton, to know of me what was meant by the
banns—sober earnest or silly joke.

Margery was not at home.   She always frequented
St. Mary Tavy Church, because she had a dislike to
Brentor ; it was associated in her mind with two
centuries of chilling and repellant associations.
Margery was a regular church-goer.   That was part
of her bringing up.   In her young days, if anyone
missed church, he was fined a shilling, and if he did
not take the sacrament, was whipped at the cart-tail.
These penalties are no longer exacted ; nevertheless,
Margery is punctual in her attendance.   Such is the
force of a habit early acquired.

Thus it came about that Farmer Palmer and his
daughter arrived at Foggaton before Margery had
returned from church.   I am sorry that my hand is

not expert at describing things which I neither saw
nor heard accurately. I have no imagination, which
is a delusive faculty leading to serious error. Palmer
and his daughter were attended by Solomon Davy,
who I believe endeavoured to explain the situation to
them and told them who Margery really was. I had
become so dull of hearing, and so cataracted in eye,
that I was unable to understand all that went on, and
to follow and take part in the somewhat heated and
animated conversation. If, like a modern writer of
fiction, I were to give the whole of what was said, with
description of the attitudes assumed, the inflections of
the voices, and the degrees of colour that mantled the
several checks, I might make my narrative more
acceptable, no doubt, to the vulgar many, but it would
lose its value to the appreciative few, who ask for a
true record of what I *observed.*

I believe that Solomon in time made it clear to the
dull intellects of the Palmers that the banns were for
my marriage with the great, great, great, great-aunt
of Margaret, and not with herself. What he said of
poor Margery I don't know. I strained my ears to
catch what he said, but heard only a buzzing as of
bees. I doubt not that he spiced the truth with plenty
of falsehood.

Farmer Palmer has a loud voice. I heard him say
to his daughter, "Wait here a bit, Margaret, along
with George Rosedhu, and bide till t' other Margery
arrives; I back one woman against another."

"Oh, father!" exclaimed the pretty creature,
"where be you a-going to?"

"My dear, I shall be back directly. This be Fifth

o' November, and bonfire night. The lads wiil be all collecting faggots for a blaze on the moor. I'll fetch 'em here, and they can have the pleasure o' burning the old witch instead of a man o' straw."

I held out my hands in terror and deprecation. " You durstn't do it ! "

"Why not?" asked the farmer composedly. "Her's a witch and no mistake. Her have sucked you dry of life as an urchin (hedgehog) sucks a cow of milk."

"But," protested Solomon, "though that be true enough, what about the laws ? I won't say but that it be right and scriptural to burn a witch ; for it is written, ' Thou shalt not suffer a witch to live,' but I reckon it be against the laws."

"Not at all," said Palmer. "No man can be had up for burning a person who has no existence."

"But she has existence," I remonstrated. "That is the prime cause of her trouble ; she has too much of it ; she can't die."

"There is no evidence of her existence," argued Palmer. "You, Solomon, tell me how far back your registers go in Brentor Church."

"Back, I reckon, to about 1680."

"Very well, then they contain no record of her birth and baptism. Now you cannot be hung for killing a person of whose existence there is absolutely no legal evidence. The law won't touch us if we do burn her."

"But—but," I said, crying and snuffling, "she is your own flesh and blood."

"That may be, but that is no reason against her cremation. My own Margaret stands infinitely nearer to me, and her interests closer to my heart, than the person and welfare of a remote ancestress. As the banns have been called, Foggaton shall go to my daughter and to no one else. In three weeks' time Margaret shall be Mrs. Rosedhu." He spoke very firmly.

"Father, dear father, how can you be so cruel to me?" cried Margaret. "Do y' look what an atomy Mr. Rosedhu be come to?"

The burly yeoman paid no heed to his daughter's protest, knowing, no doubt, its unreality. He said to me, "Look y' here, George Rosedhu, you've had my daughter's name coupled wi' yourn in the church to-day, and read out before the whole congregation, without axing my leave or hers. I won't have her made game of even by a man o' substance like you, so her shall marry you before December comes, whether you like it or not."

"Oh, Mr. Palmer, sir," I pleaded, "how can you think to force your daughter into nuptials which must be distasteful to her?"

"Don't you trouble your head about that. Margaret knows which side her bread is buttered. She can distinguish between clotted cream and skim milk."

"Besides," I argued, "I am bound by the most solemn engagements to my Margery. I have promised to settle Foggaton on her."

"You cannot," shouted the farmer of Quether. "The thing is impossible. You cannot marry a woman who has no existence in the eye of the law. The only Margaret Palmer of Quether of whom the law has cognizance is she who now stands before you. She has been baptized, vaccinated, and confirmed. What more do you want to establish her existence? Whereas, what documentary proof can the other Margery produce that she exists? There is but one Margaret Palmer of Quether in this nineteenth century; that's flat." He slapped the table, and then, with the air of one administering a crushing argument, he added, " Now, tell me, is it possible for a man to marry a woman from whom he is removed by from two to three centuries? Answer me that."

" Put in that bald way," I said, " it does seem unreasonable; but in these Radical-Gladstone-Chamberlain times one does not know where one stands. All the lines of demarcation between the possible and the impossible are wiped out, reason and fact do not jump together."

" I leave you to digest that question," answered Palmer triumphantly. He saw I was pushed into a corner. Then he went out, along with Solomon Davy.

I do not think that Margaret objected to be left to meet Margery. I noticed her pluming and bridling like a game-cock before an encounter. She stroked down the folds of her gown, and pursed up her lips, and now and then shot out her tongue from between her lips, as I have seen a wasp test his sting before stabbing me. I was getting uneasy for Margery, and was myself uncomfortable. I said, " Miss Margaret, will you be so good as to pick me up my handkercher; it is lying there on the floor, and I be so cruel bad took with the lumbagie that I can't bend to take it myself."

She complied with my request somewhat surlily.
Then I said, " Would you mind, now, just uncorking
that bottle there on the shelf, and putting a drop or
two on a lump of sugar, and giving it me.   My hands
be that shaky I cannot put it in my mouth myself,
and I've no teeth to hold it by.   The drops be
ipecacuanha, and be good for bronchitis."

" No, I won't do it, you nasty old man."

" Then, miss, will you rub my spine with hartshorn
and oil?   You'll find a bottle of the mixture on the
sideboard, and a bit of flannel in the cupboard."

" I will do nothing of the sort," she said, testily.

" You won't, miss?   Then please to take me up in
your arms and carry me to bed.   Margery does it.
She is very kind and considerate ; she begrudges me
no trouble, and feeds me out of a spoon."

" I will do nothing of the sort," she said again, in short,
angry tones, and with an air of supreme disgust.

" I am sorry for it," said I.   That was Gospel truth.
I knew that when the two women met such a storm
of words would rage as would wreck my poor nerves,
and I wanted to be in bed and out of it, before the
hurricane broke loose.

" You'll have to do all this for me," I said, " when
you become Mrs. Rosedhu.   A very old person needs
just as much attention as a baby.   I know that, for
I've gone through it myself ; I've done the nursing.
Why will you not leave me alone, and allow Margery
to marry me ?   She will take care of me ; she kisses
and fondles me.   Will you ? "

" You disgusting old scarecrow and atomy, certainly
not."

"An atomy — scarecrow and atomy—what next will you call me?   Yet you want to marry me!"

"You fool!" said Margaret, shortly.   "I put up with you for the sake of Foggaton."

"It's the same with Margery," I said; "but she put it more pleasantly.   Her manners are better than yours; but then she belongs to the old school—the good old school!" I sighed.

What I said made her angry.   She did not like to have comparisons drawn between herself and her remote great aunt, to her own disadvantage.

"I suppose I am to have a voice in the matter," I went on; "and though I have liked you very much, Margaret, yet I like the other Margery better.   One thing in her favour is—she is older than you."

"You are not going to have her—who has drained life and spirit out of you.   Do you think I will allow it?   Don't you see I bear her a grudge?   She has turned the fresh and hale George who courted me into a shrivelled old man.   It would have been a pleasure to have young George, it is a penance to have the old one.   I owe her that, and I shall scratch her eyes out when we meet."

"Whatever you do," I pleaded, "do not hurt her. Your father has made a dreadful threat.   I hope he will not execute it."

"There she comes!" exclaimed Margaret Palmer, starting to her feet in a tremor of delight.   "I hear her step on the walk."

"Throw the hearthrug over me," I entreated, "I cannot bear to be agitated.   Toss the table-cover above the hearthrug, all helps to deaden the sound."

Margaret complied with my request. Here again
my narrative must present an appearance of incom-
pleteness. I cannot describe what I neither saw nor
heard during the interview between Margaret and
Margery, because I was buried under a heavy sheep-
skin rug and a thick, coloured, damask table-cover on
the top of that. I have no imagination, and I only
relate what I actually saw and heard. I saw nothing,
and what I heard resembled the jangling of pots and
pans when a host of maids are going after a swarm of
bees. Of words I could distinguish none, till after a
while the hearthrug and table-cover slipped off, owing
to my coughing a great deal, the dust out of the
hearth-rug having got into my bronchial tubes. Then
I saw a sight which filled me with dismay.

My room was full of men and boys, with their caps
and hats on. Their faces were flushed and eager;
savage delight danced in their eyes. One had a pitchfork, several had sticks, one was armed with a flail.
Head and shoulders above the rest stood Farmer
Palmer, keeping back the mob that crowded in at the
door. In the front of all, as if in a cockpit, opposite
each other, stood the two Margarets, red in face, blazing in temper, their tongues going, their eyes sparkling, their hands extended. I will say that poor
Margery acted solely on the defensive. She held up
her arms in self-protection. Margaret had driven her
nails into her cheek and a red streak down the side
showed that she had drawn blood.

"See, see!" exclaimed the younger Margaret, "the
witch! her power is broken. The blood is running."

This is a popular belief. If you can draw blood from a witch, her power—at least over you—is at an end.

My poor Margery gazed with alarm at the crowd of red, threatening faces that looked at her. She shrank from the sticks, the clubs, the pitchfork and flail. She drew behind me, as if I, broken down into premature old age, could defend and assist her. I raised my shrill pipe in entreaty, but my words were without effect. Those horrible faces glowered at Margery with the savagery of dogs surrounding a hare they are about to tear to pieces. The fear of witchcraft blotted all human compassion out of their hearts.

Suddenly a red light blazed in at the window. The evening had fallen fast and it was now dark.

"Look! look there!" shouted Farmer Palmer. "Look there, you witch, at the bed made for you. There are plenty of faggots to heap over you should you complain of the cold."

Margery uttered a scream of terror and clutched my chair, whilst she cowered on the floor behind it.

"Oh, George!" she cried in her agony of dread, "save me! save me! They cannot kill me, but they can fry and burn me! Then I shall live on—on—on, a scorched morsel, not like a human being."

"My darling," I answered, "I can do nothing against all these men." I, however, made a desperate attempt. "I am master in this house," I cried in my shrill old tones; "no one has any right within the doors without my permission, and I order you all to go away peaceably and to leave me alone."

The men and boys, led by Palmer, laughed and did not budge an inch. There came a shout from outside.

"Bring out the witch, and let her burn!"

There is an innate cruelty in human nature which neither Christianity, nor education, nor teetotalism will eradicate. I always thought the peasantry of the West of England wonderfully gentle, kindly, and free from brutality, and yet — scratch the man and the beast appears—here were my peaceable, tender-hearted countrymen ravening for the life of a poor woman, really pretty, and as good-dispositioned and without malice as an angel. I knew that they would gloat over her anguish in the fire, that they would poke up the fuel to make her burn more thoroughly—they would do so without compassion; not really because they thought her a witch, but because Farmer Palmer had told them they might burn her without fear of the law.

A fresh heap of fuel had been tossed upon the pyre, and the flame spouted up to heaven. A roar from the boys without. "Bring her out! Let her burn!"

Poor Margery covered her eyes with her hands to shut out the terrible light.

"Oh, George, George!" she cried, "save me, and I will give you back some of your youth and strength again."

"Stand back," thundered Palmer, as the circle of men contracted about her, and hands were thrust forth to grasp and tear her from my chair. "Do you hear me? She has offered to recover our friend Rosedhu."

"You cannot do it, my poor darling," I said.

"Oh, save me, George, and I will indeed."

"You hear her," shouted Palmer. "Stand back, and let her fulfil what she has undertaken."

Then Margaret put in her voice. She was afraid that her rival would escape. "No, father, do not trust her. She can do nothing. She is a witch, and wants to cast spells over you all. Take her away, boys, and pitch her into the fire. Don't listen to a word she says, however heard she prays to be let go."

"Into the flames with her!" shouted the men, and stepped forward. "That is the place for such as she."

"Fair play, my lads," said Palmer, and with his strong arm he drove the rabble back. "As for you, Margaret, don't you interfere. Now then, you—Margery—or whatever you call yourself, stand up and come forward. None shall hurt you if you really recover Rosedhu of his age and incapacity. But, mind you, if you fail, I swear that with this cudgel I will break every bone in your body, and then throw you into the fire with my own arms."

Margery quivered and cried out at the threat.

"Are you going to do it or not?" asked Palmer.

Poor Margery, feeling the necessity for prompt action, if she would save herself from terrible torture, rose from her crouching posture and stole tremblingly forward.

"Stand out o' the road, boys," shouted Palmer; "clear away with you," and with his stick he swept a circle round Margery and me.

"Oh, George," she said, with tears of mortification

in her blue eyes, " I am sorry to do it. I wouldn't if
I could ; I really wouldn't. But I cannot help myself. These cruel men do so scare me. We might
have been so comfortable together; I'd have nursed you
into your grave quite beautiful and convenient like,
and then I'd have had Foggaton to myself, and it
would have gone so well for all parties. But now,
you see, that blessed arrangement you managed so
nicely for me won't come to nothing because of the
wickedness of evil men, who walk about like unto
roaming and roaring lions seeking whom they may
devour. I cannot help myself, George. You'll do
me the justice to say it were against my will and under
compulsion. There, give me your two hands into
mine."

She took my hands and stood opposite me, holding
them at arms length, and looking into my eyes. Poor
thing ! her lips trembled, and the tears stood on the
lids and overflowed and trickled down her soft red
cheeks. It was a sore trial and disappointment to her,
but she bore it like a Christian, and never cast a word
of bitterness at those who forced her to it. And to
think what a sacrifice she was making ! Those rude
creatures knew nothing of that, and could not appreciate the greatness of her self-sacrifice. I submitted,
because I saw that in this way only had I the means
of rescuing her.

As she held my hands, I felt as if streams of vital
force were flowing from her up my arms into my body.
The aching in my bones ceased. My legs became stronger,
my head lighter and more erect, I could see better,
and hear better. I began to smell the peat burning

on the hearth, I felt an inclination to draw Margery
on to my knees and kiss her; but when I looked at
her, the desire passed, she was waning as I waxed.
She grew older, the colour left her cheek, her eyes became dim; then, all at once I sprang to my feet and
shook off her hands. "Enough, Margery, enough,"
I said. "You have restored to me sufficient of my
strength and health, the rest I freely make over to
you. Now for the rest of you." My voice was full
and loud as that of Palmer himself. "Everyone of
you listen to me. This is my house, and an English-
man's house is his castle. Leave this room, leave my
land at once, or I prosecute every man jack of you
for burglary and trespass. Good Lord! Do you
know where you are? Do you know who I am?
This is Foggaton, and I am a Rosedhu. Gladstone and
Chamberlain and that Harcourt fellow haven't brought
matters quite so far yet that every dirty Radical may
come inside a landed proprietor s doors and snap his
fingers under his nose." I snatched the stick out of
Palmer's hand and went at the men with it. Not one
ventured to show me his face. I saw a sudden change
of posture, and a crush and rush out of my door and
down my little passage. "You bide here, Palmer,"
I said; "and Margaret also. But as for all this rag-
tag and bob-tail that you have brought in, I'll make a
clean sweep of them in a jiffy."

'It is all very well, Rosedhu," said Palmer, folding
his arms, and setting his legs wide apart. "You have
got rid of the rabble, and you are right to do so if you
choose. But you do not get rid of me and Margaret
so fast. The banns have been called between my

daughter and you; I take no account of the other, she has no legal existence."

I was silent, and looked from Margery to Margaret.

"Besides," Palmer went on, "you may not think so much of her now. In appearance she is old enough to be your grandmother."

Certainly Margery looked aged, a hale woman, but still old—too old to be thought of as a bride at the hymeneal altar. Margaret was young and pretty; I wish she had not been quite so young and opened such an alarming vista of possibilities. But then I looked at myself in a glass opposite, and saw that I was grey-headed and on the turn down the hill of life. That was an advantage. "There is one thing," I said musingly; "in the matter of amiability there is no comparison. Margery is as good—"

"We will have no comparisons drawn," interrupted Palmer, as the girl darted a look at me that plainly said, "You shall suffer for this some day." "Hold out your fist like a man and say you will take my daughter for better, for worse, and make her Mistress of Foggaton within the month. The first time of asking took place to-day."

"Let us say in another couple or three years," said I, with the principle of the family at heart.

"No," answered Palmer curtly. "Within the month. Unless you consent to that—into the fire the old hag goes."

"Oh, Palmer!" I exclaimed, "you passed your word to her that she should be spared."

"No, no. I said that unless she restored you I would break every bone of her body and throw her

into the flames myself.   I will certainly not touch her
with my stick, nor commit her myself to the flames,
but I will let the men outside deal with her as they
like.   I see what it is, there is no security for you
from the witchcrafts of that old hag till there is another woman in this house.   That woman must be
my daughter, and when she is here I defy all the
witches that dance on Cox Tor, and all the pretty
wenches of Devonshire to get so much as one foot
inside the door."

"Father!" protested Margaret.

"My dear, I know it."

"Well, you need not *say* it."

"Give me a twelvemonth's grace," I entreated.

"No, not above twenty days."

A howl from without—a fresh faggot was cast on
the fire.   The pyre was not on my ground but on a
bit of waste adjoining the lane, and as I am not lord
of the manor I have no rights over it.   That the
rascals knew.

Poor Margery laid hold of my arm.   Margaret at
once intervened and thrust her aside.   "You do not
touch him again."

"You see," laughed the father, "it is as I said.
Come, your hand."

I gave it with a sigh.

I have written these few pages to let people know
that Margery of Quether is about somewhere—where
I do not know for certain, but I believe she has gone
off into the remotest parts of Dartmoor, where, probably, she will seek herself a cave among the granite
tors, in which to conceal herself, where no boys will

be likely to find her and throw stones at her. I am uneasy now that there is such a rush of visitors to Dartmoor to enjoy the wonderful air and scenery, lest they should come across her, and in thoughtlessness or ignorance do her an injury. Now that they know her story, I trust they will give her a wide berth.

I think that what I have gone through has taught me a lesson, but it is not one much to be recommended, though it is one largely followed : Never succour those who solicit succour, or they will suck you dry. .

TOM A' TUDDLAMS.

CHAPTER I.

JULE A' NORT A' NOWHEER.

IF I were to begin my story with the words, "Look in the map!" I am as sure as that my head stands on my shoulders that those who read so far would neither obey the injunction, nor read another word of my tale. Consequently, instead of giving that piece of advice, I say, Take my word for it, all the western border of Yorkshire, from Derbyshire to the sources of the Tees, is a region of mountains and moors. The scenery is very wild in places—rugged, picturesque, varied, and everywhere beautiful.

In parts of this region it is still unusual for a native to be known by a surname. Indeed, he is generally doubtful whether he possesses one, and has to consider and consult authorities for it when he gives in his name to have his banns called. Every one in one of these dales knows every one else, and every one's pedigree, and it is by their pedigrees that each man and woman is known, much as in Wales, where every one was an *ap* someone, and in Normandy of old every man was a *fitz*. For instance, in the parish of Kebroyd, in these Western Hills, there were, no doubt, at least two Johns and two Marys. One man would be John a' Dick's, and the other John a' Jake's; and each Mary would, in like manner, be recognised and distinguished by the name of her father. But as it sometimes happens that there may be in the same place two Johns, both sons of Richards, though of different Richards, to differentiate them the grandfathers of each are called in, and one becomes John a' Dick's a' Harry's, and the other John a' Dick's a' Jake's. But sometimes the designation of a man is not by a patronymic, he takes the territorial name when he is the owner of and permanent resident in a small farm or cot. This was how Tom a' Will's a' Joe's came to be called Tom a' Tuddlams. Tuddlams is not an euphonious name; but no name but one sounded sweeter in the ears of Tom, for Tom was proud of Tuddlams—prouder, maybe, than the Duke of Devonshire is of Chatsworth, or the swallow is of its well-plastered nest. Tom loved Tuddlams because Tuddlams had come to him in a time of great distress and doubt where he should go, and had come to him quite unexpectedly.

I have said that no name but one sounded sweeter in Tom's ears. The one name more grateful to him than even Tuddlams was that of his wife Jewel. "Jewel" was the name by which she was christened, but "Jewel" was shortened on the vulgar tongue into "Jule;" and she was known throughout the neighbourhood as Jule a' Nort a' Nowheer, or, more laconically, as Jule a' Nobbudy. This meant that she did not belong to the parish of Kebroyd, nor to any of the parishes immediately impinging on Kebroyd, into which public opinion allowed the young Kebroydians, when seeking mates, to look for them. Every one beyond that arbitrary line was esteemed as "nobbudy" and "nort" (naught), and the whole of the British Empire outside the same line was "nowheer" (nowhere). If Tom had wanted a wife, why did he not wait till he came into the parish and then look about him? Tom had not waited till his uncle died and he had inherited Tuddlams, and settled in to take a "skeen" (look) round and choose a house-wife where his home was to be. He had married an outlandish lass, of whose ancestry nothing was known and whose birthplace none had seen.

Tom a' Tuddlams pretended to pay no heed to what was said, but, for all his affected indifference, it irritated him, and rankled in his heart.

Tom's ideas were not cast in the same mould as those of the people of Kebroyd. He had seen the world—that is, a good deal more of it than they—and he was impatient at their narrowness and prejudices.

Tuddlams was a small, low farmhouse, built of limestone blocks that had turned grey with old age. The fells rose behind it, covered with heather, on which one waded knee-deep, and when one waded, started grouse. A dip in the hills carried the drainage away to the Skelf; little converging becks rose on the sides of Scalefell and Houghfell and united in a ravine below the farm, where they formed a brawling, foaming stream of some pretence. Tuddlams lay in a scoop or basin of the moors, high up, sheltered from

E

fierce winds, unless they blew up the valley from the south-east. A scramble of twenty minutes above the house brought one to Arncliff, a rock from the summit of which, through a dip in the moors, could be seen— when the sun set over it—the flaming, quivering waters of Morecamb Bay, like a vast outspread sheet of gold-leaf fluttered by the air.

There were no woods about Tuddlams, the trees began lower down the valley. Around the farm-buildings were a few fields under cultivation, which belonged to Tom; but the great advantage of the place lay in the free runs the moor afforded to the sheep kept there.

Tom had led a roving life. His father had been an unsuccessful, discontented, disagreeable man. He had gone away from Kebroyd early in life, and had wandered from town to town in quest of work, never settling for long in any place, and never settling for long to any one trade. Nature had set her mark on him as a politician, but hard necessity drove him to labour with his hands for his livelihood, instead of exercising his tongue for the subversion of his country and social order. He was a cantankerous man, ambitious to make a figure in the clubs to which he belonged, and angry at having to think of his work and tinker at that, instead of at the constitution of England. The consequence was that he neglected his work, did it badly, and was discharged. It never occurred to him that blame attached to himself; he attributed his misfortunes to the rapacity of the masters, who ground down the proletariat, and grew wealthy and arrogant and cruel on the sweat of the poor. Tom's father, Will a' Joe's, as he was called in his native place, Bill Greenwood as he called himself out of it, as already said, never stuck long to one trade. He tried wool-combing, he tried cutlery, he tried dyeing, weaving, he even for a short while cultivated liquorice at Pontefract; he went on a coal barge on the Calder canal, quarrelled with his trade when he did not quarrel with his employer, and, finally, helped to make Devil's dust in a shoddy mill at Ossett. The Devil's dust got into his lungs, and cast him on his bed in a galloping consumption. On his deathbed he threatened to prosecute the nurse who attended on him, and he argued politics with his doctor till a fit of coughing came on and he broke a blood-vessel, and died slapping at his son who ran to hold him in his arms.

His wife had died some years before, glad, poor woman, to leave a life full of change and privation, and only sorry to be obliged to leave behind her her little boy to drift about the world where that spinning, eddy-headed husband of hers carried him.

After his father's death, Tom found work in a mill, and remained at his post for several years, steady, patient, exact in doing his daily task, and doing it always well. He was a quiet, reserved fellow, who did not make many friends, because he did not seek the society of his fellows, and he had acquired in his drifting life the art to live to himself. But though he had few friends he had no enemies, for he was harmless, and ever ready to do what was kind to those who needed assistance.

As he went to his work every day and as he

returned from it, he encountered a girl who worked in another factory. This girl was Jewel, a tall lass with fresh complexion and clear honest eyes, with hair like amber, but covered with a scarlet kerchief, after the habit of mill girls. Also, like the rest, she wore a white pinafore, and carried her dinner in a tin can. She was usually attended by a brother, a poor deformed boy, with one shoulder higher than the other, and a twisted spine. This lad, almost daily, attended his sister to the factory, and went to meet her as she returned, when "the mill loosed."

Tom took to pitying the cripple, made him little presents, and gained a smile from Jewel. An acquaintance thus began, slowly ripened, and Tom thought the happiest moments of the day were those to or from his work, and the most miserable occasions those when he got away too late or too early to walk with Jewel. Tom, however, was not aware that he loved her, till a time of distress came on Ossett, and Jewel was thrown out of work.

Among the hands the greatest distress prevailed. Hundreds were discharged from the mills. Then it was that Jewel lost her work.

Tom became uneasy about her. He looked around for her, but could not see her. He feared she might suffer want, that she would be forced to leave Ossett, and go elsewhere seeking work—that Wakefield, Dewsbury, Leeds, might engulf her, and that then it would be impossible for him to trace and recover her. Then, and then only, did he wake to discover how much in love he was. A couple of weeks passed, weeks of torturing anxiety to Tom. He could endure the uncertainty, the suspense, no longer, so he went to the house where she lodged with her brother, and rapped at the door. As he stood on the steps listening for her foot, waiting for her call to enter, he heard the tones of a fiddle within, playing—

"Christians, awake ! salute the happy morn
Whereon the Saviour of the world was born ! "

Christmas was coming, but was not come. What a sad Christmas it would be to many in Ossett! thought Tom. Happy was he to be still in full work. He tapped again at the door, and went in. No candle was burning, but there was a fire of coals shedding a red glow over the "house," as the main downstairs' room of a cottage is designated in Yorkshire.

By the fire sat Jewel, doing needlework; bending forward to see by the flames, and so the light danced over her amber hair. On a low stool sat the deformed, half-witted boy, fiddling.

"Jule," said Tom, "art thou out o' work ? "

"Eh ! I am, Tom."

"And how beest thou keeping body and soul together ? "

"They hou'd together without keeping, like man and wife."

"Why, lass ! Jim addles (earns) nowt. Hast thou any savings out o' which to feed him and thee ? "

"The savings be all emptiness, Tom."

"Look thee here, lass," said Tom Greenwood. "I'm in work mysen, and the strong ought to help the weak. If thou'lt let me help thee, thou must take me altogether—me, that is, for the sake o' my savings."

Jewel considered a moment, then said—

"Who takes me must take Jim, too. I've to fend (care) for him, poor lad ; there's no one else."

"Never another word, lass ; I've a broad back, and I'll carry the whole bag o' tricks."

That was a queer courtship, and a doubtful start on the journey of life, made doubly doubtful after the banns had been put in, by Tom getting his dismissal from the factory where he worked, not from any fault of his, but because there was no work more to be done in it till trade looked up.

"Jule," said he dolefully, "now I'm out o' work too, so we sha'n't lose nothing by honeymoon holidaying. We can't be worse off together than we are apart, so we'd better link our hands and hearts."

"Very well, Tom : thou know'st best."

That was a dismal wedding on Christmas Day. They had no new clothes, a sorry dinner, and no wedding trip, though they kept, perforce, holiday. Hungry and poor they went to church ; hungry and poor, but full of love, and rich in hope, they began their united stream of life.

CHAPTER II.

TUDDLAMS

TOM had some savings, but not much. Jewel had
none at all. How could she? At the best of times
her earnings had but barely provided for her own
and her brother's necessities. Six shillings—at piece-
work sometimes eight, never ten—per week, worsted
reeling. How had she managed to support herself
and brother on from six to eight shillings a week?
She had often tried to get Jim to do some trifling task
which might add something to the little store, but he
was too unreliable, too feather-brained, to remain long
at anything : and all her efforts were unavailing.
Yet, he was always sorry that he had disappointed
her, and cried piteously over his own shortcomings.
But he was as incorrigible as a drunkard. He could
not stick to regular work. And yet he earned money
in his own way, though a way not approved by his
sister. Jim, like so many who are half-witted, had a
singularly developed faculty for music, and he could
play with rare delicacy and feeling on his violin. No
one who heard his performance without seeing him
would believe that he lacked brain : he threw so much
expression into what he played, and played with such
71

refinement of feeling. His skill on the violin led him to play in the "folds" or mill-yards to the workmen during their dinner hour; and those who heard him gave him halfpence. Sometimes he went, when invited, into the public-houses. His sister had urged him with fervour not to allow himself to be enticed into the taverns; but Jim could say no man "nay," and he went in, played, received money and drink, and now and then staggered home tipsy.

But now this small rill of income dried up. The hands were no more flush of money, the folds were empty, and Jim might play to the idle, but he received no pay in return.

"Whativer is to be done?" asked Tom disconsolately. "We must go elsewhere."

"But whither shall we go?" asked Jewel.

A rap at the door, and a letter flung in by the postman. The question was answered. Tom's uncle was dead—Uncle Nick, about whom he had scarcely heard —thought less. Uncle Nick had been a small landowner—a yeoman on a very small scale—at the head of the Skelfdale, at Tuddlams, in Kebroyd parish. Uncle Nick was dead, and left no sons or daughters to inherit Tuddlams after him, so Tuddlams fell to his nephew. This is how Tom a' Will's a' Joe's came to be Tom a' Tuddlams at the age of twenty-three.

A proud and happy man was Tom Greenwood— proud above all to have a house of his own in which to place his dear Jewel, to be its mistress and queen. Jewel looked about her.

"I'm glad—I'm fain glad," she said. "It must be

two miles from a public-house, and there'll be no trouble about Jim."

"Is that the chief good o' t' place in thine eyes?" asked Tom, a little disconcerted.

"It is one, and a great one," answered Jewel.

But every pleasure has its attendant annoyance, and Tom's delight and pride in his home were damped, and his temper nettled, when he heard his wife—his Jewel of jewels—lightly designated by all the neighbours, acting under a common impulse, "Jule a' nort a' nowheer."

It cannot be said with truth that Tom received a cordial welcome on his arrival in the parish. In the first place, he had married a foreigner.

"'Tis a pity," said some, "that he should have took that lass Jule a' nort a' nowheer! 'Tis like putting new cloth into an ow'd garment, or new wine into ow'd bottles, clean contrary to Scripture. It is as bad as Moses casting down and breaking the Ten Commandments."

Then, in the next place, Tom was regarded as a sort of renegade. His father had left Kebroyd and gone east, to the big towns, and roystered there, and had never returned to his native village, not even there to lay his bones. Tom had not been born in the dale, but at Huddersfield. However, though not born and bred under the shadow of Scalefell, he could not be counted a stranger, for he was Tom a' Will's a' Joe's a' Jake's a' Nick's—his genealogy was better known than that of Noah, and he was, in right, as he was in fact, inalienably, undeniably, Tom a' Tuddlams.

Tom speedily settled into his little farm.   He kept on in his service old Matthew, the man who had been with his uncle, Nicodemus—Nick a' Joe's a' Jake's, as he was called.   The old man's advice and assistance would be invaluable to him, ignorant of the mode of conducting the operations on a farm.   Tom had Yorkshire energy and self-assurance, and had inherited some of his father's versatility.   In a very short time he was sure, to use his own expression, he would "frame."   The life he had led since his early child-hood, instead of making him restless, had filled his soul with a longing for rest.   The incessant change in his father's condition, now in receipt of good wages, then with nothing, had made him hunger for a stable position, in which he need not be looking forward with uneasiness to the future.   To have a house not rented, but his own ; to have earth under his feet in which he could take root, certain not to be upriven and displaced, this was to him the most perfect happiness that could fall to his lot.   It had come to him quite unexpectedly, for he had never thought of, certainly never reckoned on, Uncle Nick's acres. He had never inquired whether his uncle was married, whether he had children.   He had never visited him. He had not thought of applying to him when out of work and in distress.

Tom was sensible of the beauty of the place where his lot had fallen, of the clearness and freshness of the air, doubly valued after the smoke that filled the atmosphere and sullied every object in the manu-facturing districts, where all things but water which sprang fresh from the earth were dirty, even the grass

was sooty and the trunks of the trees black as ink.
It was true that Tuddlams was a lonely spot, but
Tom did not mind that; he had his Jewel, he wanted
no other society; and to Jewel it was well that Tuddlams was remote from the village inn, for the sake of
poor, silly Jim.

Tom loved, admired, almost worshipped Jewel, with
a deeper love, admiration, and religion every day.
Tom had not had his heart unlocked as a boy. His
mother had died early, and was to him only a pale
and characterless reminiscence. His father had
bullied him, had shown him little affection, or had
shown what affection he bore in an unpalatable
fashion. No one else had shown him any regard, and
he had been brought in contact with no one to whom
he could cling. Consequently Tom had grown to
man's estate without having really loved anyone,
and now that he was married, and possessed both a
house and a wife of his own, his heart overflowed
with love for both. He had, it is true, acquired
also a brother-in-law, but Jim did not inspire him
with much affection. Jim was the fly in his
cup of happiness, chiefly because he exacted of
Jewel so much attention and caused her so much
anxiety.

Silly Jim might have done a hundred useful things
on the farm, if he could have been kept to his work;
but if he was set a task, he began to execute it eagerly,
then tired, and deserted it. Jim tried Tom's temper.
He could not believe that the poor lad was not
responsible for his actions; he believed that Jewel
spoiled him by allowing him to have his own way, by

not being stern with him, and forcing him to adhere to his work till it was done. Tom had, without knowing it, a strong sense of the beautiful, and Jim was so ugly, so untidy and misshapen, that his appearance was offensive to the eye. Tom came to dislike the boy, and he had some difficulty in concealing his aversion from the sharp eyes of his wife. But though he tried to hide his distaste, and believed he had effectually covered it, Jewel perceived it. It distressed her; it disappointed her. Her first duty was to Jim, who had no one else in the world to care for him; and, she argued, she had given Tom fair warning, when he had asked her to take him, that she would not go to him without her helpless brother. It was a pity—Jim was the spring of trouble that began to cloud—only a little, but still a little—the clear current of the life and love of Tom and Jule.

Christmas was at hand—the first Christmas since Tom had taken Jule, the first anniversary of their wedding day.

"Oh!" thought Tom, "if some excuse or contrivance could be got to send that fool, Jim, out of the way, what a happy Christmas we should spend! I'll get him a mask and send him a-mumming."

But—"Tom," said Jewel, "we're bound to have" (*i.e.*, we must have) "a Christmas-tree."

"Tree! Why!—there are no bairns, lass."

"But there is Jim; it will give him so much pleasure. And then, lad, I want to find some'ut as'll keep him at home and away from the mummers, and the carolers, and the ale and spirit drinking—poor bairn, poor bairn! Thee'll get me a tree, wilt thou not?"

Tom shrugged his shoulders, and the corners of his mouth twitched; but he said nothing.

"Thou doesn't grudge me a tree?" asked Jewel.

"*I* grudge thee anything!" he exclaimed. "Nay, I grudge thee naught. Why, lass, if thou'd a fancy for Tuddlams without me, thou should have it, and welcome."

"I don't want Tuddlams without thee. Tuddlams and thee goes farrantly (comfortably) well together. But to go back to Jim. It is a pity that the beck is being dammed up to make a reservoir for the towns below—it brings a parcel of navvies and rough chaps up near us, and they draw Jim to them, what with his curiosity to see what they are doing, and what with the fiddling, in which they encourage Jim."

"Oh, Jim, Jim—always Jim!" said Tom impatiently. "Thou hast no thoughts for nobody or nothing, but only Jim."

"And why shouldn't I? He's my brother, and a poor, silly, misshaped creature, with no will to earn his living, and no looks that nobody should like him. If I didn't care for him, who would? He's my own flesh and blood; and if there be ony truth that man and wife are one flesh, then he's now just as much thine as mine to fend for. I told thee—I never concealed it one moment—that he who took me, took Jim, too."

She was hot. A fire sparkled in her eyes, and her hand trembled as she scoured a kettle.

"I didn't mean offence," said Tom.

"Then go out and get the Christmas-tree."

"Yes—for Jim."

CHAPTER III.

THE TASTING OF THE TREE.

TOM went out and fetched first his pick, then his shovel. There was a small plantation behind the house—a belt of larch, spruce, and Scotch pines, that had been put in by Uncle Nick a few years before his death. They had not made much growth, for the situation was cold; still, they were sturdy, green trees, well rooted. Several could be spared, as they had spread and incommoded one another. The larch had shed its leaves, the Scotch boughs turned up, clad in spines all round, but the spruce would serve the required purpose.

Snow had fallen, and had to be shovelled away, but the ground was not frozen. Tom chose a tree, and then began to clear the snow from about it. Tom was not only fond of, he was proud of Jewel. He wondered at her cleverness. She fitted into the house as if the house had been made for her, like a set of clothes. She fell into the duties as if they had been familiar to her from infancy; she seemed to know by instinct what should be done in a farmhouse—she who had lived in a cottage in a row all her girlhood! But, love and admire her as he did, he could not love Jim;

and he felt jealous of the poor idiot because the boy occupied so large a share in the thoughts and affections of his wife. Men are said to be most selfish animals, and Tom was no exception; he was very selfish in this one particular: he wanted his wife to think, and consider, and work for himself alone. He was not a man to analyse his feelings, and he was therefore supremely unconscious that he was jealous. The boy annoyed him—he disliked him; but he did not attempt to account for his repugnance.

"Jule wants the tree for Jim. Shoo" (she) "never for a moment thought I might like it. I never had a Christmas-tree in my life—no, never. Father wasn't the man for that. He never thought of one. Why shouldn't I have my tree? I suppose I'm to find the tree, and the trouble, and the candles, and the gimcracks, and the gilt nuts and apples for that Jim. And I know that Jule is knitting him a muffle for his throat, and warm gloves, and stockings, and shoo hasn't a thought for my comforts no more than for my pleasures. Why should not Jule think that I might like a tree? 'Tisn't the tree itsen," said Tom, impatiently driving the pick into the ground— "'tis the consideration. Why, if Jule were to light a tallow-candle-end in the lantern, and say it was done for me, I'd kiss her and be pleased. And now, here I be digging and pulling up a tree only for Jim. She said it—'only for Jim.' 'Tis unhuman."

He was unjust; but is not jealousy always unjust? Does it not always jaundice the eyes that they see falsely, black spots dancing in clear air, and lines crooked that are perfectly straight?

Tom was working himself up into an angry, resentful mood about nothing. The day was cold enough for him to have thought coolly of the matter, and seen how absurd it was of him to be in dudgeon over so small a thing. Was it possible that Jewel could for a moment entertain the thought that her husband, a man standing six feet, with hair on his face, with a gruff voice, aged twenty-four, very nearly a quarter of a century old, a landed proprietor, could fret for a Christmas-tree? If he had considered the matter impartially, he would have perceived that he was making himself ridiculous. He vented his ill-humour on the roots of the spruce; he hacked through them. "Of course," he said, "I'm expected to spoil one of my beautifullest trees—just for Jim!" Then, after another peevish dig at the roots, he growled, "But I won't. Why should I spoil my tree, that Uncle Nick planted, just for that lout? I'll dig all round it, and have it up roots and all, and plant it again when Jule has done with it. I won't have even a spruce spoiled for Jim. He ain't worth it; a fiddling idiot?"

Just as he had got the tree up—a pretty, well-built tree about three feet six inches high—he heard a cough behind him, and turning, saw Matthew by the hedge.

"Aught fresh, old man?" asked Tom.

"Over-fresh," answered Matthew, laconically.

"What do you mean? Am I wanted?"

"Eh! I should just think you were."

"What has happened?"

"Fine laikes wi' Jim."

"What has Jim done now?"

"There's nort like a fellow seeing the unpleasant through his own eyes."

Tom threw down his pick and shovel, and, grasping the little fir-tree just above the root, walked to the house, after signing to the man to bring in the tools after him.

As he came in at the back door, and stood holding the same, knocking the snow off his boots, he heard voices in the front kitchen or "house."

Carrying the tree, he pushed through the door, and saw a couple of men standing in the room, broad-shouldered fellows, and Silly Jim cast at their feet. Tom looked first at the men, then at his wife for an explanation. Jewel was sobbing.

The case was not one that needed much explanation. Jim had been down to the reservoir, had fiddled to the navvies there employed, had been treated by them to gin and water, and had been made tipsy.

The men had brought him up, and they looked at Jewel and Tom with a pleased and also expectant expression. Their consciences told them they had done a good thing in bringing Jim home, and said no word of reproach to them for having brought him to a condition in which he was unable without assistance to reach his home. The glow of a contented, approving conscience beamed in their rough faces. A good deed always deserves, and almost demands, a reward, and the two navvies in their warmth of self-satisfaction waited for the feel of money in their palms and the offer of brandy neat, or, at least, ale and cake, as refreshment after their exertions.·

Tom took in the situation at a glance. Of course he must reward the men, though little deserving. He signed to Jewel to bring out the cake and the " haver-bread " (oat scones), and to put butter on the table, whilst he filled a jug with beer.

" Sit you down," he said sulkily to the men. " There's a shilling a-piece for you, and it is the last I'll spend in this way. The lad would not be drunk unless you'd given him the liquor. I'll teach him not to go near you again."

He said no more till the men had done eating. The haver-bread is oatcake thin as biscuit, baked on a girdle, and hung up on strings in the ceiling. The men ate heartily, voraciously ; bread, cake, and butter flew, and they drank the ale as though they had drunk nothing for twenty-four hours and had fed on herrings and salt pork. Then they drew their hands across their lips, and each, thrusting his plate before him, said, " I'm full "; and one said condescend-ingly :—

" I don't think, now, as I've iver enjoyed myself more, not even at a hanging."

Tom said nothing. He waited till the men were gone, then he called angrily to the boy :

" Get up ! "

Jim was somewhat recovered ; the jolting of the journey, and the time it had taken, had combined to somewhat sober him, and he obeyed. He had a great mouth, like that of a fish, and he grinned at Tom; but the grin died away as he saw the expression on Tom's face, and the boy had sufficient mother-wit to understand what that meant. He began to whimper.

"Come, Jim, get to bed," said his sister, going up to him. She was engaged clearing away the remains of the men's meal. "Do, to please your Jule."

"Give me a drink first," pleaded Jim.

Tom said roughly, "Stand up!" and he caught the lad by the collar of his coat and pulled him to his feet. Jewel was back in the kitchen.

"Jim," said Tom, "I won't allow these goings on. Thou'rt not going to bring discredit on my house, and unhappiness on thy sister, and stir me to anger, not if I can help it. If thou doesn't learn mastery over thysen, I must teach it thee. Look here, Jim. Dost thou see this tree? 'Tis a Christmas tree Jule made me go and dig up for thee. A Christmas tree hung with apples and nuts is for good chaps, and not for bad. It's not for them that demean themselves, and make beasts o' themselves, as thou hast a' been doing. I don't wish to give thee a hiding, lad, but I must, to teach thee what thou must not do. And so—I'll make thee taste o' this tree o' knowledge of good and evil, wrong way on, sour end, afore Christmas comes."

And with that he brought the Christmas tree whishing, slashing, crackling, about the boy's back. It did not hurt him. It could not hurt him. Tom knew that very well. It made much noise, and there was a great deal of it, but it could not raise a welt in his skin anywhere. Tom did not design to hurt him, only to frighten him, as a parent chastises his young child with a newspaper. But the shrieks that Jim uttered, the leaps, the writhings he made, would have led anyone to suppose he was being scourged with scorpions.

Jewel rushed from the back kitchen into the room, and stood for a moment paralysed with horror; then, with a cry of wrath, she rushed on her husband, her cheeks flaming, her eyes flaring, and wrenched her brother out of his hand. She trod on the end of the spruce, and, clutching it, tore the root away from his grasp.

"How dare you!" she gasped.

Jim staggered back, howling and sobbing.

"How dare you—you coward! you base, mean coward!" she cried, facing her husband, without a spark of love in her face, without a token of relenting in her tone. Her blood boiled, and every scrap of control she had over her tongue was lost. She was like a tigress defending her cub.

"Jule," said Tom, "be reasonable. Jim must be punished if he does wrong."

"But not by you!" gasped Jule. "Not by you. Is this what I and my poor brother are to expect in your house?"

"I have not hurt him."

"You have. Do not add a lie to your wrong. Cruel and false—that is what you are! I curse the day that ever I came under your roof! I curse the day that ever I saw your face—if this is what is in store for me and Jim. Come to me, Jim; come to your sister. She will take care of you, and defend you with her arms against brutal men. And—I tell you th's, Tom ; if ever you dare—you dare—you dare" she quivered with rage, she panted for breath, she stamped her foot—"if ever you dare lay hands on my own poor afflicted Jim again, I'll carry him in my arms, and run away, and leave you for ever. Thank God, I have hands, and can earn my living. It may be only six shillings a week, but I'd rather live on crusts with Jim, and drink water, and toil eight, or nine, or ten hours a day than stay here to be slave-driven by you—you, a strong man, beating a defence-less, helpless innocent!"

Tom was speechless with astonishment. In a moment his loving, his true Jule was converted into a savage, hostile virago.

To reason with her was impossible. She was not in a condition to listen to reason. She was not her-self ; she was as one possessed.

"Jule," said Tom, looking sadly at the Christmas-tree that lay on the floor, "if I have done wrong, I am sorry ; but I think I am not to blame."

"No," said she scornfully ; "men will never allow they're to blame. It is we—we feeble lasses—who're in the wrong."

He went up to her.

"Jewel, I do not understand thee."

"I am sorry I have not spoken plain."

She threw herself into a chair, and folded her arms.

"Jewel, forgive and forget. Give me thy hand, lass. This be Christmas eve, when there should be 'peace

on earth and good-will among men,' most of all in a
home between man and wife."

"No," she said; "there shall be no peace between
us, no good-will."

Then he turned, opened the door, and went out.

CHAPTER IV.

A PEACE-OFFERING.

Tom a' Tuddlams left the house. He walked away down the valley without any clear idea whither he was going or what he wanted to do. He left the house because he could not breathe in it; he could not endure it, whilst his Jewel was in this new and wondrous mood. His temples throbbed, his hands were clenched, and a sombre flicker was in his eyes. He had been married for one year, a year less a day, and had been perfectly happy—so happy that he had sometimes felt that he could not bear an accession to his happiness. We do, at times, become aware of a happiness so acute that it almost touches on pain—so supreme that we cannot laugh, we are disposed to cry. It had been so with Tom; his cup had brimmed. Jim, as already said, had been the fly in it; but a small fly, only a gnat floating in a very brimming cup. And now that gnat had tilted the goblet and poured forth all its contents! Tom had been so happy that he now felt his disappointment, his misery with double poignancy.

How cruel, how wicked, how unjust Jewel had been! He had not hurt that odious, yelping idiot, he had not meant to hurt, only to scare him. He had chastised him for his good—to deter him from again drinking with the navvies and becoming drunk. Jewel was spoiling the boy; she remonstrated with him, but remonstrance was thrown away on him: he was not rational, he must be made to feel, like an ass or a dog, when he did wrong. Jewel would, in the end, be the sufferer unless Jim were corrected and disciplined.

How unfair it was of Jewel to stand in the way! How short-sighted she was! Her conduct encouraged the boy in wrong-doing. A sense of anger against Jewel simmered in Tom's heart.

He walked fast, his feet stamped in the snow, he set them so hardly, firmly, as he trampled his way down the valley. The simmering wrath in his heart rose and boiled over. Let her go! He clenched his hands and teeth. Let her go! How dare she insult him by such words as to call him a coward and a liar! A coward—he a coward! he laughed out. He knew his own heart, his strength of purpose. He a liar! He, who would be torn to pieces rather than speak a word that was not true! It would have been bad, had a man called him cruel and false; bad for the man who had thus designated him. He would have taken him by the throat and shaken him, and shaken him till he shook the teeth out of his mouth, the hair off his head, the nails from his finger-ends, and the eyes from their sockets. Tom stood still; he was trembling with emotion—with wrath. His knees smote together. He was thinking how he would deal with the man who spoke to him as his wife had spoken. But there was the terrible rankle of the words: he could not resent them, for they were spoken *by his wife*. Those dear lips he had so often kissed, that heart in which he thought he reigned sole and altogether—they had poured forth the wicked words which entered into him as a searching knife cutting his heart.

He came to the reservoir, then to the dam; at that point there was a tavern recently built, and opened for the entertainment first of the navvies engaged on the works, and then was to serve for the refreshment of the visitors who came to fish and boat in the reservoir, or Scalefell lake, as it was called.

When Tom came opposite the door of the tavern he halted. A strong impulse came on him to go in, sit with the navvies there, drink, smoke, laugh, sing songs, and tell tales, and forget his misery. He was conscious of his utter loneliness. He had shown himself indifferent to the society of the neighbours, because he was perfectly satisfied with that of Jewel; and now that Jewel had turned on him, and stung him, he was alone, he had no friend. But the impulse to enter and drown his grief was but momentary. He was angry with Jim for going there, he had chastised him for drinking, and should he do the very thing he had objected to in the idiot?

He shook his head and walked on.

"Yes," he said, "there is some excuse for the fool, but none for the sane man!"

And then, strangely, the wheel of his mind went round and his mood altered. He had been accustomed to his father's bad humours, had made allowances for them, and had schooled himself to patience under them; and now the old discipline began to tell on him, and his wrath faded away. What gave his mind the turn were those words he used about Jim, as he

went past the tavern.   He began to think of Jim, and
he admitted to himself that Jim was not seriously to
blame.   Then he thought how that Jewel had not
been in the room when he laid hold of the boy and
struck him with the Christmas-tree.   Jim had howled
ear-piercingly.   Jewel came in, frightened by the cry,
and thought her brother had been more hurt than he
really was.   After all, it was natural that she should
take the side of her brother—that she should defend
the weak and suffering.   What would he have had?
asked Tom of himself.   Would he have had Jewel
stand coldly by and tell him how many cuts the lad.
was to receive?   No, that would be unlike Jewel.   No,
by ginger! he would not have endured that in Jewel!
Why, that would have been worse than her firing up
at his laying his hand on the boy.   There was something grand, womanly, in Jewel defending Jim—Jim,
who had no other protector in the world but she.
There was really something noble in the way in which
she threw in her lot with the poor, fond creature; she
was ready—she said it—rather than that he should be
maltreated, to leave her comfortable, beautiful home,
and trudge back to a factory town, and work again in
a worsted mill and earn her six shillings a week, which
she would freely divide with her brother.   Give up
Tuddlams!   Tom considered.   Really Jewel was a
wonderful woman ; he had never hitherto realised her
greatness of soul.

And then Tom remembered his own train of thought
as he dug up the tree, how jealous he had been of the
poor idiot, how absurdly vexed he had been because
the tree was destined for Jim and not for himself.

"Why, Lord!" said Tom, standing still; "all the trees
in the plantation are mine. Tuddlams is mine, so are
the fields and the pastures, so are the sheep and the
cow, and the grey mare. Everything is mine. Shoo
couldn't give me what was my own! Shoo simply
axed me to give that darned boy one out of the
hundred or two hundred, or may be five hundred, trees
in my plantation, and I begrudged it him! Gor!
what a chap made up of selfishness I be!"

But, although Tom a' Tuddlams thus debated with
himself, and extenuated Jewel's fault, and stood her
advocate against his outraged feelings, he only half
convinced himself that she was in the right and he in
the wrong. He threw the cloak of forgetfulness over
her bitter words. Yet they worked their way through,
scratched and bit and tore their way through, and
were again before him in all their unkindness and injustice.

"I suppose there was wrong o' both sides," said
Tom uneasily. "I'm sure there must ha' been wrong
on mine." He had had no experience of women's
anger, of female temper, and he did not know how
long the storm at home would last; whether, when he
went home, he would find Jewel subdued with self-
consciousness, in tears, and ready to kiss and make
up the breach, or whether the evil temper were
still tossing and threatening, possessing and unex-
pelled.

"There can be no harm in my bringing her
summat," he said. "It is Christmas eve, and I'll give
her a Christmas present, and—by George I will!—
I'll get a packet of yellow, and green, and red, and

blue tapers for the tree. Shoo'll be fain at that, and ready with her forgiveness."

He was now in the village of Kebroyd. When I call it a village, I do it a dishonour; it was one of those hobbledehoy villages that are almost towns and yet not quite towns. There was no gas in the streets.

As Tom entered Kebroyd he saw a cluster of men and women about a cottage, and beside the door, on a table, stood a man haranguing.

"A political lecturer, or a teetotal or a ranter chap," said Tom; but on nearer approach he heard :—

"Going, dirt cheap! What! for this beautiful looking-glass no higher bid than one shilling? I'll tell you what it is, the gentlemen don't want to look at their faces, and so they won't bid, and as for the ladies, they are provided already, and think the most beautiful of mirrors are the eyes of their admiring husbands and lovers. But nevertheless, I urge you not to be shy of making a bid. Why, this looking-glass cost 15s. 6d., if it cost a penny, when it was new. Real mahogany, and not a scratch, and—see the size of the glass. It is too ridiculous, only one shilling. Thank you, marm, eighteenpence. Are we to strike it down to you, marm, for that absurd sum? Two shillings. This gentleman with a red tie" (he was a navvy) "has bid another sixpence that he may be able to tie a stylish bow every day when he goes out courting."

An auction was in progress. The occupants of No. 14 Reservoir Road had failed, and were leaving, and their furniture was being sold before the house.

"I daresay," proceeded the auctioneer, "many of you ladies have been disappointed in your looking-glasses. The knobs on which they swing have a tendency to come off, and the screw gets loose, and when you want to look at your beautiful hair and eyes, then the mirror is swinging so that it shows nothing but your toes. Now I beg you all to observe how—thank you, marm, half-a-crown—how, I was going to say, how easily this turns on its pivots, and how it always stands at the angle at which you want it. Three shillings, yes—going for three shillings. Now, let me see, this is Christmas eve; I'm sure for certain there are some of you who want to make a Christmas present to your wives or sweethearts. There's nothing a woman likes better than a looking-glass. It is meat and drink to her. Let us suppose you've had a domestic breeze or a lover's quarrel. Do you want to make it up? To lay the storm? Buy the looking-glass, and present the lady with it; and you will see the waves go down and become smooth as though oil were poured on 'em. Eh? sir!"

"Three and six."

"Three and six you are, sir. I beg pardon, is it Tom a' Tuddlams? Tom a' Tuddlams it is. Tom a' Tuddlams has bid three and six for a mirror for Jewel a' Nort a' Nowheer, and a more beautiful and smiling and sweet face than hers to look into it is not to be seen. Or, do I stand corrected? If any gentleman thinks he knows a beautifuller one, let him bid four shillings, or for ever hold his silence."

"Four shillings."

" Right—four shillings ; now, sir ? "

" Four and six," said Tom.

" Five shillings."

" Five and six," said Tom.

And at five and six the mahogany swinging look-ing-glass was struck down to him.

Tom went on into the village and visited the grocer's shop, where he purchased some coloured tapers for the tree, and nuts and oranges, and sweet-stuff; and also some little tin or lead ornaments to hang on the tree and make it glitter.

Thus supplied, with his pockets stuffed, he put a bit of cord around the mirror, fastened it to his large pocket-handkerchief, where it passed over the wood, to prevent chafing, and so slung the great looking-glass across his back, and trudged up the glen home-wards to Tuddlams.

The trouble was gone from his mind now, the weight from his heart. Now he was bringing home to Jewel a beautiful Christmas present, which would delight her, and prove to her that he bore no ill-will for the cruel words she had launched at him.

He chuckled as he strode along. He thought how pleased she would be. He pictured her waiting im-patiently for him, longing to make up the little quarrel, of her flying to his arms and clinging to him, and cuddling into his breast with sobs of penitence and of love, as he opened the door when he came in.

He was rudely undeceived.

As he came unexpectantly into the house, Jewel started up—

"Tom! there! this comes of your cruelty! Jim is run away and we cannot find him. What have you got there? A looking-glass! What folly and waste of money! Put it down and run—see if you can find where Jim is."

CHAPTER V.

ON THE FELLS.

Yes, Jim had run away, and taken his fiddle with him. At first Jewel had not thought much of his disappearance. She had sent old Matthew down to the reservoir; but Jim had not gone in that direction. Night had fallen and the boy was not returned.

There was nothing for it but to search for him. He could not be left straying about the fells all night. He would be dead before morning.

"You must go after him," said Jewel. "Put on a great-coat and take a lantern—Jim must be found."

"You do not know in which direction he has gone?"

"Matthew said he saw footprints in the snow going towards Arncliff."

Tom saw that it was necessary that Jim should be pursued. Matthew was too old to do that. He must go after the boy himself.

"The night will be bad; there's a bank of black cloud over Houghfell full of snow, ready to shake out its feathers."

"Then, make haste," urged Jewel. "If the snow comes on thou'll not be able to trace him."

She took a shepherd's-pouch and put into it a

flask of brandy, a box of lucifers, and a second candle.

"If he is lost," said Jewel, "I will never forgive thee. Unless thou had ill-treated him, he'd never have run away."

Tom heaved a sigh—he was disappointed ; still, he made an excuse for Jewel. She was alarmed for the safety of her brother. His heart was heavy when he went forth in the night with the lantern in quest of the missing lad.

The tracks noticed by Matthew as diverging from the road were a little way down near a stone called the "Loaf," from a fancied resemblance to one.

Matthew accompanied him thus far. "I thowt," said the old man, "he'd a' gone after liquor and fire, and not up into the fells, which shows he's more of a fool than I believed."

The old man offered to accompany his master in the search, but Tom declined his assistance. "In the dark one pair of eyes are as good as two," he said. Then, holding the lantern to the snow, he followed the traces. "Mind the pot-hoyles!" shouted Matthew. The Yorkshire moors are dangerous, in parts, to traverse by one unacquainted with them, and even dangerous to go over by one who knows them, in the dark, for, in addition to the usual risks of loss of way, there is the special peril of falling into the so-called "pot-holes." These are natural shafts descending into the bowels of the mountains, often of great depth, and all gaping with assurance of certain death to anyone who should incautiously fall into their treacherous jaws.

The mountains are built up of limestone, and in the limestone are numerous caverns running horizontally, through which, at one time, streams were discharged. But all the caverns are not horizontal; some are vertical, caused by the fall of the crust above a sub-terranean vault, but the water has worked its way to a lower level, and now runs out at a considerable depth beneath the deserted and dry channel, or else the shaft has been worked through some fault in the limestone by a descending stream, and it precipitates itself into the well that engulfs it and conceals its further course.

If Jewel had but greeted him lovingly, put her arms about his neck, and entreated him, as he loved her, to go in search of her brother, Tom would have started on his quest with alacrity and a hopeful heart; but her reception had been chilling. She had taken no notice of his looking-glass, she had been too much engrossed in her anxiety, and her ill-humour had not spent itself: she charged her husband with having driven the poor fool forth—perhaps to his death.

If Jim were to die, to fall into a pot-hole, to sink in the snow, Tom feared that Jewel would never forgive him—that it would totally destroy his married happiness. To escape such a contingency, it was necessary for him to find Jim, and this urged him on as much as his desire to help the unfortunate, half-witted creature.

Jim's course had been erratic. He had gone along without any notion whither he would direct his steps. His traces led in a zigzag course, now up the hill, then at a slant to the north, then they turned downwards, to where were rocks, among which Tom lost them.

He was obliged to search long before he could pick up the trace again. He looked up at the sky. The clouds were black above, but then his eyes were dazzled with the glare of the lantern on the snow, and he could not tell whether they had spread and were about to discharge their burden.

He stood still and shouted. He waited; he received no answer. He shouted again and again in vain. Then he went on, bent, holding the lantern to the snow, following the course of the steps. Suddenly he stared and shrank aside. There was a broad, black, snowless disc near at hand. He held up his lantern over his head. It was a pot—he believed, but dared not approach nearer. The traces of the boy led along the verge. A foot to the right would have precipitated him down the abyss.

"There is a providence over bairns and fools," said Tom. "If God were not bound" (going) "to save him he'd have gone down there. But—wherever can I be?" When he had passed the dangerous spot he stood still to consider. He was out of his reckoning altogether. He had not the smallest notion where he was. He had gone on, looking intently at the traces, without considering whither they led; and, indeed, the night had become so dark that he might have lost himself soon had he not been thus preoccupied. "Let me see," said Tom, "there's Hull Pot, and there's the Ox Hole, and there's Scale Pot, and the Boggarts' Well—whichever of all these was it that I've gone by?"

He went on, shaking his head.

"I'm flayed" (afraid) "I've lost mysen," said he.

"There'll be nowt for it but when I've found him we must come back the same way."

He considered.

"I must be certain not to go down the pot-hole with him here." He took out a red pocket-handkerchief and threw it down on the snow. "There, when I come to that, I'll remember to walk more cautiously, because we'll be close to the pot."

Again he stooped and walked on; and now saw flakes of snow sail lightly as eider-down into the flare of the lamp. First a solitary flake, very large; then several; and, after a minute or two, the snow came down fast and thick.

"Now I'm beat," said Tom. "In a varra few moments all the foot-taps will be covered over, and how shall I find my way on after Jim, or, missing him, find my way back? That was a bad hour for me when I dug up the Christmas-tree; if I hadn't had the tree I shouldn't, maybe, have whacked him with it. And now we shall both be lost on the fells all along of it. However, it is no use considering; I must go on after the lad while I can mark where he's set his foot."

There was little or no wind. In the still, dark night the flakes came down thickly; they came into the depressions made in the old snow, blurred their edges, and began to choke them up. Fortunately, the boy had dragged his feet heavily, as if weary; and so had drawn a furrow; and this furrow was traceable for a while. It went in the same random, doubling, zig-zag, purposeless way as before. Where a dark rock had appeared, the boy had made for it in the dusk;

and then had turned away from it again, finding it to be only a rock affording no shelter.

The way became steep, steeper; a sharp, scrambling ascent—to what could it lead? Then came a slip or shoot of snow where the boy had gone down; and below, a trampled mass, where he had rolled about, struggled up, and at length gone on again. Whither? Tom hunted about and could not find. There was a tract of rubble on which no footprints could be distinguished, and what snow lay on it was dotted on the lumps of stone.

What was Tom to do? He began to be uneasy about himself as well as Jim. He had been walking a long time; how long he could not tell—he had lost the count of time. He had gone a long way; how far he could not tell—the direction had changed so often. He might have crossed the neck between Scale and Hough fells and be in Lancashire, or he might be near his home; he could not tell. He put the lantern behind him, and covered his brow with his hand, and looked through the night and falling snow to see if he could distinguish anywhere a light. If he saw a light he would make for it—it might be his home; if not, it did not matter—he would ask for help, and a party would scour the moor for the poor lost boy.

Not a light could he see. Had there been an illumined window a mile away he could not have seen it, for the snow thickly descending formed an impenetrable veil.

"Blow that Christmas tree—that's done it!" said Tom, and suddenly turned. He heard something far above him—a shrill strain. In his sudden turn he struck the lantern with the lappet of his coat; it went over and bounded down the steep—for a moment as a flying rocket, and then was dark.

"Here's a worse go than all!" groaned Tom. "Now I'm without lantern, and whativer in the world shall I do?"

Then, again, above him, he heard the same weird, shrill sounds—the strain:

> "Christians, awake! salute the happy morn,
> Whereon the Saviour of the world was born."

"That's Jim!" shouted Tom; "and like his mad ways: fiddling in a winter night—in the snow—lost."

He resumed the scramble, guided by the sound, and soon found himself against the face of a rock. Still he could hear the notes of the violin more now to his left, and he groped his way slowly, cautiously along, now almost sliding down or falling over a projecting stone, till his hand pressed against nothing, and here the strains sounded so articulate and loud that Tom was sure he was close to the boy.

"Jim!" he called, "are you under shelter?"

"Eh, be that thee, Tom?"

"Yes—come after thee. Where art thou?"

"In a sort of a hoyle."

"A cave?"

Tom felt with his hands and feet, then he groped his way forward; the boy had ceased fiddling.

"Go on playing, Jim; I can see nowt."

Again the instrument twanged.

"It is a cave thou art in. Is it large?"

" I dun' know."

Tom put his hand in the pouch and produced the candle and the match-box. He struck a light and kindled the tallow candle. He was obliged to hold his hand over the flame, for there was enough air stirring to blow it out if unprotected, and thus imperfectly he reconnoitred the place.

Jim had taken refuge in a small cave in the face of a limestone scar—a cave rounded and smoothed with water, but dry. It ran some way in. As Tom looked about, he saw that there was dry fern and heather piled up against the side. Others before Jim had gone there and had used it for shelter—perhaps from sun or wind—and had collected material to make soft cushions.

" Why, Jim," said Tom, " we're in luck's way. I've a light and here's fuel. We'll have a fire, lad ; I'm sure thou'rt cold."

" Eh ! I am, Tom. I fiddled to keep my fingers warm."

Tom put a light to the bracken, but it was damp and would not readily burn. He swealed the tallow over it, and at length coaxed it into a blaze ; then it flared up, and he looked around. The light and the smoke alarmed some birds or bats—he could not make out which—in the recesses. They fluttered and danced about, and then, as the smoke became thicker, rushed forth.

" It's boggarts !" said Jim ; " that's why I played a hymn. I heard them before you came."

" They are gone now, Jim."

Tom considered what was to be done. There was

a possibility of rescue, if he could keep the fire burning ; it would guide searchers to the spot where he
was. But, supposing no searchers came out or came
that way, and Jim and he had to remain there till
morning, they would need the fire to keep them from
being frozen.

"Jim," said Tom ; "we must have more heather.
Where can we get it ? "

"There's that near the mouth of the hoyle," said
the boy. He crept out, and soon returned with some
heather. There was plenty without that could be
ripped up.

"That will do, Jim," said Tom ; "anyhow, for a
bit." Then he took the brandy flask and uncorked
it. "Open thy mouth, lad." He gave him a draught
of the spirit. "Now keep by the fire and warm thy
limbs. I'll fend the fire."

Tom sat over the glow, raking it together, adding
fresh fuel as required, and did not speak. He was
now thinking of Jewel. He knew that she must be
anxious about him, and in great distress. What
would she do when she found that he did not return ?
She would send down to the reservoir for some of the
navvies. Jewel had her wits about her, and would
not lose her head in an emergency. "She don't lose
her head," murmured Tom, "but she's got a way of
losing her temper."

"I say "—Jim interrupted his train of thought—
"thou won't take away my fiddle, wilt thou ? "

"I—I ?—no ! "

"Jule said thou wouldst if I got fresh. That's why
I runned away."

"That is why you ran away," repeated Tom. "Not because I beat thee?"

"No," the boy giggled; "thou didn't hurt much. But I hollered and Jule came up. Thou won't take away my fiddle?"

"No—certainly no."

The boy was satisfied, and said no more.

Then again Tom sank into a train of thought. So Jewel had been scolding and threatening Jim; and it was her doing that he had taken flight.

But this consideration did not occupy him long. He was relieved by it. It would simplify the reconciliation. He was cold, very cold, for the frosty, snowy air breathed in from the entrance. The fire was a poor affair. He must husband his material, burning a little dry heather along with some of the wet and fresh, so that there issued from his fire more smoke than flame. Still, he must be thankful to have any fire. Occasionally he put on some bracken to produce a flare, in the hopes of attracting attention. The smouldering damp heather did not emit much light. Then he went to the entrance of the cave and looked out. The snow was not falling as thickly. In half an hour it might cease altogether, and then through the darkness he would be able to see lights. That would be a comfort; though he could not venture to leave where he was till the day dawned. Lights at night are treacherous. They may be very far off, and gulfs and impassable rivers may intervene.

Tom came back to the fire. Jim had sunk beside it, and was asleep. The flicker of the fire was on his pale face. Tom leaned over to observe it. Poor boy, he was to be pitied, not blamed. As Tom looked, he saw that the upper portion of the lad's face was very like Jule's—the same forehead and delicately-drawn, gold-brown eye-brows. What long lashes Jim had! In his sleep the feebleness was effaced from his countenance, and there was a delicacy in the features, and even a beauty, which was not perceived when he was awake. "How like Jewel! How like Jewel!" said Tom, and his heart grew soft and warm and loving within him towards the poor boy.

"He'll take cold. He looks deadly white," said Tom, and he pulled off his great-coat and laid it over the sleeper. "Poor Jim! I wish I'd noticed before he hadn't his overcoat."

And, as he drew off his warm garment, he noticed by a flicker of the fire a long amber thread—long, a yard long—caught in the rough cloth.

"One of Jule's hairs," he said, and took it and twined it round his finger, and kissed it and smiled, and held it to the light, and kissed it again. "Dear Jule! dear Jule!"

CHAPTER VI.

THE JOVIAL HECKLER'S BOY.

A SHOUT ! Tom started from his reverie, threw on a handful of dry fern-leaves, and ran to the entrance.

Men with lanterns were below, apparently a long way down, and they called, and he replied. Then Tom ran back into the cave and roused Jim, who with difficulty rallied his scattered dream-laden wits ; and Tom noticed that when he opened his eyes and great mouth, at once all likeness to Jewel disappeared. He was again ugly and loutish. But Tom had a pity for him, and a love he had not felt before. He had felt what it was to have to care for a poor, helpless creature ; and he had seen in the dull face the underlying likeness to her who was dearest to him in the world.

He helped the boy to his feet.

"What is't, Tom ? Thou'rt not going to take away my fiddle ? "

"They are come," said Tom eagerly. "Come along ; they are here."

"They—they'll leave me my fiddle ? I won't go unless thou swears to me that I shall keep it."

The clouds of sleep and of suspicion were not off the boy's brain, and Tom had to be patient with him.

Presently, up the steep ascent came some of the searchers, scrambling.

"Whatever brought you up here?" they asked.

"I do not know where I am."

"In Arncliff."

What! in the great grey crags above his own house? Tom was amazed. He had wandered strangely. He could be down at home now in ten minutes. It took twenty to reach Arncliff from his door, but half the time to descend.

"There comes the moon," said one of the men. As he spoke the disc of the moon rose above Sowton Down into a space of clear sky, painting white and ghostly the fringe of snow-cloud that hung across the sky from north to south. The cold light flared over the moors deadly white, palled in snow.

Below, the lights of those who had come out in quest of Tom and Jim seemed, by contrast, not yellow, but orange. Below, beyond was something— no, someone. Surely not Jewel!

It was Jewel, indeed—come forth in the track of the men who were seeking her husband and brother. When Tom saw her he flung out his arms and away he went down the steep descent, plunging through the snow, shouting, sliding, recovering his balance, and then bounding over a snow-capped stone.

Presently one of the navvies nudged his fellow and said:

"It's not Jule a' Nort, but Jule a' Tom's, and Tom a' Jule's: they seems to belong to each other and to none beside."

"If they are so glad to see each other again," said

the man addressed, "and we've had the finding and the bringing together, we shall be tipped handsome for our trouble, and be given to drink."

"Eh! to be sure," said Tom, who overheard the remark, made purposely as an aside to be overheard. "Drink and meat and cheese you shall have. 'Tis Christmas eve. Peace on earth and good-will, and the making-up of quarrels and the patching of strife, and the sowing again of love in the field where weeds had sprung up and nigh choked the corn."

Then the whole party went to the farm, where a blazing fire filled the "house" with warmth and light and laughter. The white plastered walls, the ceiling, the floor, flushed as with pleasure at the return of the master; and the crickets were shrilling behind the jambs and back of the great fire-place, as if they also were rejoicing that he was not lost on the wold, but come home again. On the table were the trifles Tom had bought for the Christmas-tree: sparkling tin ornaments that twinkled gleefully, and oranges that asked to be eaten, and nuts that cried out to be cracked, and the great Yule candle, which every grocer in Yorkshire sends on Christmas eve to his customers, expecting to be lighted. And, more, beside the fire was a great pan of fermity—wheat and currants mixed with water and milk, and stewed— ready to be eaten, for on Christmas eve every York- shire Christian makes his supper off fermity. Now was the time for Jewel to show her powers, and she showed them, and the long deal table was rapidly spread and laden, the bowl of fermity was placed smoking on it; cheese, and "cake" (bread) and butter, and oat-scones, cold beef, smoking potatoes, and jugs of home-brewed ale—everything that was needful to furnish a good Christmas eve supper was ready to be attacked in a very short while, Jewel getting all ready whilst the men and Jim and Tom crowded about the fire to thaw themselves, and melt off their boots and breeches and coats the snow that still clung.

Then Jewel set the Yule candle on a brass candle-stick, and planted it in the midst of the table, and bade—

"Come, lads, you as have a mind to 't, fall to."

Not one was indisposed to do so, not even those two who had previously partaken of Jewel's hospitality. Their appetites had not been satisfied—only stimulated, and they ate now as lustily, as omniverously, and as long as the rest. Verily, a navvy is like a caterpillar, that eats its own weight in four and twenty hours.

When supper was over, and every bowl and plate and dish had been cleared, the wonder was that bowl and plate and dish had not been eaten as well, with the steel two-pronged fork and the knife to boot, as pickle and Yorkshire relish to the rest ; and the cauldron, and the saucepans, and the stone ale-jars on top of the rest as stomachics and digestive pills, and the red-hot coals off the hearth after them again, as stimulants to torpid livers. Then the men groaned, and thrust back from the table, and Tom said :—

"Let's all draw about t' fire, and have some hot brandy and water, and a bit of fun."

The suggestion of the master of Tuddlams was

complied with, with equal alacrity to that displayed when the call came to table from the mistress.

Then they lit their pipes and held their steaming glasses, and Tom said—

"To begin wi', lads :—

> " 'The King of Agripp
>   Built a varra great ship,
>   Ann' at the one end
>   His sweet daughter did sit.
>   If I had to tell her name,
>   I shu'd be varra much t' blame.' "

"But thou'st told it for all, lad," shouted one of the navvies, Ben by name.

"How so ?" asked another ; "I didn't hear it."

"He has, though—i' t' third line.   Her name were *Ann*.   I can cap that, though :—

> " 'As I were going over London Bridge
>   I saw a man stealing pots,
>   And the pots were his own.' "

"Yes," said Weatherall, another man.   "Thou'st told that too often, Ben.   The pot-steals were his own, and he was putting the steals " (handles) " on the pots."

"Right," said Ben.   "Black and breet, and runs without feet."

Then Jewel, looking into the circle by the fire, answered, as she carried the dish with the beef-bone away, " A flat-iron."   She halted in the doorway to the back kitchen, and asked :—

> "' A houseful, a hoyle' (hole) ' full,
> An' I can na' catch a bowlful.'"

Then said Tom, "It's t' same as I am blowing out betwixt my two lips now—reek" (smoke), and he sent forth a long spiral puff of tobacco smoke into the air above him.

"Eh! to be sure it is," said one of the men. "Come, then answer me this :—

> "' Under the earth I go,
> But on oak-leaves I stand.
> I ride on a filly that never was foaled,
> And carry a collar that never was bleached.'"

No one was able to guess this. The riddle was new to the company. Then the teller said, "A man was on his way to be hanged, and he put earth into his cap, oak-leaves in his shoes ; had the hempen cord round his neck, and rode the gallows tree."

"That's rather far stretched," said Weatherall.

"So the man thought who was dancing at the end o' the cord," answered the propounder of the riddle, and elicited a laugh. "Wick" (alive) "at both ends and dead i' t' middle ; Tom a' Tuddlams, what is that ?"

"A plough," answered Tom. "Come, tell me this :—

> "' The King of Northumberland
> Sent the Queen of Cumberland
> A bottomless vessel to put flesh and blood in.'

No one could divine the answer, so Tom sprang up, ran after Jewel, caught her round the waist, drew

her into the circle before the fire, held out her hand
on one of his, divided the rosy fingers, and pointed
to the wedding ring. "Do you see, lads? A ring o'
gou'd."

"Stay, lass!" shouted Ben, "and I'll make thee
laugh, wi' a lying tale. There was on a time five
men: t' one had no eyes, t' second had no legs, t'
third had no tongue, t' fourth had no arms, t' fifth
was neck't" (naked). "T' blind man said, 'Eh!
lads, I see a brid'" (bird). "The dumb man hollered, 'I'll shoot it!' T' man without legs said, 'I'll
run after it!' T' man without arms said, 'I'll pick
it up;' and t' neck't man said, 'Darned if I don't
pocket it!'"

Chorus of revellers, "Eh! that *is* a lee!" (lie).

"Here, Jim!" shouted Ben, "here is a riddle for
thee :—

> "'It whistles i' t' wood, it rattles i' t' town,
> It addles' (earns) 'its master many a crown.'"

Jim had been standing away from the company,
attending to his violin, wiping tenderly off it the
drops of water into which the snowflakes that had
rested on it had resolved themselves. He did not
understand riddles. He could not think, it made
him dizzy to be asked to exercise his wit. When the
trial of ingenuity in guessing conundrums had begun,
the boy had retreated from the circle to be away
from something that was teasing to him.

Now he was drawn forward, holding his violin and
looking alarmed. Why would the men worry him

and make his head spin with asking him questions he
could not answer?

"Come, now," said the men, "thou'st been out
there i' t' cold.   Take the little stool and play us
up a tune."

" But first answer the riddle," said the propounder :

> " ' It whistles i' t' wood, it rattles i' t' town,
>   It addles its master many a crown.'

" Dost thou give it up ?   Why, lad, it's a fiddle."

" Si' there, lad, sit down on the stool and play up."

" What shall I play?" asked the boy.   " ' The
Knight and the Lady'? or 'The Fish and the Ring'?
or 'Saint Joseph was an Oud Man, and an Oud Man
was he'?   No ; I'll play you ' The Jovial Heckler's
Boy.' "

" Eh ! that's right.   Give us the ' Heckler's Boy.' "

Then Jim sat on the stool, tuned his violin, and
fiddled, and as he fiddled, one of the men sang :

> " I am a jovial heckler's boy,[1]
>   And by my trade I go,
> I trudge the world all over
>   And get my living so.
>
> " I trudged the world all over,
>   A pretty fair maid I spied ;
> I axed her if shoo would go wi' me
>   And be my bonny bride.

[1] This ballad, which I believe has never before been printed,
with its curious old English air, is traditional, and was· taken
down from the lips of some " mill-lasses " in Calderdale, as well
as the riddles and stories already given.

"The pretty fair maid denyed me
 And said, 'If I do so
I shall be ruined for ever-a-day,
 And shall be loved no mo'.'

"'O how wilt thou be ruined?'
 The heckler's boy replied,
'For I am sure I will marry thee
 An' work for thee, my bride.'

"'Now hou'd thy tongue from chattering,
 An' tell me none such tales,
For thou'rt a jovial heckler's boy
 And naught thy word avails.'

"'How dost thou know me so, my dear?
 How dost thou know my trade?'
'I know thee by t' fringes o' thy apron,
 Of thy apron,' she said.

"'By t' fringes of thy apron, lad,
 And by thy slender shoe;
Thy stockings they are as white as snow,
 So that's how I know you.'

"I could not help for laughing out
 To hear the lass say so.
I threw my arms around her waist,
 And away we both did go.

"Shoo brought a glass all in her hand,
 An' filled it to the brim;
'My love shall drink good den to me,
 An' I'll drink like to him.'"

When the song had proceeded as far as the pen-
ultimate verse, all the voices took it up:

"I could not help for laughing out
 To hear the lass say so!"

Then Tom sprang to his feet, passed his arm around his wife's waist, and sang lustily:

> " I threw my arms around her waist,
>   And away we both did go."

And suiting the action to the word, he spun Jewel about, and danced round with her in the contracted circle before the fire; then scattering it, he broke through, and danced about in the kitchen with her, waving his glass of hot grog above his head, then putting it to her lips and to his own, and spilling it over them both.

"Have done!" said Jewel. "Thou a'most sent my skirts into t' fire and set me in a blaze."

"It's Christmas eve!" exclaimed Tom. Then to Jim: "Strike up a dance, lad, and me and Jule shall dance in Christmas day."

The men cleared a space, thrust back the table; some jumped upon it, and seated themselves thereon. Ben caught up Jim and the stool together, and heaved him up on the table, where he could fiddle as from a gallery. The boy was in his element now. He struck up a waltz, and played first slowly, but gradually quickened his pace.

Jewel had hesitated, shrunk away at first; but the strong arm of Tom was about her, and his heart was beating against her shoulder. He put his chin on her head and drew it against his breast. She moved it away to utter a word of remonstrance, and, looking up, her eyes met those of her husband, and such a flood of love streamed from them, that her heart gave a leap, she forgot her objection, rested her head where he had drawn it, and danced with him. The navvies clapped their hands, and sang or trumpeted through closed lips the air of the waltz, and kicked the table to the time.

Then Jim played "heel and toe," and Tom and Jewel danced that; and Ben on the table, who set up to be a wag and a clown, began to throw out his legs, heel and toe, as he sat, and to torture his body and face and arms into grotesque postures, and to emit absurd noises. Also Weatherall got the iron empty kettle, in which the hot water had been boiled for the grog, and put it between his knees, and hammered on it as if it were a gong or a drum.

Suddenly Jim changed the tune to a polka, and the two wheeled round faster and ever faster. Jewel's face was on fire, her neckkerchief had fallen, and as she danced she entangled it with her feet, and danced over it, and caught it in her shoe, and kicked away her shoe and the kerchief together. How well they danced! How they whirled and kept the tread! Her skirts flapped past the fire and made it blaze up with the sudden draught, then they were flung round the legs of Tom as he spun along. Her hair came loose behind, and she disengaged her hand to put it up; but down it came, and, as the amber tresses flew about with the firelight on them, the men jumped off the table and up from their stools, and came caper-ing, dancing around them, catching the end of her locks, circling round the circling pair, and then—stopped short; for, from outside came the song of the carolers :—

> " Christians, awake, salute the happy morn,
>   Whereon the Saviour of the world was born."

Tuddlams was the last house they visited that night, and already the grey dawn was showing.

CHAPTER VII.

THE HECKLER'S BOY, IN MINOR.

"AMANTIUM iræ amoris integratio est." That we learned in our old Eton Latin grammar, and we always believed, on the strength of that adage, that the quarrels of lovers are the renewal of love. So it is popularly asserted that thunderstorms clear the air. Our acquaintance with thunderstorms teaches us that this assertion is not based on experience, but on desire. When the weather has been bad, and a tempest comes on, we trust that the nasty weather, having reached a climax, will give over being nasty and will smile. But is it so? We doubt it; we are even positive that this is not the case. Our experience proves the contrary—that a thunderstorm unsettles the weather for an indefinite period after it, and that blue sky and laughing sun do not succeed it; or, if they do, they appear fitfully between squalls and cloud.

Now, if a quarrel were the reintegration of love we should rather hail a quarrel. When we found love growing cool, and little breezes blow, and tears begin to rain about trifles, then, just as Franklin sent up a kite to attract lightning and showers, so should we provoke a quarrel for the pleasure of having it over, and for the sake of the reintegration and restoring and reblazing up again of languishing love.

But it is not the case. A quarrel between lovers, so far from reintegrating, goes far to totally disintegrate love.

"Well," said Jewel on Christmas day, "this is the first time that I've not been able to go to church at Christmas. I don't feel any other than a Jew or a heathen; and you know why I cannot go. I daresay there will be no blessing on the coming year, as I've not asked it this day."

"But, Jule," argued Tom, "why should you not go to church, if you wish, this evening?"

"This evening! Thank you—in the night and cold. I had enough of going out of a bitter winter night after you last night. No, thank you! I have not been able to go to church this morning, so I suppose I must be a heathen."

"But, Jule—"

"It is all your fault. I couldn't pray if I went to church after last night. I should shame to be seen by decent folk. What did you take me for—to make me dance, to pull me about before all those men? Do you think I married thee to practise to become one of them little figures that go round on a barrel-organ?"

"I thought thou liked it, Jule."

"I like it! Thou never asked me."

"Jule—" said Tom, anxious to change the topic, "haven't thou looked in the pretty mirror I bought thee yesterday?"

"Mirror!" exclaimed Jewel. "You brought it here to insult me. You made me dance before all those men, till my kerchief came loose and fell off, and then my shoe went away, and, last of all, my hair came down, and there were all of them dancing and capering round about me, holding on to the ends of my hair. I never was so ashamed in my life! And you, my husband—you who ought to protect and care for your wife—you expose her to this shame." Jewel began to cry. Tom was alarmed. It was a bad sign when she began to address him with "you" instead of "thou."

"And when you've almost danced every rag off my back, you say, 'Go and look at thyself i' t' glass.'"

"I did not say that, Jule!"

"I saw thee look it in thy eyes. And all those men staring at me, and me with scarce a stitch o' clothes on."

"Jule, you had lost a shoe, that was all."

"And my kerchief."

"But that you only put on when you went out of doors after me."

"Do you call it naught having my hair all down, and the hair-pins sanding the house-floor?"

"Jule," said Tom, "I wish thou'd look in thy new glass I bought thee now, and thou'd see thy beauty gone; thy eyes arn't bright, thy cheeks are red, and thy lips—"

"Oh, I know I'm a fright in thy eyes. I never was much, except just for a week or two, and then thou wast ready to cast me aside. No, I will never, never look in that glass. Some day, when thou'st lost me, thou can'st ask some other lass—some one with a pretty face, whose eyes are bright, and whose cheeks are lilies and roses, and whose lips are worth kissing

and full o' smiles—thou can'st ask her to look in it—
I will not.   Keep it for her."

"Thou art tired, poor lass," said Tom.   "And because thou'rt tired, thy temper is ruffled."

"Of course I'm tired.   How should I not be tired ?
First, I have to be rambling over the wolds and fells
after thee, because thou can't bide at home."

"Eh ! Jule ! I went after Jim at thy bidding."

"That may be so ; but what made Jim run
away?"

"Thou didst flay" (frighten) "him with making
him think I'd take away his fiddle."

"It was not that.   It was because he was in
dread for his life.   Thou didst poise" (kick) "and
beat the poor lad—"

"You are unjust, Jule."

"I know I'm all that is bad in thine eyes.   Other
folk may think better of me.   I wish I were dead ! I
wish I were dead !   I'd like to cast myself into the
reservoir, or down one of the pot-holes, to be out of
my wretchedness and away from thee."

"From me, Jule ?"

"Eh ! I've had enough of thee, after last night,
putting me to shame before all those men, after thou
hadst beaten nigh to death my poor brother.   Oh,
that ever I married thee ! That ever I did ! I curse
the day !"

"Jule ! Dost thou mean this ?   Hast thou ceased
to love me ?"

"Long ago.   I hate you."

He heaved a long sigh ; stood thinking.

"Very well, Jule, I'll trouble thee no more.

"' Shoo brought a glass all in her hand,
　　An filled it to the brim ;
　' My love shall drink good-bye to me,
　　An' I'll drink like to him.' "

He was gone.

CHAPTER VIII.

JEWEL dished up the roast beef, and saw that the
plum-pudding was ready in the pot to be dished up
when noon struck—the hour of the early dinner in the
farmhouse, but Tom did not appear. She waited till
half-past and then sat down with Jim and ate her
Christmas dinner in gloom, and with a tear of vexation
gathering in her eyes. When evening closed in, snow
began to fall thickly.

"Now, Jim," said Jewel, "Tom brought in a beautiful tree yesterday, and nuts, and oranges, and candles ;
but we could not have the tree on Christmas eve, so
let us amuse ourselves together with dressing it, that
we may have it on the evening of Christmas ; and,
Jim, I've knitted six pairs of the most beautiful warm
socks for Tom, and he knows nowt about it, and
will be pleased when he finds that sort o' apple hanging for him on t' tree."

But after the tree was made ready with all the
beautiful contrivances provided for its adornment, Tom
did not come. Jewel went to the door, and looked
out into the snow that fell in blinding fleeces, large
and fast.

"Wherever can he be ?" she asked.

At dinner-time she was angry, because she thought

he stayed away to annoy her ; now she became uneasy, thinking he was staying away too long. Annoyance might be carried too far ; well—the night was bad, and to trudge home through the deep snow would be a labour—up hill, too, for no doubt he had gone to Kebroyd. Perhaps he had gone to church ; in that event he would not be home till late. The night would be pitch-dark, the moon did not rise till late ; he had not the lantern with him. Well, he would have a tedious and unpleasant walk. She was glad of it, the more tedious and unpleasant the better. It would serve him right for staying away. She would not give him the socks now. As he did not come home in time, she would have the Christmas-tree without a present for him, and so punish him. He would feel that, and he must be made to feel uncomfortable if he gave his wife occasion to be anxious.

As the night drew on and Tom did not return, Jewel became alarmed ; but she was far from supposing that he had taken mortal offence at her words.

"I did speak a bit sharp," she argued with herself ; " but men don't mind that. They've their consciences thick-skinned as rhinoceros hide, and unless one speaks sharp they don't feel. I'll give him the six pairs of socks when he comes home, and he'll forget all about what I said. Men ha'n't got much o' memories."

She had removed the socks from the tree ; now she hung them on it again.

Ten o'clock struck and Tom had not returned. Jim was nodding by the fire, wearied with not having had proper rest the night before.

Jewel went to him and touched him.

"Is t' tree alight and ready?" he asked, starting up.

"No, Jim. We shan't have it till Tom comes back. He is out. He went down to church at Kebroyd, and the snow has come on so thick, and he not having a light, has thought best to stay there. He'll be home i' t' morning"—she spoke what she hoped and believed, or tried to believe—"Jim! go to bed, lad, thou needst sleep."

It was unlike Tom, always thoughtful, leaving her in uncertainty. Why had he not made an effort, got a lantern from an acquaintance, and made a push to get through the snow? If he could not come himself, why did he not send some one to tell her he was detained?

She slept as little that night as she had slept the night before. All next day snow fell, and the moors were deeply buried. There had not been much wind, so there were no heavy drifts, but the white sheet lay pretty evenly, and very deeply over everything.

Jewel consulted Matthew next morning. He had not seen his master. She despatched him to the reservoir, and, if he heard nothing of him there, to Kebroyd. After several hours spent by Jewel in suspense that would not let her remain quiet in the house, Matthew returned. No one that he could learn had seen or heard anything of Tom a' Tuddlams on Christmas day.

Not a trace, not a report of his having been seen reached Jewel on that day, or after.

Then Jewel remembered Tom's last words to her—

> "My love shall drink good-bye to me,
> An' I'll drink like to him."

Did he mean that seriously? Did he mean a long good-bye? Her heart stood still at the thought. But though Jewel began, reluctantly, to fear that Tom would not return, she was very far from supposing that she had driven him from his home. She racked her brains to think what had become of him. She supposed that after the quarrel had broken out again on fresh grounds, he had flung away in a huff, and had, perhaps, gone over the moor and lost his way—perhaps had fallen into the reservoir, perhaps into a pot; there were quaking bogs on those moors to engulf the wanderer who treads incautiously upon them. She turned faint at the thought that he might be dead.

Some one suggested that he might have gone to Ossett to see some of his old acquaintances there at Christmas. She wrote to a friend there to inquire, and learned, so far as her friend could find, he had not been seen in Ossett. Old Matthew asked whether it was the way of Tom to go for a spree to one of the big towns, because old Uncle Nick did that occasionally, and drank for a fortnight till he had spent all his money, and then came back.

The fortnight had passed and Tom had not returned. January passed and still no tidings of Tom. No tidings all February. The Christmas-tree was put in its pan, outside the house; there was earth with the roots, and the old pan had holes in it. The tree would live. As for the tapers and gewgaws Jewel thrust them out of sight in a drawer.

In March came a thaw—a rapid thaw—and the white world, in a day and a night, under pouring rain and a westerly wind, became black.

A few days after the thaw, old Martha a' Samuel's —an aged, very poor woman, who was thought to be a witch, who blessed white swellings, and took away warts, and discovered lost articles, and removed spells—came one day to Tuddlams holding a red kerchief in her hand.

"Dost 'a know this?" she asked of Jewel.

"Yes," answered the mistress of Tuddlams; "yes; where didst thou find it?"

"I found it at the very edge o' the Boggarts' Well Hole, one end caught in a bleg" (bramble) "bush, or it might have been washed or blown away."

"At the Boggarts' Well!" Jewel's head swam. She put her hands to her temples.

"Eh! to be sure. And if that be thy man's, how came it there?"

Exactly—how came it there? Jewel could not speak.

"To my mind," said the old woman, "it seems that Tom a' Tuddlams must have gone that road, and what with the snow and the darkness coming on, he may have slipped and fallen down into t' pot-hole. But the bleg, wi' its thorns, caught the handkerchief and held it. He wouldn't cast a good handkerchief away. He lost it somehow. And how came it caught by a bleg unless he were falling, and it held to the kerchief as were sticking out o' his pocket?"

"The pot must be searched."

"Eh, dear life!" exclaimed Martha. "However

I

wilt thou do that? Why, if thou goes nigh it, and listens wi' thy ear over t' hoyle, thou canst hear water running and roaring far below. If a chap was to fall in, he'd be swept away—the Lord knows where —for nobody yet has found out where the water comes to daylight that is heard running below the earth in the Boggarts' Well."

"I'll ne'er believe it! I ne'er will!" cried Jewel, wringing her hands. "It would be too dreadful; and my dear, good Tom! The Lord is merciful! He would not suffer it."

"Then where be he?" asked Martha.

Jewel threw herself down on the bench beside the table, laid her arms on the table and her head on her hands, and burst into a storm of tears.

"I cannot bear it!" she cried, choking with sobs; "I cannot bear it! If I only knew where he was! But not to know if he be alive or dead!"

"Not to know," said old Matthew, who came in, "whether he mayn't be still on the spree in Halifax, or Huddersfield, or Sheffield. Why, bless thee, he was brought up i' towns, and this was too lonely for him. He'd money i' his pocket when he disappeared. Take my word for it, he's laiking at one o' the towns where he used to be wi' his father when a boy."

"Oh, Matt!" she cried, "I'll. give thee brass" (money) "if thou'lt go to Doncaster, and Pontefract, and Sheffield, and Huddersfield, and Ossett—wherever I can call to mind that Tom has been in former days—and ax if he has been seen there."

"Nay," answered the old man, "I must look after the farm, and I should never know how to begin that road. Get some younger man to go. There be Ben, the navvy. They've just about finished the new reservoir, and the water is to be let in to-day and out o' the oud one. Then Ben's occupation will be gone. Send him. He's a shrewd chap."

A rap at the door, and in came Ben himself.

"Mistress Jule a' Nort a' Nowheer," said he, "thou must come down directly to t' reservoir. The water ha' been let out o' t' oud pond, and a dead man ha' been found i' it ; but the eels ha' played the deuce wi' his face, and nobody can make nowt out o' him, except by the clothes, and them as does must be his kin. Come along and see if it be Tom. Whomsoever he be, t' folks as drink water out o' this reservoir ha' been drinking soup for some time made out o' dead man and oud clothes."

Sick at heart, wild with misery, horror-struck at the discovery, Jewel went with the man, and was led into the parlour of the little tavern, where the corpse was destined to lie till the coroner had come and sat on it, and an intelligent jury had decided who he was and how he came by his death.

Jewel came away with face livid and eyes dilated with horror. No, no; it was not he. It could not be he. She could identify nothing. The hair was the same colour as that of Tom or near about, but the clothes were not his—at least, she thought not. No, no; that was not he.

Accordingly the coroner and jury sat on the dead man and pronounced that he was unknown, and that the occasion of his death was unknown. Nevertheless, a strong impression remained in the minds of the people of Kebroyd that this was the body of Tom. For—they reasoned—one man disappears, and a body is found, and nobody knows of a second man having been lost—it stands to reason that the corpse belongs to the man we know was lost. As for Jule, poor thing—well, it's natural she should cling to hope that her husband is still alive.

There were times, nights—long sleepless nights—when Jewel doubted whether this were not really the body of her husband. It was true that she could not identify the clothing ; but that had been sodden in water and mud, and was so disfigured and dis-coloured that she might have been deceived. The hair—the hair was the same colour. But no! Those were not his boots. She could swear he had no boots such as were worn by that horrible corpse. No ; that was not Tom—unless he had changed his boots somewhere.

Then, on other nights, she thought of his red hand-kerchief by the Boggarts' Well which lay on the flank of Scalefell. How could it get there unless he had been there ? How could it be caught in a bramble spray, unless it had been caught from his pocket as he lay on the ground ? She would rather think of him drowned in the reservoir than carried under-ground by the mysterious stream whose exit was unknown. Again, at other times, mostly at night, she considered the suggestion of old Matt. Was it likely that he had tired of the loneliness of Tuddlams, tired of *her*, and gone away to a more stirring, gay life, such as he had, or might have known, of old ? Oh, rather than that, in the Boggarts' Well—rather the drowned man found in the reservoir—rather dead than alive and unfaithful to her.

The summer passed.

Jewel, with the assistance of Matthew, carried on the farm with prudence.

No tidings of Tom, except a letter from her friend at Ossett, that someone had said he had heard somebody say that Tom had been seen somewhere. But next week came a letter from the same friend to say that it was a mistake. Someone had heard somebody else say that someone very like Tom Greenwood had been seen somewhere.

Autumn passed, and the suspense was the same. The uneasiness, the unhappiness of Jewel grew greater, instead of diminishing. And now a new name was given her—" Jule All Alone."

CHAPTER IX.

IN THE MIRROR.

SUCH is the perversity of mankind, Jule acquired the title of "Jule All Alone" just as she ceased to be all alone, for in September she became a mother of a dear little son, who was christened Thomas, and who was destined to be the future Tom a' Tuddlams, or Tom a' Tom's a Will's a' Joe's. Consequently Jule was not alone; yet she was in another sense more alone than ever, for she felt doubly desolate in having a child without a father to show it to, to think of and care for the little one. She tried to trace the likeness to the old Tom a' Tuddlams in the face of the young Tom a' Tuddlams, and fondly fancied that she found it.

One day, shortly before Christmas, old Martha, the witch, arrived at the farm; she had come to remind Jewel, by her presence, that on the former Christmas she had received a widow's dole.

Jewel bade the old creature be seated by the fire, and she showed her the babe.

"Eh!" said the hag, "I've brought him salt, and an egg, and matches. As thou didst not bring t' bairn to my house, I've brought t' puddening to t' bairn."[1] Then, when the three gifts had been disposed of, with thanks from the mother, "Si' there, lass," said the old woman, "I've brought the weeds and onfas," and she offered her some blue woollen threads. "Thou must wear these about thy neck all the time thou'rt nursing t' bairn."

Jewel accepted the threads.

"Whativer thou does," said the old woman, "don't let t' bairn see into a looking-glass afore he's a year old."

"What would happen?"

"Thou'd best not ask," said Martha shaking her head. "But there, Christmas eve is coming, and if thou wants to know how to be sure where thy Tom is, whether he be alive or whether he be dead, I can tell thee how to discover."

"Doest thou know anything? Hast thou heard?" Jewel gasped, her colour went, then flushed her cheeks, then she again became deadly white. "Oh, Martha! if thou knowest aught, tell me."

"Nay, lass," replied the hag, "it's none for me to tell thee. It is for thine own sel' to find out."

"But how can I find out? I've been trying every way I can think of all this twelvemonth, and not a word about him can I hear. I cannot tell if I'm a widow and my bairn an orphan, or whether Tom be alive. He may be ill somewhere—I shall go mad if I do not know."

---

[1] These three gifts are made to every child when visiting a house. It is called, in some places, "Puddening." Sometimes silver—generally a threepenny-piece is added—or takes the place of the matches.

"I tell thee, lass, it is for thee to find out."

"How can I, Martha ? Tell me the way."

"Hast thou never heard o' looking i' t' glass on Christmas eve at night ? On Christmas eve the spirits of the dead are all about in the wind, and if thou looks i' t' glass, and thy husband or thy true love be dead, thou'lt see him looking over thy shoulder ; and if he has been drowned, he'll be dripping with water; and if he's been burned, he'll be all in flames; and if he's been killed wi' a knife, thou'lt see t' wounds bleeding."

"And if he is alive, and elsewhere, and—and—happy and has forgotten his home ? "

"Then thou must say t' Lord's prayer three times again, thou'st said it already three times, and lighted the Yule candle. If he don't come then, then thou sayest t' prayer over three times again, and backwards, and then thou'lt force him to come and show hissen, just as he is."

"And if—"

"And if he's been untrue to thee, and forgotten thee, then thou'lt see his face over one o' thy shoulders, and the face of that other over thy second shoulder."

Jewel shuddered and covered her eyes. "I had rather know nothing than risk it."

"Nay, lass, there's no risk. And, there—I'd forgot. Thou mun take a sprig o' mistletoe and set it over the mirror, and then light the Yule candle. An' thou must be alone, and nobody must disturb thee or know aught about it."

Again Jewel shuddered ; it seemed an unholy venture to call the spirit of the dead to appear to her, to force the spirit of the living to come at her call and show itself in the mirror, not face to face—that would be horrible enough—but looking over her shoulder, with the eyes fixed on her eyes, in the glass !

But however she busied herself, the thought of the mirror and the vision haunted her. A year had passed —a year all but a day, and an opportunity presented itself which could not be seized again for twelve months. She might at last learn what had become of her husband, her suspense might be brought to an end. It would be a satisfaction to know the worst ; but which was the worse ? Which would she rather see ! the double of the living man, perhaps alone, perhaps not ? or the ghost of the dead ?

She thought about the suggestion of Martha all the day on Christmas eve, and when evening came, she had made her mind to the adventure. As she nursed her babe, she stooped over it, and whispered in its ear, "To-night thy mother shall know all, and whether thou'rt a fatherless bairn or no. It mun be, it mun be ! I cannot bear the doubt any longer."

When the darkness had set in, Jim was troublesome ; he was fidgeting about the house, going up stairs and then coming down.

"What is it, lad ? What dost thou want ? "

"Jule," said the boy, " I'm looking for Christmas. Matt said I mun have my tree to-night."

"Tree !" exclaimed Jewel, then thought. " Aweel, lad," she said, " there's the tree still living and green, outside the door, that Tom took up last Christmas. Thou canst have that, and in yonder drawer are tapers and sparkling things, and thou canst take

them out, and do what thou likes with them, only "—
she said emphatically—" thou mun be quiet, and not
disturb me. Si' there, t' baby has gone to sleep, and
I'll lig " (lay) " him i' t' cradle, and don't thee disturb
him whatever thou dost. I'm going upstairs, and
don't thee come up, mind."

Jewel had procured a sprig of mistletoe, and this
she took in her hand. She took in the other the
Yule candle sent her by the grocer at Kebroyd. It
was green. She went upstairs to her room in the
dark.

Now Jewel recollected the looking-glass that Tom
had brought her that same night a twelvemonth ago,
and which she had put aside on a shelf, with a towel
thrown over it. She had never looked into it since he
gave it her.

She struck a light with one of the matches the hag
had given to the babe, and with it kindled the long
green Yule candle, which she set on a candlestick
upon the dressing-table. Then she went to the shelf,
withdrew the towel, and, taking the heavy swing
mirror, placed it on the table. With a strong pin she
affixed the sprig of mistletoe above it. The green
candle she set beside the looking-glass.

Her heart began to fail her. Was she right in
venturing on this experiment? What if the vision
she saw were to send her mad? She had heard of
such things occurring. If she did see something
dreadful, whom could she reckon on to assist her?
Were she to shriek out, there was no man in the
house but Jim.

She had heard that if on Christmas night, in the

dark, one walks round the room, one can hear the
steps and feel the brush of the clothes of another
walking in an opposite direction. Who that other is
none could tell.

This day—twelve months ago! Jewel knelt down
before the glass and turned it, so that, looking up, she
could see her own face in it, and also—when it
appeared—that other face she desired, yet dreaded,
seeing. No, that would not do. She could not bear
the glass thus. She turned it up again, so that kneel-
ing she could not see into it, but must rise to her feet
and stand before it to see what she sought.

Then she knelt, and waited a moment.

How hushed the house was! Jim hardly stirred,
so engrossed was he with his treasures.

She said the "Our Father" in a low and tremulous
voice. Then she paused.

This day—twelve months ago!

She remembered how angry she had been with
Tom about the tree, about his beating Jim. Yet—
had he not acted rightly? The boy must be broken
off the trick of going among the navvies and drinking
spirits. Did the chastisement hurt him? Jim had
himself told her it did not ; he had howled to awake
her sympathy and provoke her interference. What
had she said to Tom? She remembered now every
word—every cruel, cutting word. She remembered
the look of pain that came in his face as she spoke.
What—what were the words he then said? She
recalled them now—now for the first time ; "Jewel,
forgive and forget. Give me thy hand, lass! This
be Christmas eve, when there should be peace on

earth and good will among men, most of all in a home between man and wife."

And what had been her answer ?—

"There shall be no peace between us, no good will."

Jewel put her hand to her brow and wiped the cold drops of sweat that ran over it. Then she stood up, trembling as she rose, and looked into the mirror, and saw her own face, white, with the sweat-drops forming on the brow, and the eyes, large, full of fear, and with dark rings about them.

That was all she saw—herself.

Then she remembered that she had said the Lord's Prayer but once, and the apparition did not appear till it had been repeated thrice.

She knelt once more, and slowly, and with a broken voice and trembling lips, said " Our Father " again.

That night—a twelvemonth ago !

Tom had gone forth, after she had spoken so un-kindly, and had brought her this mirror, and the little candles and tin ornaments for her tree ; he bore her no ill-will, though she had spoken so cruelly to him. Then she had not thanked him, but sent him forth after her brother. Oh, he had been well-nigh lost on that snowy night, along with her brother ; but he had saved Jim. Without him Jim would never have been recovered. He would have slept in the cave and died as he slept.

How had she acknowledged what he had done for Jim and for her ? He had been merry that night, and she had yielded at the time to the spirit of joviality that sprang up; but next morning had regretted it, being angry and ill-humoured because tired, and had vented her ill-humour and anger on her husband.

She had read of David dancing in his joy of heart, and of Michal his wife sneering at him. What followed? David put away Michal. And she—Jewel—had been like Michal: she had scoffed at her husband because, in the gaiety of his heart, and in his gladness at having come safe home and to her, and in his love and delight at being able to clasp her, he had spun her about in waltz and polka to Jim's fiddling. Now the same fate had fallen on her that fell on Michal: she had lost her husband; she was bereaved—Jule All Alone, Jule the Desolate.

She staggered to her feet once more, and again looked into the glass, and saw herself, and herself only.

She struck her head with her hand.

"I am distracted! I have forgotten; I have said the prayer but twice."

Then she fell on her knees again.

That night—two years ago!

Two years ago! Why, then she was a poor mill-girl, almost starving, and seeing her brother nearly starving, too. Then Tom had come and offered to stand by her in her need; and two years ago to-morrow they were made one. What would have happened to her had not Tom then come to her aid? There had been nothing for her—or at least for Jim—but the workhouse; and it would have been misery for her to have to part with that poor silly brother. Tom had kept Jim by her. Tom had been very good to Jim for her sake, because he loved her ; and how he loved her now she saw plainly. On six shillings a week she had maintained her brother and herself, so scantily ; and now she and Jim lived in plenty; but Tom, who had brought them into the land that flowed with milk and honey, Tom was cast out from it, cast down, may be into death, by her hand, by that hand he had taken to lift her out of poverty.

Though she was shivering with cold and fear, yet a rush of blood mantled her brow and cheek, and dyed her neck, and in her shame she laid her head on the ground. Then she heard her blood beat like hammers in her ears ; there was a bounding of pulses in her temples, and noises as of tramping feet behind her, on the stairs, in the room.

With a cry of terror and shame and yearning un- utterable, she leaped to her feet, and looked once more in the glass and again *saw herself.*

Yes, she had seen herself that night as 'she had never seen herself before. And in her agony of self-remorse and longing for pardon she cried out :

"Oh, Tom ! oh, Tom ! oh, Tom !"

And suddenly, at the word, saw his face looking over her shoulder in the glass.

She stood frozen to the spot ; her heart ceased to beat. She could not speak. Her wide, distended eyes were riveted on the mirror; and lo ! there was a third face reflected there, looking over her other shoulder. Her bosom heaved with a spasmodic sob. A cloud came over her eyes, but cleared again, and she saw that other face was the face of her babe.

"Jule!"

With a cry she turned.

In the mirror under the mistletoe were three clasped together.

CHAPTER X.

ON EARTH, PEACE.

How long did they thus remain, those three, clasped together? Not long, for the babe protested.

"Oh, Tom! oh, Tom! where have you been?"

"In Lancashire."

"Lancashire!"

No one had for a moment dreamed of his crossing to that side of the fells.

"And what hast thou been doing?"

"Never mind, lass: working and waiting, and wishing to come back to thee."

"Why didst thou not come?"

He hesitated a while, then he said:

"I thought it best to keep away a bit."

"And how didst thou hear of the babe?"

"As I was coming here I spoke to Matt, and he told me. When I entered I saw the cradle, and took up the bairn; then I came on to thee, upstairs. Jim said thou wast here."

"Oh, Tom! I am fain thou'rt back. Yea, lad, it were right. I'm glad thou went, and I'm glad thou'rt come. Tom, I'll never drive thee away again. I've seen that to-night I never knew before—I've seen my Real Self."

Then they heard Jim calling, and they went down

the stairs, holding hands, and holding the babe between them ; and as they passed through the door
into the room, their eyes, that had been in the dark,
were dazzled by the light, for Jim had kindled all the
tapers on the tree, after he had set them up ; and now
he caught his fiddle from the nail where it hung, drew
the bow across it, and began to play—

> "Christians, awake ! salute the happy morn
> Whereon the Saviour of the world was born."

And, as he played, the carolers from Kebroyd, who
had come up to Tuddlams, burst forth in the song :

> " Christians, awake ! salute the happy morn
> Whereon the Saviour of the world was born."

And Tom and Jewel tried to sing, also, but their voices
failed. He had his arm over her shoulder, and she
hers about his waist, and with her other arm she sustained her babe, which looked at the sparkling tree
and crowed.

The voices of the carolers died away. Jim ceased
playing, but the wind blowing up the vale wafted
on its breath the music of the Kebroyd Christmas
bells.

K

AT THE Y.

CHAPTER I.

THE FOOT OF THE Y.

ONE dreary evening late in November, a "dry drizzle" enveloped hill and vale in grey haze. A dry drizzle would be a wet drizzle anywhere but in Devon: there the term is comparative. It wets to the bone in two hours, whereas a driving rain drenches in half-an-hour, and a thunderstorm in five minutes. Therefore a drizzle is dry. Q. E. D.

The young woman plodding forwards with a babe a few months old in her arms had been out in it many hours, and the dry drizzle had consequently saturated her garments as thoroughly as if she had been plunged in the river.

The evening was fast falling. The mist hung so thick over the hills and clung so tenaciously to the trees that there was no saying where hill and tree ended and sky began. Already here and there a cottage window was flashing with light and making a halo about it. One bright and glorious halo irradiated

the darkness at the bottom of the valley where four
cross roads met, bright and glorious as that surrounding
the head of a saint.   It surrounded, however, nothing
other than a shop window exhibiting tins of Colman's
mustard and Reckitt's blue.

The young woman was so wet and weary that she
could scarce drag herself along.   She stopped at the
shop door and asked the way to Longabrook, learned
it, and with a sigh went on.   She had descended the
great moorland ridge of Heathfield from the direction
of Tavistock, and had entered a coombe, in summer
sweet with pines, and pleasant with the rippling of a
falling brook.

Her direction lay through a lane, deep between
dripping trees that wept on her cold tears as she went
by, and over stones that threw stumbling-blocks before
her feet.   Presently she came out on a widening in
the lane, and saw a barn built on a bit of slaty rock,
the wall of slaty stone, so that one could not say
where the rock left off and the wall began.   Against
the end of the barn the rock fell away abruptly, and a
gate gave access to a farmyard on a slope, and was
so contrived that all the drainage, rich and dark as
treacle, ran out at the gate into the road and was
wasted.   Within the yard was the farmhouse, low, of
stone with granite windows, and thatched.   The
traveller stood at the gate and looked hesitatingly at
the lonely house.   It lay with its back to the south
against a wooded hill; no sunlight could ever enter its
gloomy rooms.   There was nothing inviting about its
appearance, and the young woman's heart trembled

as she opened the gate with numb fingers and crossed the road.

Before she reached the door she was intercepted by a tall, bony woman, who emerged from one of the "linneys" or cowsheds.

"What be you a-wanting here?" she asked, in a hard voice.

"Is this Longabrook?"

"It be; what next?"

"Does Mr. Doidge live here?"

"I reckon he does."

"I want," said the young woman, timidly, "I want to speak to Ephraim Doidge."

The woman eyed her from head to foot; her grey eyes contracted and stabbed like steel daggers. She did not speak. She was gathering ideas. She drew her own conclusions at last, and said :—

"You'm a stranger in these parts, I reckon?"

"I am. I come from Ireland."

"And what be you asking after Ephraim for? What has he to do along of the likes of you?"

"I knew Ephraim when he was a soldier in Ireland.'

"If you are come all the way from Ireland after Ephraim, you've got a long road to go back."

The strange girl looked at the hard woman with supplicating eyes. "You are not his mother," she said faintly, "I know you are not. He told me his mother was dead—glory be her bed. Where is he? I must see him myself."

"No, I am not his mother," answered the woman, sharply. "I thank the Lord as has delivered my soul out of the paw of lovers and from the mouth of marrying men. I've never had a man to rule me with a rod of iron, nor a child to break my heart with fermented liquour. This comes of Ephraim not taking the pledge. If he'd been a teetotal he'd never hev gone to the Stag's Head and met with a 'cruting sergeant, and taken the Queen's shilling and been shipped to Ireland and met with you."

The woman had worked herself up to white fury. She turned abruptly and ran to the mow-hay, where a young man was cutting hay from the rick for the horses and cows.

" Come here, Eph ! " she cried, in discordant tones ringing with anger. " Come here, and see what comes of it all."

" Comes of what, Aunt Judy ? " asked the young man, composedly. " Don't excite your bile over nothing."

" Comes of drink, man, of drink ! "

" Drink, drink ! " echoed Ephraim ; " one would suppose I were a toper to hear you talk. I never take more than is good for me, and you cannot deny it."

" Ah ! you moderate drinkers are a worse curse to the county than confirmed drunkards. Follow me, and see what comes of moderate drinking." Then, controlling herself for a moment, she said, bitterly ; " There be two in the yard afore the house calling for you as never ought to be there. Go and pack them off whence they came."

" I am cutting hay, aunt, I will attend presently."

"You must come now and drive them off the premises, or I'll tell your father to load the gun and fire buckshot at 'em." Then she grasped him by the arm and drew him through the gate and confronted him with the traveller. There was still some light in the sky, and by the light Ephraim saw the anxious, dejected face and knew it. He started back.

"Bridget! you here! my God! what brought you ——?" he hesitated, and did not conclude his question.

She threw back her shawl and exposed the sleeping infant at her breast, then raised her heavy eyes and looked him full in the face. That was her answer.

Ephraim put his hand to his brow, and looked unsteadily from the young to the old woman. He was so taken by surprise that he did not know what to say or do.

Ephraim Doidge was a tall, strongly-built, young man, with fair hair and frank blue eyes. He had a healthy colour in his cheeks, and was a good-looking, honest, and manly fellow, as every one who saw him admitted. But his lips were weak and his eyes wanting in steadiness, so that his aunt had some reason for saying to her brother, "You should not have called him Ephraim, the fruitful, but Rueben, because that, unstable as water, he will not excel."

Bridget's knees shook under her, her face was deadly pale, but two hectic spots burnt in her cheeks for a moment and then went out like extinguished candles. Her large, dark eyes were brimming with tears. The old woman was also pale, her brows were knitted, and her teeth clenched as with lockjaw. Her hands also were contracted spasmodically. She did not withdraw her stabbing eyes for a moment from the unfortunate girl who tottered and shivered before her.

Ephraim had been a soldier. His time had been up some six months ago, and he had returned home, had thrown off the scarlet and donned the fustian and corduroy. With that admirable genius for doing the wrong thing which characterises England, she has substituted short for long service in the army. In other words, she spends a huge sum of money in training raw bumpkins and turning them into soldiers, and, as soon as they have been manufactured into serviceable articles, breaks and throws them away. Thus it was that a sturdy young man in the prime of health, intelligence, and youth was sent home to unlearn at the plough-tail the lessons of the drill-yard.

Presently Ephraim recovered himself sufficiently to say :—

"Aunt Judy, I know this young person. I have met her in Ireland, and—and—I suppose she is travelling in England, and, being near this place, she has called to see me as a friend, and—"

"You are a liar, Eph!" exclaimed the old woman. "The devil marked you for destruction when you refused the pledge. This is but one step on the road to death."

Then suddenly flaring up into lambent fury, she rushed on the girl with her great hands open and the fingers crooked, "Out of the place with you! you

Irish vagabond ! you kinkered heifer ! you—" and she cast at her the grossest and most insulting word that leaped from her heart to her tongue. The girl, who had cowered before her, recovered with a start, flame shot out of her dark eyes, her whole frame quivered with rage, and she clenched her disengaged hand in the face of her antagonist.

" Leave her alone, aunt," said Ephraim, interposing his broad person. " You have the knack of saying that which would wake the dead. Do not touch her. She has done you no harm. Do you not see she is exhausted with weariness and wet and cold ? Come with me, Bridget, I will help you to a lodging." Then he drew the young woman out of the yard into the lane. .

The lane was dark, muddy, stony, and narrow. Ephraim walked first, silent, with bowed head, and the girl followed. Presently he came to a gate opening west. The drizzle had ceased ; the clouds had curdled into shape and lay in ribs on the horizon, and the evening light pierced between them. The sun had set ; but his rays lit clouds high above the lower raindrift, and tracts of unblurred blue, and these luminous clouds and illumined skies shone between the stripes in the west. Ephraim leaned against the gate, with his elbows on the top rail, and his chin on his hands, looking at the dying light. The girl stood behind him, pressing the child to her heart.

" Ephraim," she said timorously, " I can go no farther. I have been walking since daybreak, carrying my babe through rain. Sure it is killing me, and I can go not an inch beyond this at all."

"Why have you come? What do you want with me?" He knew why she had come, and what she wanted, but he spoke thus because he must say something, and could think of nothing else to say.

"This is your child," she answered reproachfully.

"Humph! a bad job. What is to come of it?"

"Ephraim, you swore to me that you would return to Dublin and marry me—you swore it before you left. I waited all the summer, daily expecting you; but as you never did come, why, I came to you."

He uttered a low perplexed whistle that vibrated between tones and semitones. "I've been an ass, a solemn jackass," he said. "Confound it all, what is to be the end?"

"What is to be the end?" she repeated. "This, and only this, that I become your wife, and that you undo what you did amiss. Eph! here in Protestant England I dare say it's not thought so much of as it is with us in old Catholic Ireland, when a girl trusts too far the promises of the man she loves. But with us it's a bad thing, and an unforgiven thing, entirely. My father has turned me out of his house, and bidden me go and find the man I loved, and who deceived me."

Ephraim withdrew his hands from the pockets into which he had thrust them when whistling. "Curse it all," he said, "I reckon I've got myself into a queer kettle of fish."

"Ephraim!" sobbed the girl, "I cannot stand. I

shall sink and die at your feet unless you give me hope to hold by. And the poor babe too ! Sure but my arms are broken. I've carried it all day. Will you take it ?—it is yours." She almost forced the child upon him. He looked at the tiny face. The cloud bars had gone, and in the west lay a great golden dome of sunlit vapour rising high into translucent emerald ether, and by this reflected light the baby face, with the tears like dewdrops on the lashes, was irradiated. "It has your eyes and hair, Ephraim."

"Is it a boy or a maid ?" he asked, almost sullenly.

"A girl, just four months old. O Ephraim ! where will you put me ? I am streaming with water, and sick with hunger and cold."

"Follow me, I will find a place where to lodge you." He turned from the gate and walked on. "Curse it," he muttered, "this comes of trusting women."

"Ephraim," sobbed the girl, drawing her weary feet with difficulty through the mud and over the stones, "how can you speak thus ? What have you to resent ? Have not I a thousand times more cause to complain ? I trusted you, I relied on your word, your sacred oath."

"Why did you ?" he asked discontentedly. "Don't you know that men promise and swear, and mean nothing by it ? You should have known better than trust a soldier."

"A soldier !" echoed Bridget. "Sure but who else is one to trust but a soldier, who is everything that is true and honourable, and not a taste of a rascal in him? Would you have all the world think that because a man is a soldier therefore he is a liar, and perjured?"

Ephraim did not answer. He walked on with his head down. Then the child he bore in his arms uttered a feeble cry, and a tiny hand was thrust forth from the shawl and touched his lips. Ephraim turned his head aside, but again the little fingers sought his face, and the palm rested on his mouth. Then he kissed it, and a warm gush, as if a fountain had broken in his heart and was welling up, made his cheeks glow and his eyes grow dim.

"The little one has my hair and eyes," said he; "it will be a pretty maid. But, Lord! how heavy she be."

"I have carried her all day," said Bridget.

"I cannot think how you did it." His mouth twitched, and the little hand played about it. When he spoke he moved his face on one side. He stood still and looked at the girl. She was tall and graceful, with black hair and dark eyes. A handsome, noble-looking girl; the tears were rolling down her cheeks, and her mouth was quivering.

"Well, well, Bridget," he said, and his voice shook, "it is true that I swore to marry you, but I did not mean that you should take me at my word. There— as you have come, I suppose I must do it. That is— I will think it over."

"Ephraim, I cannot go home again. I have spent every penny that I had, and my father will not receive me unless I return as your wife. Fulfil your words,

or my death will lie at your door, and that little one
—that little one—have you the heart?" She burst
into a storm of tears and sobs, and sank, broken by
grief and fatigue, at his feet.

"Get up. For heaven's sake, get up! Lord! what
if some one were to pass and see you thus! Get up.
There, there, I passed my word, and so I suppose I
must keep it. Of course I will."

He lifted Bridget with one hand, holding the baby
with the other. He put his arm round her and kissed
her, and her head sank on his shoulder. "There,
there, you are over-tired."

"I cannot go any farther. I cannot, indeed. My
heart feels as if it would stop entirely."

"Only a few steps farther, Bridget," he replied
tenderly. "I am taking you to an old widow woman,
Betty Spry, who will receive you and make you comfortable." He kept his arm round her to stay her up,
as her knees yielded under her, and the weight of her
sodden garments.

Presently they came to a cottage built of "cob"—
that is, clay kneaded with straw, and whitewashed.
It was covered with thatch, and looked warm under it,
as a mole in its brown fur. A friendly light shone
through the little window. "It be small," said Ephraim, "but snug. You'll not fare badly within."

He knocked at the door, and Betty Spry opened.

"What, Mr. Eph! You! Loramussy, and who be
you a-bringing along of you?"

"Betty, I want you to do me a favour. Here is a
poor young woman with her baby, tired and wet; she

has walked all the way from Plymouth, and is a stranger to these parts. She will be thankful for a night's lodging. You will take her in, and I will pay you what is reasonable."

"Surely, sure-ly," answered the old woman. "It be a poor living I can make out of half-a-crown a week and a loaf of bread, which is all the Boord of Guardians allows me, and out of that one shilling for rent of my house. I reckon the Boord won't be down on me and reducing the half-crown if I take in lodgers?"

"No, certainly not. If they do, I'll make it up to you."

"They did with Martha Balsdon; her went out washing to Varmer Vallance, and they cut her down next meeting of the Boord. And Rebecca Kite, her took in a woman as was sick, and they docked her of everything but a loaf."

"Set your mind at ease, Betty. I will see you do not suffer."

"Boords be hard things," observed Mrs. Spry. "Deal is softer than oak, and oak is deal to Guardians." Then to Bridget: "Come in, my darling, and sit you down by the fire. Loramussy! you be streaming wet. I reckon I've got some of my daughter's clothes upstairs in the hutch. I'll bring 'em down and air them. They'll fit 'ee beautiful." Presently, as she returned with clothes, she said, "I reckon you be hungry, but I've no meat for supper. I've not tasted meat this five week. I get but half-a-crown and a loaf, and out of that goes a shilling for rent."

"I will run to the village, and see if I can get some bacon. You have some eggs?"

"Eggs—! well, yes, out of a mere chance the hens have laid, but they don't use to. How can they on half-a-crown and a shilling out for rent? 'Taint in their constitution to do it."

"I will fetch what is necessary," said Ephraim. "Now, Bridget, get off your wet things and warm yourself before I come back."

When Ephraim returned from the little shop with meat and sugar, tea and bread, and a bottle of British brandy, he found Bridget seated by a bright fire of wood that flashed and leaped and laughed on the hearth. She was seated in the chimney-corner, and the rosy light illumined her graceful figure and beautiful face, and flickered in her large dark eyes. Her wet hair was loose, and hung over her shoulders. Old Mrs. Spry had thrown a scarlet shawl about her, and the reflection gave colour to her pale face. On the little round table by the fire was a white cloth, and on that were cups and a brown teapot that glowed in the firelight like copper. The widow was pouring boiling water into it from the kettle, and the steam rose from it. She had been making buttered eggs, and the fragrance of the toast filled the room.

How comfortable the cottage kitchen looked! How pretty was Bridget!—and see! the little child was on her knees laughing at the flames, and extending the tiny feet and every tiny toe thereon to catch the pleasant heat. Is there a more lovely and moving sight in the world than that of a young mother with her babe on her knees?

Ephraim's brow cleared. His heart grew soft and

weak.   He went over to Bridget and kissed her, then each little foot and hand, and then the lips of the child.

"Oh, Betty!" he said, "give me the frying-pan.   I will do the bacon myself, and lay me a plate and a cup.   I must have supper here also, with you and Bridget and the baby."

CHAPTER II.

THE LEG OF THE Y.

WHEN Ephraim returned to Longabrook it was dark,
dark as pitch, and the lamp was lighted in the kitchen
where his father was seated smoking before the fire,
and his aunt, Judith, was engaged ironing at the table
by the window, with the lamp by her. The old man
was tall and bony like his sister, with the same hard
face. He wore a bushy grey Newgate collar about
the jaws and under his shaven chin. His long legs
were like tongs, and were expanded with a great foot
on each side of the fire. He sat back in his chair,
sat at a joint in the middle of his back, and his head
was sunk between his shoulders, which were elevated
by reason of the elbows resting on the arms of the
chair.

Old Noah Doidge was a yeoman, owning his own
little farm, which had belonged to the Doidges for
several generations. He was a proud man, proud of
his independence, proud of his savings, proud of his
stubbornness, proud of his pride. Stubborn he was,
stubbornness he regarded as an hereditary virtue.
When he had formed a resolution he would stick to
it at the risk of running to his ruin. There was once
a gentle family of his name lived at Hurlditch, not

five miles off, and over their door stood carved the
Doidge arms, a woman's breast distilling milk.   The
Doidges of Longabrook may possibly have been
related remotely to the family that owned Hurlditch,
but if so, all reasonable claim to the armorial cognis-
ance had gone from the family.   There was no
feminine tenderness, no drop of the milk of human
kindness, in the Doidges of Longabrook.   All his
weakness and wavering Ephraim derived from his
mother.   Noah Doidge had bushy grey tufts for eye-
brows, and grey eyes keen and cruel as those of a
hawk.   His wife had died early, leaving him two
sons; the elder was Ephraim, now at home with his
father, the younger, Cornelius, was in a drapery shop
at Tavistock.   Ephraim and his father had never got
on well together, and Cornelius, Noah despised as a
milksop.   The father was despotic and obdurate.
Ephraim had enlisted after a quarrel with his father,
and Cornelius had gone behind the counter rather
than work on the farm and endure the sneers and
blows of the old man.   Now Ephraim was back.
He and his father had come to disagreement, but the
old man had constrained himself, as he found the
value of a son at home.   Ephraim, moreover, knew
that he was to succeed his father; he therefore threw
his heart into the work of the farm, and avoided
doing anything which would needlessly exasperate
old Doidge.   When Ephraim returned from the army
a man full of vigour, broad-shouldered, hale and
florid, with iron sinews, a military bearing, and military punctuality, Noah felt proud of him; he recog-

nised in him one worthy to maintain the dignity of the family.

For a moment after Ephraim had entered he stood uneasily at the door, looking from his father to his aunt. Noah drew a long whiff and puffed it slowly before him; he did not turn his head. Judith beat the iron down with an angry thud on a shirt she was smoothing, set her brows, glared at him out of the corner of her eyes, and then went on vigorously with her work.

"Father," said Ephraim, "the pigs have been out over the orchard wall again. I've put up a rail, but I reckon naught will stop 'em. They are mad after the beech masts, and where a rat will run a pig will follow."

The old man gave a grunt.

"I opened the pie," said the young man again; "I found the potatoes cruel took with the disease."

To this remark no response was vouchsafed.

"Be you going to sell the heifer to Thomas May, father?"

"No," with a growl.

Ephraim came over to the settle and seated himself on it, and began to drum with his fingers on the seat.

"Be that rats?" asked the old man, sitting suddenly up and thrusting forth his head.

"No, I was playing a tune with my fingers," explained Ephraim.

"Have done then," said Noah, and relapsed.

The young man saw that it was useless to evade speaking on a subject uppermost in all their minds.

"I see, father," he began, " Aunt Judy has, as usual, been drawing a bramble between us. I suppose she has told you that a strange girl has been here asking after me."

"Yes."

"Well—that poor maid has come a long way, and I—I have asked Betty Spry to give her a shakedown till—"

"Till what?" asked the old man, confronting him.

"That depends on you, somewhat, father."

"Then it needn't depend another minute in uncertainty. I have and will have naught to do with her. Pack her off whence she came. What's the sense of a foreign hussy coming here and asking after you, eh?"

"The sense of it ain't far to seek," threw in Judith Doidge, leaning both her hands on the iron and glaring maliciously at her nephew. "The sense is obvious enough, I reckon."

"Yes," said Ephraim, whom his aunt's vindictiveness had spurred into resolution and defiance. "The sense is plain enough. The maid has a claim on me. She's a good girl, and a handsome one, too, and I've passed my word of honour to her—that I can't go from."

"Your word of honour!" sneered Aunt Judith. "What is a word worth when the deed is deficient? Suit the word to the deed, and make a pair of 'em."

"Father," said Ephraim, his colour deepening, "it is time for me to marry. You and Aunt Judith are getting old, and you need a young woman in the house to see to the cows and the maidens."

"What is that?" cried Judith. "I be old and fit for naught but the graveyard. You'd shovel me in there and sit down on me, that I mightn't kick off the mould and rise again, you would. I be old? Can't I mind the cows and make better butter than any young maid in the three parishes?"

The old woman dashed her iron aside, and, going up to the side of her brother, said, placing her arms akimbo, "Noah, is the young man to bring kinkered cattle into the family to corrupt the breed? Be I to be driven from under this honest roof to make room for a slut Eph have picked drunk out of a ditch?"

The yeoman was undisturbed by his sister's vehement appeal. He did not look at her, or notice her.

"Quite so, Eph," he said, answering his son. "It is right that you should marry. I reckon the sooner the better, and none so pleased as I. Never you mind the squalling of cats."

"Thank you, father, thank you."

"Stay, Eph. I've not spoke of this before, but there be Farmer Jeffry's daughter, Susanna, out to Hurdwick, is worth three thousand pound. Her'll have three thousand pound paid down the day you marries her."

"But, father—"

"There be no choice in the matter, Eph. It is almost a concluded affair. Farmer Jeffry and I have spoken about it already."

"I do not love her."

"We can't have all we want in this world of woe," said Noah, sententiously. "That were the re-mark made by the rabbit when he found his burrow invaded by the hedgehog."

"Father," said Ephraim, firmly, "I will never consent to this. My word is passed to Bridget, and she shall be my wife."

"And who may Bridget please to be?"

"The—the Irish girl who came here to-day."

The old man drew a long whiff, and let the smoke escape leisurely from his nostrils.

"I—I—" Ephraim hesitated, then added in a low tone and hung his head, "I am the father of her child."

"Well, what of that?"

"What of that, father? My conscience will not allow me to desert her. For good or for ill I marry her."

"As you like, it don't concern me," said Noah, coldly.

"What's that?" cried Judith, in quivering wrath.

"You please to mind my shirt," said the yeoman, composedly.

"Father," said Ephraim, "do you consent to my marriage?" He spoke doubtfully; he did not like his father's manner, he mistrusted his composure.

"I neither give consent nor withhold it. Did you not hear, that it naught concerns me?"

A constrained pause.

"Three thousand pounds would buy Cott's Meadow, Furze Park, and Longlands, and them we want cruel bad to round off the estate," said the yeoman.

" I have promised to marry Bridget," said Ephraim.

"Ah!" burst from the old woman. "It be a plant! Eph put her up to coming here. He thought if once she could put her foot in, all her body would follow."

"Silence, Judy," said Noah, gravely. "Her shall never cross this drexil " (threshold).

"We shall see," said Ephraim, rising. His blood was up, excited by his father's coldness and his aunt's venom.

"We shall see," repeated the old man, composedly. "You are not master here to open the door to whom you will; no, nor ever shall be, if you marry that wench. I have, God be praised, another son. He bain't all I could wish, but he be better than you."

Ephraim stood by the settle, with his hand against the back, disconcerted. "Be reasonable, father," he said. "The maiden is the daughter of honest parents. I would have gladly fulfilled your wish and married Jeffry's daughter, but, as you must see, it is now impossible. I have done what was foolish, what was wrong. Bridget has come here after me to remind me of my duty. If I were to be false, I could never have a happy home, and hold up my head among honest men."

" And I reckon her be a Catholic, too," threw in Judith. "You'd be bringing an idolator into this Christian house, would you ? "

"I cannot break my promise to Bridget, father," said Ephraim, firmly and gravely.

"Very well, keep your word. I have nothing to

do with it.   That is your affair.   Cornelius shall give up counter capers, and come here and learn to be a man.   Perhaps, with the prospect of having Longabrook after I am dead and gone, he will fall to farming with some zest.   He shall marry Susan Jeffry and buy Cott's Meadow, Longlands, and Furze Park.   One man is as good as another."

"He won't object to that," threw in Aunt Judy. "Corny is a dear fellow, and docile as a lamb."

"You will not, you cannot, do this injustice, father."

"Injustice?" echoed the old man.   "Hoity-toity! I reckon I must put on my spectacles to see it. Isn't Corny my son as well as you; and may I not leave Longabrook to which I will?"

"Hah, hah!" jeered Judith Doidge.   "Now, at last, Corny will come by his rights.   I always said it wasn't fair to favour one son at the expense of the other."

"Silence, sister!" enjoined Noah.   "Mark this, Eph! You know me.   When I say the word, the word is sure as the everlasting hills.   If you marry that piece of Irish baggage, neither you nor she ever crosses my drexil, and Cornelius becomes my sole and exclusive heir."

"Father!" Ephraim passed his hand over his eyes; "this is hard; it is cruel.   I must consider what you have said.   But it is hard—bitter hard. Good-night, father."

With slow and faltering steps he mounted to his bedroom.   He shut and bolted his door.   Then he seated himself at the window, and looked out into the night. The rain had come on again, and was driving against the panes. The night was dark and cheerless as his prospects. He knew that his father could do what he threatened. He had a little money of his own—very little—that he had saved whilst a soldier. He was a strong man, able to earn a livelihood as a day labourer on a farm or in a mine, and live on fourteen shillings a week. But he was not born to this. He had some Doidge pride in him, and he shrank from the prospect. He might become a gentleman's groom or gardener, and his wife do-washing. But here again his pride rebelled. Independence was dear to him ; it was his birthright. Then he thought of his brother, whom he had always looked down upon, as weak in body and narrow in mind. "I know Corny's dirty little heart," he said bitterly. "He will grasp greedily at the offer. He won't concern himself about me and my wrongs. Here he will be master, and drive his trap, and I shall be a poor miner at Hogstor, black with manganese, and glad of a scrap of meat on Sundays, dining all the working-days on dough pasty." But then he recalled the figure in the firelight of the ingle nook, with the beautiful black hair and lustrous eyes, and the innocent fair child laughing on her lap. Ephraim rose and stretched himself; he was stiff and cold. He crept to his bed. "After all," he muttered, "what must be, must; and as one sows, so one reaps. Bridget is here, that settles the matter. I'll go to sleep. Maybe with morning, light will come into my affairs."

When Ephraim woke next morning he woke with

an idea in his head.   A gleam had broken over his dark look-out.   He thought that, under the circumstances, delay was desirable.   Why should he precipitate the breach with his father?   He would persuade Bridget to go into service, and leave the neighbourhood.   He would give her a written promise of marriage, and tell her the reasons why he must postpone fulfilment of engagement.   Widow Spry would take charge of the baby..   Two or three years' delay might save everything; his father's mind might change, he was old and might fail and be ready to yield when he saw how set his son was on marrying Bridget.

Ephraim had a friend, a schoolmaster, about five miles off.   He resolved to visit him and get his help in the composition of an advertisement for the "Western Daily News," for a situation as nursemaid or general servant, "where no footmen are kept," said Ephraim.   "I could not bear to think of Bridget in a place where there are footmen."   The schoolmaster would not be disengaged till four o'clock, so he had the morning before him in which to assist his father in getting in the turnips.

The old man said nothing to his son, but when, after dinner, Ephraim changed his clothes, both he and Judith looked hard at him.

"Where be you a-going to?" asked his father.

"I'm going to set all square with Bridget," he answered evasively.

"I don't see how you can square what's all askew," said his aunt spitefully; "nor why you need put on your Sunday suit for that."

Ephraim vouchsafed no further explanation. He took his hat and stick and went forth. Judith watched him, and saw that he did not take the turn to Betty Spry's cottage. "He is gone elsewhere," she said: "but Lord help me if I know whither."

When Ephraim had left the room, his father's face lost all look of resolution, and his bearing became hesitating. "I shall never abide Cornelius," he said, "and Eph will be no good till that wench be got rid of."

"Give her money, and she will go fast enough," said his sister, contemptuously. "Ephraim is so weak that she thinks she can do what she likes with him. She came and looked round the farm to see if the nest would suit her, and she has settled near it. She'll turn Eph to do her will unless she be got rid of. Give her money, and don't stint. It is worth dropping a few pounds to be rid of her."

"How much?"

"Well, I reckon, about what a half-Guernsey is worth—twenty pound."

The old man went upstairs to his bedroom, unlocked his strong box, and took from it a leather bag, into which he put twenty gold sovereigns. He thought a moment, and put ten more, loose, in his pocket.

Then he came down, put on his hat, went direct to Widow Spry's cottage, and asked to see the foreign woman who was lodging there.

"She is in the upstairs room. Do you want to speak to her?"

"Yes, I do, Betty, and, what is more, alone. Go to

my sister, she has some hog's puddings for you. We killed a pig Wednesday. Tell her I sent you for them." He waited by the fire till the widow was out of hearing, and then went upstairs.

The young mother could not doubt for a moment who the stern, grey old man was who entered her room. She rose from her seat timidly, and cast an appealing look into his steely eyes, then hers fell with the sense of hopelessness that came over her heart. She stepped aside and caught the back of the chair on which she had been seated near the bed and the babe that lay on it.

"Be you the maiden who wants to marry my son?" he asked, in a harsh voice. She coloured.

"I trusted him when he promised me marriage," she said, in a low tone. "I never thought but that he was true as gold."

"Eph is a fool," answered the old man, impatiently. "He had no right to ask you to trust him. He had no right to make any promises. He is engaged to be married to Susanna Jeffry of Hurdwick, who brings with her three thousand pounds. It stands to reason he can't marry both of you. We are Christians here, and not Turks. It's against the law. So the question is, *which* woman he is to take, and *which* word he is to break?"

"Your son is under oath to me. He cannot bind himself to another."

"Can he not?" the old yeoman laughed. "Does the law bind him to you? Try the law if you will—it will prove weak as an elder twig. If he chooses to pay his addresses to another, and snap his fingers in your face, all you can do is to learn patience and bear it."

Bridget trembled, and put her hand to her bosom.

"Ah!" pursued the old man, "take my advice and go home whence you came. If you made your way here thinking to force him—"

"I had no thought to force him at all," said Bridget—"I will have nothing to do with the law. If he has not the honour in his heart to keep his word to me, then God help me, I am a lost soul."

"That is right, and sensibly spoken," said Noah Doidge. "Have nothing to do with the law. The law is like dog-grass, you take it between finger and thumb, and it cuts both. But I'll deal fair by you. My son has been a fool and must pay for his folly. Look here; I have brought you twenty pounds, all in gold, good as was ever minted. There's not an Australian white-faced coin among them. There's ten of them have the man and the horse, and the rest have the royal arms on their backs."

He opened the bag and poured the contents on the table. Bridget turned white and put both her hands to her brow, shading her eyes—farmer Doidge thought—the better to see and count the sovereigns.

"What is the meaning of this?" she asked hoarsely.

"Meaning? why, maiden, the meaning is clear enough. You have mother-wit to understand, I reckon. Look at the gold, count the sovereigns, there be only two ten-shilling pieces among them. That is a deal of money, and takes a lot of sweat to earn. Why," argued Noah, "if you were to swear the child on Eph, I reckon you'd get eighteenpence a week, or maybe two shillings, not a penny more."

Bridget was motionless, frozen to her place.

"Look'ee here," said the old man, in a coaxing tone, "there's many a man will sell himself for twenty pounds. I've a young chap working on the farm. He's a bit tottle (silly), but that don't matter. I reckon he would marry you right on end for that twenty pound, if I were to propose it to him ; and so I'll get a licence, and in a week you shall be made an honest woman."

At last Bridget realised what was said. Her bosom heaved, her cheeks flamed, and fire leaped from her eyes. She trembled so that the furniture in the room shook. She dashed her hands against the table, so as to send some of the coins upon the floor.

" I won't stick at twenty," said the old man, " though it is enough, heaven knows, and hard-earned. I'll make it five-and-twenty, and at that I stand."

" I ask but one thing," said Bridget, mastering her emotion with difficulty, and fixing her glittering eyes full on the old man's face. "Did your son send you ? "

"Eph? Yes, he did." Coldly, without wincing under her gaze, Noah replied.

Then Bridget uttered a piercing cry. " Away, away with the money!" She struck the table, and the money danced upon it. " The price of blood, the price of a soul ! "

" There, do not be excited and unreasab!e," said

Noah Doidge; he stooped to pick up the fallen sovereigns. "Take the money; these heroics are useless. I will pay no more; take it, and begone."

"False, false!" cried Bridget; "your son is a cowardly liar, and you are his abettor. Old man, you should have red hair instead of silver, like Judas, who betrayed the Innocent. I will not stay. I came here trusting to the word of a Christian, and the honour of a soldier. I did not sell my soul for money. God forbid!" She beat her bosom and her brow, and stamped on the floor. The wild Celtic blood in her was boiling.

"I pray you do not shout your wrongs so that all the parish may hear," said Noah, angrily. "There is the money. I leave you to get cool and consider. The money is all there but a half-sovereign, which has rolled under the bed. Good-bye. In an hour I shall return. If you want a lift to Tavistock, I will harness the mare and drive you there myself, and"—he stood at the head of the stairs—"compose yourself and be reasonable; when we part at Tavistock, I'll give you another five. That will make thirty pounds—a fortune for a maid."

He went slowly downstairs, shut the door, and walked home.

When he was gone, Bridget cast herself on her knees by the bed, threw her arms over the child, and tossed and writhed in shame and grief. The babe woke and began to cry, and, when its mother did not regard the feeble appeal, the cries intensified to screams. Then, with an expression of despair, Bridget started up, snatched the child to her, seated herself on the bed, and rocked herself and the babe together.

Without, the wind moaned, and drifts of ash-leaves were swept by the window. Darkness fell fold on fold over the landscape and over Bridget's heart.

CHAPTER III.

THE FORK OF THE Y.

WITH the assistance of the schoolmaster, Ephraim had concocted his advertisement, and walked home fully impressed with the advantages of a liberal education, which had enabled the schoolmaster to see that "general servant, where no footmen are kept," was an unsuitable expression. The advertisement was written, and put in an envelope addressed to the publisher, not editor, of the "Western Daily News," with four shillings inclosed, in penny stamps. The envelope was not sealed, for Ephraim intended to read the inclosure to Bridget before posting it, and explain to her his motives for desiring a delay, and that she should go into service.

"If she remains in service a twelvemonth or two years, and father shows no sign of relenting, I shall have time to turn round and look out for a place myself. If I could get a situation under a parson as groom and gardener, that might suit me, or a cottage at park gates, where Bridget can open to carriages, and I can be coachman. I should like to have to do with horses. That comes natural to me. But, who can say? the old man may see that his best interest lies in keeping me, and may come to take me on my own terms. What good could Corny be to him, with his white hands and pigeon breast? Father has an eye to his own interest, and won't cut off his nose to spite his face, I reckon."

Ephraim did not enter Longabrook—he passed the gate and went on to Widow Spry's cottage. The night had fallen dark, so dark that he might have gone by the cottage without seeing it, but for the flicker of firelight through the window. A smile lit up the young man's face, and his heart was light. His conscience was easy. He was going to do what was right, and his fear of the consequences was allayed. Indeed, he held up his head with an heroic self-confidence. Was he not risking the loss of his birth-right by following honourable principle? If that does not elevate a man, what will? He opened the cottage door without knocking, and went in. Bridget was not by the fire. Widow Spry was moving restlessly about the little room.

"I be glad you'm come, Mr. Ephraim," said she.

"Where is Bridget?" asked the young man.

"Surely you'm come a bit late, just a bit too late," said Betty Spry. "Her be gone this hour."

"Gone!"

"Yes, I reckon. Her tooked up the baby and made a bundle and went back to foreign parts, right on end. That was what her minded to do, so her said."

"Bridget gone with the child!"

"Her ha'n't been a very paying sort of a lodger," said the widow. "I thought her'd a stayed longer, and been a comfort to me, but now, if the Boord hears I've harboured a tramp, and comes down on me!"— she shook her head—"If the Boord came down on me, it would knock me all to scatt, I reckon."

"Bridget gone!" Ephraim could not realise what was said. He ran outside and looked up and down the dark lane, no one was to be seen, no one could have been seen. He came back with nervous twitch‧ing of the lips and hands, and pale cheek. "What, what is the meaning of this?" he asked. "Why has she gone? Have you been unkind to her?"

"I reckon you ought to know best why her be gone," answered Mrs. Spry. "You sent her the money to pay her off. Her've left it all on the table upstairs—twenty-four pound ten. I reckon it were twenty-five when you sent it, but ten shillings rolled away, and can't be found nowhere. It have gone between the chinks of the floorboards, I reckon, and you must tear up the floor to find it. But 'taint worth doing that."

"I do not understand," said Ephraim. "I sent no money to her."

"You did, though, by your father. He've a been here and seen the young woman, and paid her over the gold, which he said you'd sent by him, as you didn't like to come yourself, and thought it best ar‧ranged between you by a third party."

"I never sent a penny."

"It's no odds to me," said Widow Spry, "but if you'm set on having back the ten shilling, don't go charging me wi' having took it. It may be that her thought better of it, and kept that to pay for a night's lodging elsewhere, as her wouldn't bide by me."

"Good heavens!" gasped Ephraim, "my father was here!"

"He came from you, so I gathered from the poor young woman, and left the money as from you, though I doubt not it came out of his own pocket. If you don't find the ten shilling under the floor, don't lay it on me. There be rats in the cottage, and they carry away anything they chance to find falled between the boords."

"I never sent my father here."

"He told her you had, and her was like one mad, and went off right on end."

"It was a lie, a cursed lie!" cried Ephraim, blazing red as fire. "I had nothing to do with it."

"Why, then, did you keep away all day?"

"That is another matter. How long is she gone?"

"An hour, I said."

"Which way did she go?"

"The way she came, back to foreign parts."

He asked no more questions, but set off in pursuit. His teeth were set, and his brows knit; his breath came short. He was very angry. When his blood was up he was stubborn. No, now there should be no delay of a year or two. If his father played him such underhand tricks he would not spare him. He would have the banns put up next Sunday, and within a month Bridget would become his wife. He snatched the envelope from his pocket, and tore the advertisement, and with it the postage stamps, and scattered the fragments in his path as he went along. No; he would show his father and his aunt that he was in earnest.

A long two-mile hill was before him, ascending a wooded valley to Heathfield. The ascent was too steep and the hill too long for Ephraim to maintain the pace at which he had started. He consoled himself with the thought that Bridget, burdened with the babe and her heavy care, must necessarily mount it with slow tread. He must catch her up before she emerged on the moor.

The ascent made him hot. He wiped his brow and took off his hat. He had left his stick in Betty Spry's cottage. He regretted it now, it would have assisted him. As he approached the head of the hill the cold north-east wind caught him. He had heard it rushing in the pine-tops, but the coombe he had come up was sheltered, and he had not felt it. Near the summit was an old turnpike house, disused as a turnpike, and converted into an ordinary cottage. It was clothed roof and walls in slate, and the windows were protected by shutters in which two holes were cut. Through these the light from within shone. They were like red eyes glaring on him as he went by. He proceeded half a mile before he got out on the open moor, eight hundred feet above the sea, swept by every blast from every quarter. The road had been fresh stoned, and was irksome to walk on, advance was slow, and did not keep pace with his impatience. No sign of Bridget anywhere. Here on the moor the night was not so black as below in the valley among the trees. When the fresh-stoned piece of road ended, Ephraim ran and called, but was forced to cease, he had lost breath in mounting the hill. Then suddenly—he came to a dead stop. Ephraim was *now at the* Y. He had come to a point where the roads, equally good, diverged, one to the S.E., the other due S. There was a sign-post at this spot, and a clump of wind-torn, headless spruce and larch. The night was too dark to allow the directions to be read, and no signpost would say which road Bridget had taken.

At the Y, Ephraim stood perplexed. Which road should he elect to follow? Both led to Plymouth, one by Tavistock, the other by Beer Alston. Both ran for many a mile over desolate heath without a habitation on it, both were circuitous. Which should he take? Everything depended on his choosing aright. If he went awrong he lost Bridget for ever. If he did not overtake her within an hour, the possibility of finding her again would be gone. She would disappear in Plymouth past discovery. She could not return to her father. Whither would she go? Where seek shelter?

No marvel if his head span, and his heart turned faint. He put his hands to his temples and pressed them, and tried to find a reason for preferring one road to the other.

He could find none. There were no data on which to form an opinion. There was nothing but chance to determine him.

" This is the way with men," said Ephraim, bitterly, despairingly. " Again and again in life we arrive at a Y, and everything depends on our choice of the road—fortune, happiness, content on this side; misery, poverty, ruin, moral and social, on that : and there is nothing to guide us which side to go. Reason can only act on grounds, and it is precisely at the Y that grounds fail us. In such a predicament there is no choice but to toss up." He took a coin from his pocket, and spun it in the air. " Heads to the right, tails to the left," he said, as he clapped his right hand on the shilling in his left palm. Then, discontentedly, "Confound it, there is not light by which to read face or reverse." He repocketed his coin, and stood a few minutes brooding and irresolute.

" What was that my father taught me as a child when I began to drive? Was it not this ?—

> ' If you go to the right, you are sure to go wrong,
>   If you go to the left, you go right.'

Well, I'll chance it. To the left. If wrong, I can but turn and try the other road. So—*To the left.*"

CHAPTER IV

THE LEFT ARM.

To the left. The wind came stronger, colder, and more cruel. Utter blackness to the north-east, as though an avalanche of snow were threatening to fall and bury the entire world. To the west and south, here and there a star sparkled feebly. Ephraim feared lest, in his haste, he might pass Bridget. It was likely that she, hearing a step on the road, would stand back against the hedge, hoping to remain unobserved. Therefore, at intervals, he called her by name.

Every now and then he stood still and listened. He could hear nothing but the moan of the wind among the grass, and the distant roar of the moor. "The roar of the moor" is a familiar token, in these parts, of approaching storm from the north-east. It is occasioned by the wind among the granite tors and furzy brakes of Dartmoor. The roaring is like the roaring of the sea. Every now and then, when he stood still, he felt impelled to turn back and take the road to the right. Perhaps he was wrong. Perhaps Bridget was speeding, head down, along the right branch of the Y. If so, every step he took, every step she took, were separating them more certainly, more fatally. But then the thought arose also, if he were to turn back, the chance was much the same that he was missing her. He had elected the left road. He must pursue it, and abide by the consequences.

Presently he heard the tramp of a trotting horse, and then the sound of wheels behind him. He looked back and saw a pair of widening lights approaching. He resolved to stop the conveyance, and beg a lift of a mile, or ask the driver, if unable to take him, to k ep his eye open for a young female, and to tell her that Ephraim Doidge was behind. As the lights came up, the young man stepped forward and held out his hand, and shouted.

"Hallo!" exclaimed a familiar voice. "Eph Doidge here! Why, what the deuce has brought you out on Heathfield on such a night as this?"

The driver had recognised the young man as he stood in the halo of the carriage-lamp.

"What! Farmer Jeffry! Will you give me a lift for a mile or two?"

"To be sure. Jump up behind, beside Susanna. My old woman is at my side, and takes up her proper seat and half of mine—you couldn't thrust a straw between us."

So Ephraim got into the seat in the cart behind, beside the young girl worth three thousand pounds, whom his father had determined he should marry.

Ephraim was on the left, to windward.

"Will you mind opening the big umbrella, Mr. Eph?" asked Susan Jeffry. "The wind nigh cuts my head off, and my ear feels like a thing dead. I reckon we shall have hail or snow before many minutes are by."

"If you particularly wish it," answered Ephraim; "but I am on the look-out for some one whom I want to overtake, and with the umbrella open I might miss —the—party."

"Oh! as for that," said Susanna, "father will keep his eye open. Won't you, father?" She nudged the farmer in his back. "Mr. Eph is expecting to overtake a gentleman, and he wants you to look out for him along the road."

"I think I should be happier looking out myself," said Ephraim.

"Oh! if it be too much trouble for you to hold the umbrella over me, never mind. I dare say my ear will get frost-bitten and drop off. I've heard of such things, and it feels like it."

Ephraim was obliged to unfurl the huge gingham umbrella.

"Not that way, Mr. Eph. It will be turned inside out unless you put him with his nozzle to the eye of the wind."

The great screen cut off all the left side of the road, and Susanna sat on the right and obscured that. Ephraim sighed. He must trust to Farmer Jeffry's keen eye. He was depressed, and turned over his difficulties in his head.

"You are mighty diverting I must say," observed Susanna. "And it's snug here behind, with father and mother in front of us as a wall of flesh, and the great umbrella against the wind."

Ephraim cast furtive glances over his shoulder. If they passed Bridget, he might see her thus.

"You haven't dropped anything, have you?" asked Susan.

"No, miss."

"Because I thought possibly you might have lost your tongue."

"It is not that," said Ephraim; "but I am so much afraid of passing my—my friend in the dark."

"I'll keep my eyes open for you," said Susan; "I shall have nothing else to occupy me. I suppose now your thoughts are mighty agreeable, and I shouldn't object to pay a penny for them."

Without paying our penny we may read them.

Ephraim was thinking that almost certainly he was on the wrong road. He could not be quite certain. Bridget might have obtained a lift. If he was on the wrong road, and every step of the horse were carrying him farther from Bridget, then his fate and hers were decided. Providence had interfered to separate them for ever. It would be in vain for him now to retrace his steps with any hope of finding her. Should he return to the Y and take the right road, she would by this time have got on so far ahead that he might not hope to overtake her. That choice of the left arm of the Y had sealed his fate. Bridget was not to be his wife. Had Heaven intended him to take her, he would not have gone astray to the left. Then he considered that the only commandment with promise is that which bids a son honour and obey his father. If he took Bridget, he went against his father's wishes,

and how could he hope that God's blessing would
rest on the disobedient son ?   His intention when setting out had been right.   He had desired to undo a
wrong once done.   At the Y stood the choice between two rights, as he now perceived—the right due
to Bridget, and the right due to his father.   He could
not fulfil his duty to both when they conflicted.
Providence had decided for him, and had given him
his direction which was to determine his future.

He was sorry for Bridget, very sorry.   He grieved
that she should be exposed to the storm with a sad
heart and a heavy load.   But what could he do?
Nothing.   The possibility of doing anything was
taken from him when he turned to the left.   The
part of a wise man is to take advantage of circumstances as they arise, and to accommodate himself to
the situation into which he has dropped.   That five-
and-twenty pounds lying on the table !   It was really
too bad of Bridget to refuse it.   If she had accepted
the money, then the score against him would have
been wiped out, and he need no longer have felt uneasy.   It was inconsiderate of Bridget ; it was
unkind, it was wicked.   A bitter emotion rose in his
heart against her.

"There comes the hail !" cried Susanna, drawing
closer to her companion.   "Do please, Eph, hold the
umbrella with a firmer hand !   Before long we shall
be at Hurdwick."   Ephraim grasped the umbrella-
stick shorter.   The hail rolled over them, the road
whitened in a minute.

Suddenly Farmer Jeffry drew up, and turned his face.

"Now, Eph Doidge," he called, "where are you bound for? Here we are at the gate of the lane down to Hurdwick. If you are going on to Tavistock, I must set you down. But I recommend that you come in, and have supper with us, and stay at least till the storm has swept past, if you will not bide the night."

"I must go home," said the young man, hesitatingly; "I have not passed the person I wished to overtake. So I must return."

"Nonsense, man!" exclaimed Jeffry; "walk all way back to Longabrook in the dark and hail, and at this time! Pshaw! you do nothing of the sort. You come in and have supper and a glass of toddy. I'll tell you what you shall do. You shall sleep here; to-morrow I must be going your way—I am about to buy some bullocks of Farmer Tickle—and I'll drive you to your own door."

The hail tore down, hard and heavy as bullets.

"Well, don't keep us waiting," said Jeffry impatiently. "There, I decide for you." He whipped the horse, and drove down the lane to his farm through an avenue of stunted ash.

All were glad to escape out of the biting cold and driving ice-bullets into shelter, and light, and heat.

A good supper by a blazing hearth off hot beef-steak-pudding, with a bowl of steaming punch, completed the work of soothing and satisfying Ephraim. This was the reward of right doing, of honouring his father, and taking the road towards fulfilment of his commands. Ephraim's spirits revived; he no longer thought of Bridget save as a misguided, inconvenient person. He became chatty, told a good story, cut a dry joke, chaffed Mrs. Jeffry, and became sentimental towards Susanna ; the more punch he drank, the more certain he became that he was morally right. Jeffry was a jolly farmer of the old school, who liked his grog, and hated radicals and blue riband ; he replenished Ephraim's glass as often as it was emptied. After a while he rose. " A good man cares for his beast," he said ; " one secret of my success in life, young man, is that I never trust anyone to do anything without running my eye over his work. Now I've had my supper, I'll go and see that Turpin has had his."

After that, Mrs. Jeffry went out to see that the rare stone-china bowl in which the punch had been brewed was washed and put away. She believed it was a marvellous piece and of fabulous value. A gentleman had all but offered her £50 for it. Simple soul, it was not worth more than five shillings. Believing it to be valuable, it was bequeathed by codicil to Susanna and her heirs and assigns for ever.

Thus the two young people were left together by the fireside in the settle. A rod ran across the room, and a green curtain hung over it. This curtain was drawn so as to exclude all draughts from and include every element of coziness about the fire. Mr. Jeffry was away for half-an-hour. His wife did not return. The cleaning of the punch-bowl led to other cleanings, and the cleanings to polishings, and the polishings to putting away. When Farmer Jeffry's red face appeared through the curtains, Ephraim and Susanna were seated so close beside each other on the settle that, to use the farmer's own expression, "you could not have thrust a straw between them."

Then Ephraim, looking very red, what with the punch, and the heat of the fire, and proximity to Susanna, said, "Farmer Jeffry, if you've no objections, we two here will put our horses together for life's journey."

"That's well," answered the burly father. "If Susanna is agreeable, I'm not particular. What! the punch gone? We must have another brew to solemnise the occasion."

The cold drive, the warmth of the kitchen, the good fare, combined to make Ephraim sleep soundly that night. He dreamed that he came to Longabrook in a cart, and pulled up at the door and shouted to his father that he had brought home a wife. Then he drew a sack out of the cart, and put it down in the kitchen, and thrust his hand in and pulled out a plump, apple-cheeked wife, and put her down on the settle. Then he thrust his hand in again, and pulled out another plump, apple-cheeked wife, and put her also on the settle ; then again, and again, and again, till a whole row occupied the settle, and still he went on pulling them out of the sack. The next lot he arranged upon the mantelpiece, and when that was full, he drew out more and more, and set them all in order, side by side, on the window-sill, and still they were not done ; he kept on diving with his arm and drawing out more, and these he ranged on the shelves of the dresser, and yet he had not done. He stood and rubbed his eyes, and put his hand in his pocket for his handkerchief, and when he drew that forth, there fell out of it another apple-cheeked wife. He had a plug of cotton-wool in his ear, and he pulled that out, and stood looking at it with bewilderment— he had drawn out with it another apple-cheeked wife. Then he went to the sack again, and continued drawing them out and putting them in all the rooms—in the parlour which was never used, on all the little glass-bead mats on the parlour table, in the cupboard where his aunt kept her cordials ; in the back kitchen he put one into each of the saucepans and empty jam-pots, into the brown jar for the salt, into the bread-pan, and the cake-pan, and the vegetable-basket. There was no coming to an end of the wives, and they were all alike, indistinguishable from each other, and all exactly like Susanna. Then—as he was becoming hopeless of accommodating more, and weary to death of the endless apple-cheeks—all at once another face looked in at the window, a sad, beautiful face with large dark eyes and black hair, and instantly all the apple-cheeked wives shrivelled up and squealed and were gone.

After that his dream changed. He thought he was in the village shop, that he leaned across the counter and ordered one yard and three-quarters of wife. " How will you have her cut ? " asked the shopman, " on the square or on the cross, and cheap or the best article we have in stock ? " " On the square, of course, and of the very best." Then the shopman took down a roll and began to measure wife out against the brass

measure let into the counter, and cut and gave it over to
Ephraim, who looked hard at it and said, " I fear it is
all dressing." " Shake and see," was the answer.
Then he began to shake the yard and three-quarters
of wife, and clouds of dressing flew out, and he shook
and shook, and more and more dressing came out of
her, and the substance became momentarily thinner.
The shopman remonstrated ; it was not fair to try
the nature of wife so—nowadays they are dressed up
to the extreme, and there is none to be got of un-
sophisticated sound warp and woof. Then all at once
a hand came and tore the flimsy gauze from top to
bottom, and before him stood Bridget.

Ephraim woke with a start, and found that he had
slept late. He rose and dressed, and came downstairs
with a feeling of depression weighing on his spirits,
the effects of the dream, he supposed. He did what
he could to make himself agreeable at breakfast, and
during the morning he hung about Susanna under
pretence of helping her in her work, but actually
hindering her. The feeling of chill on his heart
remained, he could not shake it off.

After dinner, Turpin was put in harness, and
Farmer Jeffry was ready to drive him to Longabrook.

The day was bright, but the wind was still in the
east, bitterly cold. The moor was cased in a panoply
of icy granules. In the road the wheels had crushed
the hailstones into dirty ice. The sun was powerless
to thaw the frozen envelope. Dartmoor was one
white dazzling range, and the granite crags rose out of
the hail and snow black as coal.

Ephraim and the farmer conversed together all the way on the prospects of the young man and the merits of Susanna. As they spun down the hill they emerged from the hail coating upon dark moist earth. In the valleys all was thaw and water. There Eph saw the roof of the shop where last night he had purchased a yard and three-quarters of wife. Involuntarily he looked behind him into the bottom of the cart to see if the sack of apple-faced wives was there. Then the trap whirled into the village street.

"Hallo! What is up here?" asked Farmer Jeffry, drawing in Turpin sharply. A good many men and a great many women were assembled about the door of the "Stag's Head."

"Anything wrong? What's all this about?" asked Jeffry, pulling up at the tavern door.

Some of those addressed looked hard at Ephraim and said, with a shrug of the shoulders, "It be no concern of ours. Ask he."

"But what is the matter, Tooke?" inquired the young man, descending from the cart.

"You'd better go in and see with your own eyes," answered the man addressed.

"Can no one tell me?" asked Jeffry. "Be you all tongue-tied?"

"Her be lying in the parlour," answered Tooke, "and Widow Spry has the baby."

"Poor thing, I doubt if that will live after a night in the storm," said another man.

"He ought to be tore in pieces," muttered one woman.

"I'd like to scatt his head with a cleaver," said another.

Ephraim's blood curdled. Jeffry was elbowing his way in at the door; the young man followed him.

"Us have telegraphed for the crowner," said the landlord. "It's a crowning case, and no mistake."

"Who is dead? Is it an accident?"

"A sort of accident done of purpose, I should think," said a man. "If you drive a dog into water too strong and deep for him to swim, you don't reckon it an accident if he drowns. If a young woman and a babe be sent out of house at nights in a storm, to wander on Heathfield, I reckon it be hardly an accident if they both starve of cold."

"But who can she be?" asked Jeffry, pushing up to the table, on which lay Bridget, stiff and dead. "Poor thing, poor thing, she don't belong to these parts by the look of her."

"Mr. Eph Doidge can tell y' best who her be," said the landlady.

"Who is she, Eph? How do you know anything about her?"

Then the women's tongues were loosed. Ephraim stood white, stunned, speechless, beside the form of the dead girl. In the window was Mrs. Spry, trying to pour warm milk down the throat of the child.

"Can't you speak, Eph?" asked the farmer.

"No; I reckon he can't," said the landlady; "he can't for very shame. Ask Betty Spry. Her knows most about it."

"Then, for heaven's sake, tell me," exclaimed Jeffry, turning to the widow.

Betty told the story in her own way, with exaggerations and suppressions. She told what she had learned or guessed, proud to be of consequence for a day, proud of possessing information shared by none of her gossips, and, in her eagerness to give herself importance, accentuating, aggravating every painful detail.

"Do y' want to know who her be?" she asked. "Well, I tell you, true as Gospel. I'm not one to make up lies. I'm not so daring as to do that. Not on half-a-crown a week and a shilling out for rent. I couldn't do it on the money. It ain't expected of me. Thicky [yonder] poor maiden be one as knew Mr. Eph in Amerikay or Ireland, or some of them foreign parts, and her came after him with the baby, because they'd been married out there. But Mr. Eph, he wanted to have some one else nearer home, so he wouldn't let her bide here, but drove her out of my house, which be comfortable enough for one shilling a week rent. It mayn't be grand as that of some folks, but it'll keep out rain and cold."

"Her came to my door yesterday," said a woman, "and axed the way to Longabrook, and whether Mr. Doidge lived there. I put her in the road, poor soul, but she looked then ready to drop with starvation and weariness."

"It were not yesterday, but the day afore," threw in another.

"Was it? Well, it may have been. I can't say, but—"

"Mrs. Spry, go on with your story," said Jeffry, whose face had become crimson as a peony.

"I reckon them hardhearted ones at Longabrook wouldn't take her in," said the second woman, who would have her say. "And her'd have perished of cold that night if Betty Spry hadn't had the bowels of compassion to take her in and give her something to eat."

"I've but a loaf of bread a week from the Boord," observed Mrs. Spry. "If I've done good, I'll be rewarded for it, I knows. The promise is in Scripture for a cup of cold water, and I gave her a cup of hot tea, and to that buttered eggs and some rashers of bacon, though, the Lord knows, I'm not one to afford such luxuries."

"How came she to leave your house?" asked Jeffry.

"Mr. Eph Doidge and his father turned her out last night when it was dark and threatening snow. You see, they didn't want no scandal about her ; so they gave her money and threatened her with the police and Exeter gaol if she didn't go off that very night."

"Good heavens ! Is this true ? "

"May I die this minute if it be not Gospel truth," said Mrs. Spry. "They gave her twenty-four pounds, and old Mr. Doidge has the brazen impudence to say it were twenty-five. But it were not. Four-and-twenty, and not a threepenny bit more. I counted the money myself. The poor thing would take none of it. Her went away and let it lie, all four-and-twenty pounds, on the table."

Suddenly Jeffry turned on Ephraim, his face purple with anger, the great veins of his brow puffed with blood. He caught him by his shoulder in his vice-like left hand, and said, "Ephraim! answer me at once. Do you know this unfortunate girl?"

Ephraim's stiff lips refused a reply. He tried to speak, but could not. Everything swam before his eyes. He had only half heard what had been said around him.

"Answer me," thundered the farmer; "answer me by your cowardly silence, or by a word as a man."

Ephraim put his hand to his brow. He did not answer. He could not take his thoughts or eyes off the calm, cold face on the tavern table.

"Is that your child?" asked Jeffry, pointing with the butt end of the whip to the babe on Mrs. Spry's knees.

A cry from the widow. "The darling! the dear lamb! the pretty dove! It be dying, dying! Come, Mr. Eph, and take a last look at your own child whom you have killed."

Then Jeffry's fury mastered him. He clenched his teeth, and with his left hand grasping Ephraim, he swung him round the table where the dead woman lay, up and down the room, men and women making way for him and applauding, and lashed into him with the gig whip across back and shoulders and thighs. "You came sneaking after my Susanna, did you! you came eating my beefsteak and drinking my rum, did you! and toasting your shins over my fire, and laying your cursed head under my roof, did you!

And all the while this poor soul was wandering houseless, shivering, starving on the moor; and as you turned in on my feather tyes (bed), she laid her down in the snow to wake no more." He cut him across the face, and then, full of disgust and abhorrence, he turned the whip in his hand, and brought the plated handle down with all the force of his heavy arm on Ephraim's head. Then he let go.

Ephraim spun and staggered with extended arms, like a drunken man, down the room, grasped the table to prevent himself from falling, lost consciousness for a moment, and woke with a start to find himself at the fork of the Y, murmuring to himself perplexedly—

> " If you go to the right you are sure to go wrong,
> If you go to the left you go right."

The night was dark. The wind was raving among the distorted fir-trees behind the sign-post.

" No," said Ephraim, " never to the left. Always to the right. How could I doubt it? Right always must be right. So—*to the right.*"

CHAPTER V.

THE RIGHT ARM.

EPHRAIM ran along the road to the right. Right must be right, whatever old saws might say. And right he was in this—that Bridget had actually taken the arm that turned to the right. Along that road, leading due south, Bridget was hurrying with but one wish burning in her heart, to place as great a distance as she could between herself and the place where her faith in manly integrity had been killed, and where she had met with such humiliation. No wounds torture and canker like broken confidence.

She heard the voice of Ephraim behind her; then his tread as he ran. She stood back against the bank, sinking into a pillow of dry heath. He had seen her, however, and he stopped and stood before her. She uttered a cry of anger and contempt, and folding her arms and shawl about her child, and burying her face in them, shouldered and elbowed him off when he touched her. Then, when he drew her towards him, and tried to kiss her, she shook herself free with a gesture of indignation, and cried, "What do you follow me for? Have you not done enough to crush and kill me? Keep your gold and gild your black heart with it, to hide its villainies.

Go back! I will not be touched by you. I hate you! I despise you! Touch me again, and I will scream for help."

"Foolish girl!" exclaimed Ephraim; "you might scream yourself hoarse, and none would hear you on this moor. But what is the meaning of this temper? You run from me, you throw bitter words at me, and I am innocent of offence. Would I have come after you, dear Bridget, if I wanted to shake myself free? How came you to think so badly of me as to believe the lies my father told?"

"Were they lies, Eph?"

"Of course they were. On my honour I never sent him to you with money. I had no suspicion that he intended to see you, or I would not have been away. The old man lied because he wanted to be rid of you. There, Bridget, you must trust me again; I will marry you in three weeks. To-morrow is Sunday, and the banns shall be called for the first time."

"Oh, Ephraim! is this true?"

"True as I am alive, Bridget; I shall not be able to take you home to Longabrook, for my father turns me out of the house and alienates my inheritance to my brother because of you. But I will ask the Captain of Hogstor mine for work in the manganese, and I shall be able to maintain you, though not to give you the comfort I should desire."

"Your father turns you out?"

"Yes, Bridget."

"So did mine. Oh, Eph! we shall be united by

privation and sorrow, and that is the firmest of bonds. I believe and trust you now, and nothing shall ever again shake my faith in you. You have made a sacrifice for me, as I made a sacrifice for you. Oh, God, forgive me that I ever mistrusted you!"

She laid her head on his breast and wept tears of joy. He put his arm round her, and the storm had lost its violence, and the cold its keenness to her.

"Now, Bridget," he said gaily, "give me the child; we will go together through the village, and all shall see that I am not ashamed of you."

They walked back side by side down the long hill, happy as children. He took her hand, and told her of his struggle with old Noah, and of the spitefulness of his aunt. They spoke of their plans for the future. There was a disused cottage in moderate repair that he might have for a small sum. He would do the necessary work himself to make it weather-tight. When spring came they would look out for something better; but during the winter the manganese mine would enable him to keep the wolf from the door, and the thatch of the cottage would cover their heads. He asked her about her history since he had left Dublin; and her simple narrative filled him with compunction, and resolve to make amends for the past. She told him of the slights she had encountered, of her mother's grief, of her father's anger, and how she had been laughed to scorn when she spoke of her confidence in Ephraim's honour, and reliance on his promises. Now she would gladden her parents' hearts by the news of her marriage.

When they reached the village they found several men and women at their doors or in the street. Betty Spry had told all her neighbours of the girl's flight and Ephraim's pursuit.

"Good-evening, Mrs. Tooke! Good-night, Joe Crossman!" Ephraim saluted every one he passed by name. "You see I've got a bird, now I must look out for a cage in which to put her."

In less than a month Bridget was Ephraim's lawful wife, and they were settled into the little cottage on which he had set his eye. Noah Doidge and Aunt Judith took no notice of what went on. "It is no concern of mine," said the old man. "Ephraim is of age and can suit himself. I am not yet in my second childhood, and I can suit myself."

Ephraim was badly off. He had very little ready money, not enough to furnish the cottage ; consequently he was forced to run into debt. The village shopkeeper was quite content to let him do so for groceries and bread and crockery ; and a Tavistock furniture dealer let him have bed, chest of drawers, and table for a little ready money and some credit. Ephraim was a bit of a carpenter. He had tools of his own, which Mrs. Spry fetched for him from Longabrook, and with these he mended the windows, put strips of wood to the doors to keep out the cold, and made a few necessary articles for the kitchen. He bought an old sugar cask and cut it half down, and converted it into a backed chair for the fireside.

The winter crept along — dull December, dreary January, a little bright weather in February, a raw and wretched March. The north and north-east winds prevailed, there was snow and frost, and when that went, mud and rain. A dreary time anywhere, most dreary in the deep valley in which Ephraim dwelt, for it lay to the north of the great hogsback of Heathfield, and so through winter caught little sun. It was appropriately called Chillaton. When the sky was enveloped in fog and cloud, the little low room with its tiny window was dark early in the evening and late in the morning. The workmen broke off from their tasks when daylight died, and the evenings seemed interminable. Then it was that the first shadows fell on the married life of Ephraim Doidge and Irish Breeches, as the impudent youngsters of Chillaton nick-named Bridget. If it had been possible for the young couple to associate with their fellows on good terms, all might have been well, but the women resented the advent of a foreigner into their midst; the farmers and their families held aloof from the young Doidges, and Ephraim could not bring his mind to associate with the labourers. The farmers' wives and daughters looked unlovingly on the girl who had taken the place that might so much better have been occupied by a maiden of his own class and county and neighbourhood and faith; and the farmers gave him the cold shoulder because he had defied and disobeyed his father. "He has stepped out of his class," said Jeffry, "and as he has made his bed, so must he lie." Ephraim paid a visit now and then on Sundays to old acquaintances, but was not received with cordiality and invited to a meal.

Hurt and dissatisfied, he returned home in a sulk. He had found work at the manganese mine, but it did not suit him. It was hard, and of a nature to which he was unaccustomed. He was a cleanly man, particular about his personal neatness, and the grime of the manganese was a daily offence. When he returned home in the evening he grumbled at his work, and was impatient because the soil would not wash out of his neck and hands.

Nor did Bridget find her situation pleasant. She made no friends. She had always lived in a capital town, she was reserved and dignified. The women of Chillaton regarded her as proud and contemptuous ; she was better educated than they, and had no interest for the only thing that interested their narrow, empty minds, the scandal of the parish. Some few looked in on Bridget with the intention of making acquaintance with her, but her coldness repelled them. Had she been a Dissenter, the chapel would have brought her into association with others, and religion served as a flux to unite ; but she would not go near their meeting-house, nor attend the parish church. She set up a bracket in her kitchen on which was an image of the Blessed Virgin ; and before this she hung her rosary and a pendant perpetual lamp. This alienated the neighbours from her more than anything else, and the local preacher fanned the dissatisfaction into a flame by preaching against the idolatries of Babylon and about the fires of Smithfield. The result was that one evening a stone was hurled through the window ; it smashed the image and extinguished the light. Ephraim was in the house at the time. He rushed forth, caught the delinquent as he thought, and in a paroxysm of fury so mauled him that he was summoned and fined for the assault. The young man who had thrown the stone was, however, not he who was maltreated by Ephraim ; by ill-luck Ephraim had attacked the son of the captain of the mine, and this assault led to his dismissal. Then, for a while, he was without work or money : at last he went on the road, under the surveyor, breaking stones and clearing the water-table.

There was a superiority in Bridget, due in measure to her town education, which the women recognised and resented ; and they revenged themselves for their consciousness of inferiority by saying that she had driven Ephraim into marrying her, that she had shown want of decency in pursuing him to England, and that she ought to have known better than make him quarrel with his father. If she went into a neighbour's house where the women were talking, her appearance occasioned a dead silence. As she passed along the street or entered the little shop, she overheard offensive asides, and returned home in a fever of indignation. Ephraim did not sufficiently sympathise with her trouble. "Pshaw!" said he, "that is the way of folk. You don't belong to their set, so they spite you. That will wear off in time."

"I won't go near them again."

"Then stay at home."

Ephraim began to weary of the discontented mood of Bridget, and the resentment she harboured towards those about her. Nothing pleased her. The hills were too high and close, they shut out the light. The clouds were perpetually over the sky. The weather was intolerable. The mud never dried up. No one passed along the lane ; they might as well be planted in the Bog of Allan. There was no Catholic chapel near, and what would become of her soul cut off from all the sacred rites ? The Devonshire people were odious. There was no fun in them. She had not heard a joke since she left Ireland. Ephraim himself was dull and tedious when he came home from work ; he had nothing to say except that he disliked his work. It was not pleasant for her to have hints thrown at her in this way that she had turned him out of his inheritance.

"I never hinted anything of the sort," exclaimed Ephraim, surprised and indignant. He had sufficient of a soldier's honour and manly generosity in him never to reproach her for the past. He took the blame entirely on himself.

" You do so every day. If you do not speak it, you look it."

Ephraim rose from his seat ; the injustice nettled him, already predisposed to irritation. " Upon my word," he said, " the people are excusable if they avoid you." He went out of the house and slammed the door behind him, so that the diamond panes in the window rattled. " This is intolerable," he said to himself ; " if I cannot find peace in my own home, I shall go to the Stag's Head." He was as good as his word. From that day he was often of an evening in the tavern. He did not drink much; he was never inebriated, but he sought his pleasure elsewhere than at home, and made companions of labouring men instead of seeking the society of his wife. She now saw much less of him, but when he did return he was in a better mood than formerly. He had taken enough to cheer him, and the experiences and anecdotes of his companions about the tavern fire had enlivened him. Bridget was angry at this, and reproached him whenever she saw his mood blithe, so that he began to dread his house door, expecting to have a wet cloth thrown over his heart the moment he passed through it.

Bridget, unfortunately, was of a jealous temperament. Her loneliness and dissatisfaction furnished the suitable elements for jealousy to spring up and overmaster her. Now it fell out that old Betty Spry's daughter, who had been in service, came home soon after Christmas. She was a remarkably pretty girl, with that exquisite complexion of white and rose which is seen nowhere in such perfection as in Devon. Her hair was like spun-gold. Ephraim had known her since she was a child, and in his genial nature spoke to her kindly whenever they met. He had been wont before her arrival to go occasionally into Betty Spry's cottage and help the old woman with little jobs beyond her powers. He continued doing this after Christmas. Bridget watched him with suspicion and jealousy. He had the indiscretion one day to remark to his wife how pretty Lucy Spry was. He spoke in all simplicity, but Bridget fired up and answered, " She had no doubt he thought so, as he was always dancing after her."

Ephraim's eyes opened wide. He did not take in at first what Bridget meant ; when he did he burst out laughing. The idea of her being jealous of that little scatterbrain Lucy was too ridiculous to be entertained seriously. One Sunday morning Ephraim had been to church. Bridget sat at home by her window looking out discontentedly. Here was she in a land as good as heathen, without having heard mass since she left Ireland, or a prospect of hearing it again. How could she die in such a place ?

There had been much rain whilst her husband was away; indeed it seemed as though a waterspout must have broken over the hill, for a torrent swept across the lane ankle deep, where usually there was but a dribble. Dinner was ready : the little table was laid, but Ephraim did not arrive as early as usual. He would pretend that the sermon was long. She knew better. He was loitering in the churchyard, gossiping with the men, or sauntering along the lane with Lucy Spry. As this thought came into her mind, she heard voices, and, looking out of the window, saw Ephraim with old Betty and her daughter in the lane, arrested by the stream. The three were laughing, and Ephraim was evidently making a proposal to carry Betty over on his back, for the old woman drew back and slapped him on the arm. Then without more ado, Ephraim caught Lucy up, and carried her in his strong arms through the water. When he got in the middle, where the current was most rapid and the water deepest, he made pretence that his strength was exhausted and he was going to drop her. Thereat Lucy screamed and threw her arms round his neck, and clung to him. Bridget's eyes flashed, her cheeks flamed, and she dashed her hand against the window so that it rattled, and the noise woke the child in its cradle. It began to cry. She ran to it, snatched it to her roughly, and stood with glaring face, panting bosom, and threatening brow in the midst of the room. The stroke on the glass must have been heard by those without, but as Bridget was no longer at the window, they paid no regard to it.

A minute after, Ephraim entered, smiling and fresh in colour, without a suspicion that he had offended Bridget.

"Well, dear wife! Dinner ready? I'm hungry as a hunter."

She did not answer.

"Why, what is the matter now? Stepped out of bed wrong foot foremost again?" Then he went up to her to kiss her.

"Don't touch me!" she cried, hoarse with rage and flaming jealousy. "Run after that pretty Lucy outside whom you have been tossing and kissing. Shame on you—you, a married man."

"Good heavens!" exclaimed Ephraim, "you would not have me leave two women on the wrong side of the water to wait till the stream ran away. Is it a misdemeanour deserving of transportation that I carry an old woman and her daughter through a torrent they must cross to reach home?"

" Indeed ! Do you think I am not well aware why you are now never at home ? You are glad enough that I do not go about to neighbours' cottages to see your proceedings. No wonder the idiots here look at me as they do, and burst into titters behind me when I pass. Would that you had let me go my way when I ran from this place, and that I had not been such a fool as to listen to you. Then you might spend your time in helping the girls over the water, and taking off them what toll you liked."

" I have done you no wrong," answered Ephraim, commanding himself. "Be not unreasonable, Bridget; serve dinner and have done."

" I will not have done," she cried. " I have been with you long enough, insulting me, holding me up to the mockery of your boon companions. I know what happens when you are at the tavern. You laugh and jest over my foreign ways and Catholic faith."

" Bridget, you are mad !" exclaimed Ephraim ; and to avoid further recrimination he left the house, and went without his dinner.

Such scenes became more frequent. Ephraim was inconsiderate ; it was his nature. He loved Bridget dearly, but a bitterness lay at the bottom of his soul which he could not get rid of, the bitterness of feeling himself unjustly suspected and treated. He thought to himself, " Winter will soon be over, and when summer comes we will leave this place, which has become hateful to me. I will get a situation where Bridget can take in washing, and then she will not brood over her diseased fancies."

A new trouble fell on them ; the cold March winds brought on congestion of the lungs to the child, and it was very ill. Then the religious sense in Bridget, which had slumbered, woke up in all its intensity. She knelt in agony before her crucifix and said her beads. But her prayers were in vain. The child died, and Bridget was frantic with despair. This was God's judgment on her for having married a Protestant. How could she expect the Saints to hear her prayers in an alien land ? "Come, come, wife," said Ephraim, "Catholics lose their little ones as well as Protestants, and the Saints are bigger fools than I supposed if they won't listen to one under a Devonshire sky."

When he attended the funeral, a friend accompanied him, and said to him, " Well, Eph, I hope you will soon have another to console you both for your loss."

" I don't know," answered the young man, " I reckon the Saints are in too blue a sulk to give us one."

His companion did not understand him. He looked at him, and was puzzled with the expression of his face. Bridget's words had stung him to the quick, and the barb remained rankling in his heart. He could not withhold sneers at the Saints who had to be wheeded to this, and might be offended by that. He had not the instinct to see that by these gibes he was still further alienating his wife. Her religion was that to which she held as to the holiest and purest essence of life, and he was foolish enough to shock this, and set himself before her in the light of one profane.

One of the first to come and endeavour to comfort the bereaved parents was Ephraim's friend the schoolmaster. He was an Irishman by birth, not by parentage, and his presence gave Bridget unfeigned delight. She was able to talk to him of the dear old country; he knew Dublin, and the part of it where she had lived, and could speak of the beautiful bay, and the hill of Howth—all in her own dialect, which, when the two were together, came out in both full-flavoured.

At first Ephraim was pleased at his friend's visits, and at the pleasure they afforded to Bridget, but after a while he began to dislike them. Bridget always greeted the young schoolmaster with a smile, but he himself was met with a sullen brow. Bridget noticed his dissatisfaction and was gratified by it. Her husband was becoming jealous. He must therefore love her. He would be more attentive and kind to her for the future, she trusted. She was not aware what an edged tool she was playing with.

One Saturday, when Ephraim returned from his work, he found the schoolmaster in his house talking to Bridget. He was too proud to show the man that his presence offended him, but when the schoolmaster was gone he told his wife that he would not have the man encouraged to visit there so frequently.

"You had better lock me up in a cupboard when you are away," answered Bridget. "You are capable of doing so. You grudge me the only pleasure I have now—that of seeing and conversing with a countryman."

"You know my wish, Bridget," said Ephraim sternly. "Do not drive me to desperation."

"Drive you to desperation!" exclaimed Bridget scornfully. "As if anything I could do was not indifferent to you."

Ephraim looked at her. There was something in his face that awed her for a moment—a light in his eye, a fixity of the jaw, she was unaccustomed to. Ephraim was an easy-going, good-natured fellow, but there was below his gentleness and indifference a strain of Doidge violence. It had scintillated of late, but had never blazed up.

After this Bridget was more cautious; she did not meet the schoolmaster alone. When she saw him coming down the lane she left the house by the back-door, or retired to her bedroom and did not answer his knock. But this did not last long. She argued herself into the belief that her husband was doing her an injustice by suspecting her of having regard for another beyond her duty. Then came the Whitsun holidays.

Whitsun Monday was a brilliant spring day. The club feast was to be at one o'clock, and service in the parish church before. Ephraim had joined the club, and would certainly attend. He marched with the men to church with a brass band before them, and thence to the Stag's Head where the committee met and the men dined. This was Ephraim's first year; he must attend the dinner. Scarcely had the procession passed on the return from church, when Bridget went into the little garden behind the house; she took a bowl in her lap and began shelling peas. The day was so lovely, the birds sang so sweetly, the primroses and the bluebells in the bank smiled at her so pleasantly, that for a while the cloud of troubles rolled off her heart and the sun shone on it. She began to sing " St. Patrick's Day in the Morning."

As she sang, she heard a man's voice put in a second and presently the schoolmaster was beside her. She made room for him by her on the bench, and asked him if he would help to shell the peas. Then she struck up another Irish air, and he sang with her. Her heart was light.

" What a happy man Eph Doidge is," said the young man, "to have so pretty and bright a little wife."

" He might be happy," she said and sighed.

" Might—he must."

" He ought to be, certainly," she said.

" A most ungrateful man to Providence if he does not value his happiness."

" I wish he did value it !" She sighed again. " But he does not love his home as he should."

" Why do you sigh ? Are you not happy ?"

" Happy ?—oh—yes ;" she hesitated in her answer.

Then by degrees all her troubles, her cause of discontent, were drawn from her. No, drawn was not the word. When, after a little urgency on his part, she had begun to speak of the things that made her unhappy, the dislike borne her by the people about, the loneliness she felt, then her tongue ran on unrestrained, and she poured forth the whole tale of her wrongs. The music of the band came to them wafted on the soft, warm air ; the flies buzzed round them, a white butterfly danced about the young cabbages, the thorns were blooming and exhaling sweet fragrance.

"Poor Bridget," said the schoolmaster; "you would, I am sure, like to be back in dear old Ireland?" He took her hand, but she drew it away sharply.

Then from the door behind burst Ephraim, his face transformed with mad fury, his blue eyes flaming like brimstone. Bridget sprang up with a cry of terror. She was innocent of everything but indiscretion, and she would have answered the question of the schoolmaster with a negative; but Ephraim was not in a mood to listen to reason, to believe in her innocence. He snatched the bowl from her and dashed it to pieces on the garden walk, then, grasping her wrist, he swung her away with such force that she fell against the wall.

"Are you mad," asked the schoolmaster, "that you treat your wife like this?"

"Mad, mad!" yelled Ephraim, rushing at him; "I will show you that I am mad, as you say. Do you think that I have not heard you both? Not heard her slandering me to you? not heard you ask her to run away with you to Ireland?"

"This is all crazy folly," said the schoolmaster; "listen to reason, and I will speak to you."

"Listen to reason, indeed, when you come into my garden like the serpent to deceive my Eve! What I heard with my ears I know, and you cannot talk me into disbelieving that. By heaven!" he cried, his fury bursting forth in another paroxysm—and it was as though a sheet of fire rose before his face and eyes, blinding him. " I care not what happens to me ; my life has been wretched enough of late. I will have one satisfaction—that of dashing out your brains."

The look of Ephraim was so threatening that the young schoolmaster recoiled. Eph seized a clothes-stake and endeavoured to work it out of the ground. The others took the opportunity to dart into and through the house. Ephraim let go the post at once, and went after them. The master ran ; he saw that his life was in jeopardy, that the other was too mad with jealousy and hate to cons'der what he was doing. He ran down the lane, closely pursued. Before the inn the band was performing " There is nae luck about the house." The frightened man looked right, left, over his shoulder; in another minute he would be overtaken. Then he sprang in at the tavern door, and burst, wild with terror, into the room where the first sitting-down of the club was gathered about the table, on which smoked roast beef and boiled suet pudding. The rector was standing at the head say-ing, " For what we are going to receive—" when, with a cry, the pursued man was in the room, and in another instant Ephraim after him. There ensued a hubbub. Those present put out their arms, and threw their bodies in the way to arrest the young men. In their surprise and in the confusion they did not understand which was in pursuit ; and whether it was not a case of " Stop, thief!"

" Don't let him go. Hold him fast !" shouted Ephraim, shaking off the man who held him. " Hands off. I will catch him." Two strong miners threw themselves in the way. He sent them spinning, one against the wall, the other against the table. He grasped the schoolmaster's throat with both hands and dashed him back on the table, among broken glasses and spilled gravy. The young man, thus thrown backwards, uttered a shriek of fear and entreaty.

There was a roar in Ephraim's ears, "Will you strangle him?" "Let the fellow go!" "Are you mad?" He gave no heed to the cries. As hands were laid on his arms to wrench them from his victim, with demoniacal strength he shook them off. He threw himself to right and left, driving his assailants back, and his hands tightened on the schoolmaster's throat, whose eyes were starting and his face purple. Then, in desperate dread lest, with so many interfering, his victim might escape, he let go one hand, snatched up the great carving knife by the rector's dish of beef, and drove it into the heart of his enemy.

The violence of the blow exhausted him. He felt that his senses were deserting him. The room spun round, and he lost consciousness for a moment. The last he saw was — eyes, eyes, eyes staring full of horror and reproach at him out of a blue mist, on all sides.

Then with a start he recovered himself, to find himself standing with his hand to his head, at the fork of the Y, muttering :—

> "If I go to the right I am sure to go wrong,
> If I go to the left I'm *not* right."

He shook his heavy head. The night was dark; not a star was visible. "Which is it to be?" he asked; "which, or neither? All lead wrong. Neither."

CHAPTER VI.

NEITHER.

Epiiraim walked into the kitchen at Longabrook.
His father was smoking, and his aunt ironing. Neither
spoke to him. "Are you going to sell the heifer,
father?"

"Yes, I reckon."

"The pigs have been over the orchard hedge again,"
said Aunt Judy.

"I'll put up a bar to-morrow," said Ephraim. "That
was not enough I put up to-day."

After a while he said, "I'm unaccountably tired. I
think, father, I'll go to bed."

Never after was the name either of Bridget or of
Susanna mentioned by the three. Ephraim asked no
questions. He went about his work as usual, but he
often puzzled his head with the question, "Did I go
to the left, or to the right, or did I do neither?" He
was never able to answer that question satisfactorily.
"I'm always at the Y," he said; "I stick there, and
so I reckon do some others in this world" :—

> "If we go to the right we are sure to go wrong,
> If we go to the left we're not right."

MAJOR CORNELIUS.

ABOUT thirty years ago I was clerk in a lawyer's
office, on a very small income, and unmarried. I
then lodged in Ebury Street, Belgravia, in a lodging
and boarding house kept by an eminently old maid,
Miss Jones, who treated all her boarders with consideration, and did not exact from them more than
they were able to pay. We dined at her house only
on Sundays and on Christmas Day—that is, unless
invited out. The dinner was always early—at one
o'clock—and always followed the same order. On
the first Sunday in the month we had chicken and
bacon ; on the second, boiled beef, garnished with
carrots and turnips (alternating with parsnips), and
suet pudding ; on the third Sunday we had roast
mutton and fried potatoes ; on the fourth, roast beef
and mashed or boiled potatoes. When there were
five Sundays in a month, the additional Sunday was
supplied with beef-steak pudding, three pounds of
beef to a pudding.

I do not know how it was that the boiled potatoes
at Miss Jones's always tasted of dish-clout. I know
very well that potatoes are not boiled in a cloth ;

nevertheless the pudding, which is, did not taste of the clout, and the potatoes did. There are several insoluble mysteries encountered in life—this was one.

Our landlady was tall, pale, sandy-haired. She lived *en déshabille* in the kitchen all the morning; but at 9 A.M. at breakfast, and at 4 P.M., when we boarders dropped in from our work, she was prim, laced, curled, and stately. How she managed to become so in a few minutes, I never knew. That also was one of the insoluble mysteries of life.

When one of us stayed at home indisposed, we found that by 9.30 A.M. she was what we called in our slang "dish-shovelled:" not a curl in place, a smirch across her cheek, and her neat merino gown replaced by a ragged dress not fit for a lady to wear.

Miss Jones was the ideal maiden lady of propriety, dignity, and thrift. She was good-natured; on one point, however, she was inexorable—she never allowed her lodgers to fall into debt; we paid weekly, beforehand, one pound per head. She had an affable smile, and similar remarks on the weather for all her boarders. Each had a rasher of bacon of the same size at breakfast, and two lumps of sugar in his tea, and one spoonful of brown sugar in his coffee. Each, also, had an egg, and all the eggs tasted of limewater or sawdust alike.

All the boarders were males except one, an old lady with a false front, who never was able to get her collar to remain in position. It gyrated round her throat. She wore also a set of false teeth; both jaws were thus furnished — how contrived we never quite made out. That also remains one of the insoluble mysteries of life. They were somehow contrived to fit with springs, and were so badly contrived that in eating she did not look her best, and sometimes presented a very unattractive spectacle indeed. The old lady did not like us, and we did not like her. She often had devilled kidneys for breakfast, we never, but she paid extra for them ; and when she had them, then inevitably the teeth went out of gear. Behind her back we were accustomed to mimic her ; she knew it by some extraordinary intuition, mysterious to us for a long time, till we discovered that the maid-of-all-work had sneaked to her of what we said and did. She scarcely spoke to us at meals, except in a peremptory way, to have the mustard or toast passed to her. We took a malicious pleasure in neglecting to anticipate her wants, and force her to demand the butter or toast, &c., and not to hear her requests to have them passed, till she raised her voice angrily and repeated them very loudly, when we immediately began to serve her with mustard, pepper, egg-spoons, empty sardine tins, any and every thing, with mock eagerness to forestall her little wants. We were rude to the old lady, I admit, but she was very aggravating. However, my story has nothing to do with her, so I may dismiss her ; it concerns an old gentleman who was our co-lodger and boarder at Miss Jones's pension. He was Major Cornelius, a thin, grey-haired man, with a refined face, and the most delicately cut nostrils I think I ever saw. He was closely shaven. He was scrupulously careful about his clothes, and, though they were old and threadbare, no one could doubt that he was a gentleman by birth, breeding, and in feeling. There was something very sweet and prepossessing about his face. It was pale and grave, but a kindly smile lurked about the delicate mouth, and the grey eyes were soft. He was rather lame, from a wound he had received at Waterloo. He had his pension, and he lived on that; he had nothing besides to live on. That, however, would have sufficed to keep him in comfort had he not in an evil hour stood security for a younger brother. We none of us knew the circumstances exactly, and I cannot now say what was truth and what was conjecture in the story whispered among us. My impression is that the brother, to whom he was devotedly attached, had not behaved honourably; he had left the country, and the major's resources were strained to the utmost to meet the demand that came on him as security. We none of us ventured to allude to this topic; the disgrace rankled in the old man's heart; there was an ever-open wound there, which we were careful not to touch.

There was a childlike simplicity in the old man which rather amused us youngsters then; now, looking back on him, I find it was infinitely touching. We, however, laughed over it—we knew much more of the world than he. To Miss Jones and to the old lady with the teeth he was courteous, with an old-fashioned courtesy that flattered them and won their hearts. He paid Miss Jones the same as we, one pound per week, but he dined daily at home. We used to say that Miss Jones set her cap at the major, and that she only allowed him to remain on these moderate terms because she desired to become Mrs. Cornelius. I do not believe it was so. I think she strained a point so as to retain an old Waterloo officer in her house, to give it an air of superiority above other boarding-houses in the street.

Whenever I think of Major Cornelius I remember his hair. I have already said it was thin; it was always elaborately brushed and watered, the hair drawn forward from behind the ear, and turned in a sort of curl over the temple. His collars were always clean and very stiff, and his black cravat tight about his throat.

A kind old man! When Robbins was ill with rheumatic fever, he sat up with him night after night, and ministered to him as a nurse. When Robbins was better, and able to receive our call, he sat up in his bed, leaning on the major, who had his arm round him, and smiled and looked as pleased with our congratulations as though that vulgar Robbins had been his own son.

A kind old man! He allowed us youngsters to poke little harmless jokes at him. We called him the Centurion. When an Italian band stayed playing in Ebury Street, we would tell him his proper place was to lead it. On Sundays, when he arrived for dinner, one of us would ask, " Been to church, major ? " Then Robbins or another would answer, " Of course he has. What is the good of asking ? Does not Scripture tell

P

us that Cornelius was a *devout* centurion?" These little exhibitions of feeble fun he bore with great good-humour, but we instinctively felt that there was a limit we must not transgress. The only man among us, coarse in perception, who could not recognise this, was Robbins. When he pushed his buffoonery too far, the major would rise, bow, and leave the room. Then the rest of us fell upon, sat upon, and flattened out Robbins.

The major dined daily with Miss Jones at the lodging-house. We never knew of what that week-day dinner consisted, but we believed it was made out of the remains of the great Sunday feast. After chicken Sunday the fare must have been poor. After beef and mutton Sundays, the meat no doubt was minced, and overlaid with a blanket of potato as cottage pudding—much potato and little mince; or was served as haricot with carrot and large sippets of toast; or was lost in batter and called toad-in-a-hole; or buried in boiled dough. We did not know, we only guessed. No information could be extracted from the major when we inquired after the "cold remains," or the "venerable relics," or "Duke Humphrey's dinner." He would answer gently, without a smile, "I assure you Miss Jones and I have fared sumptuously." The old man practised the severest economy. He denied himself everything he could; he drank only water at dinner and supper. Each of us had his separate jug; one had stout, another pale ale, another bitter beer; Robbins drank brandy-and-water; the old lady Marsala. Ale meant to the major fourpence a day, or two-and-fourpence a week that is, over six pounds per annum, and the six pounds were needed for necessaries. His boots were to him a constant source of uneasiness, care and alarm. Boots come expensive, and go quickly. The same pair was soled and re-soled, till the crease over the toe on the outside roughened, then parted. Still they encased his feet. A little blackened grease filled the split, some sticking-plaster disguised it and was polished over; but these were expedients postponing the evil day, nothing more. That the major pinched and screwed to raise the money for a new pair we all knew, and we all noticed the tenderness with which the new boots were regarded, how they were spared work, kept indoors when the streets were muddy and the rain fell.

The long slender fingers—they were nearly transparent—were wonderfully skilful with the needle. The major repaired his own garments; we believed that he mended his own stockings. The maid told us his darning was beautiful. One day that Robbins stayed at home with a cold, he heard the major ask the maid-of-all-work very kindly to let him have a hot flat-iron in his room. Next Sunday he appeared in brilliant—well, clothes, and we found he had turned an old pair himself; we noticed that they bulged *in*, instead of out, at the knee for some weeks, till they accommodated themselves to their altered situation.

If Major Cornelius was self-denying in the matter of drink and clothing, it was not that he could not appreciate generous liquor, and was not particular

about dress. On the contrary, he was a good judge
of wines, and he was fastidious about garments.   I
am sure that nothing galled his self-esteem more than
to have to dress shabbily. He did as much of his
own washing as he well could with a can of boiling
water in his own basin. Washing is a heavy item in
expenditure in London. I believe that some of
the major's garments were so thin, threadbare, and
patched, that he was ashamed to send them to the
wash, lest they should be commented on, and that
therefore he did his best with them at home.

His bedroom was high up, in the attic. He paid
less than we, and was therefore obliged to put up
with inferior accommodation. In winter he suffered
much, I fear, from want of fire. The parlour fire was
not lighted till 4 P.M., so that it was beginning reluctantly to burn up when the clerks returned from their
offices. In his own room, under the slates, it was
cold ; nevertheless he sat there when the bed was
made, that is, from about noon to four. Before that
he remained in the parlour, watching the expiring of
the little fire lit for show, not warmth, during breakfast. Only in the coldest weather would he descend
to the kitchen for a few moments, to stand by the
stove and warm his hands, whilst Miss Jones, "dish-
shovelled," hid in the pantry. If the day were frosty
he walked out, to put his blood in circulation, and
then his cheeks warmed into colour—a bright colour
in his clear skin like the roses in a child.

That old cat with the teeth and the false front and
the rotary collar rented the first floor, and had her own

sitting-room, and a fire there; but, from motives of delicacy, no doubt, and for fear of establishing a precedent, never invited the major to it.

He was so modest that it was only casually we learned that he had once moved in the best circles, and had acquaintances high in military positions and titled. He visited and was visited by none of them. Since that affair of his brother he had withdrawn himself from his fellows; he shrank from meeting those who knew the circumstances, and he suspected more of being aware of them than really did know. He was very proud—not haughty, understand—but with a sense of his honour and breeding which made him reserved.

One luxury he would not give up, the luxury of giving gratuities to all who served him. I believe that the half-crowns as "vales" to the footmen who took his greatcoat, hat, and gloves had much to do with his refusing the invitations he at one time received weekly from old brother officers and friends. He could not be mean, and to avoid the wound to his self-respect of seeming mean he would not go to his fellows. At last invitations, always declined, ceased to come in.

The winter of 1852 was cold. On November 18 the Duke of Wellington was buried in St. Paul's Cathedral, with great display of military pomp. Our old friend was one of the veterans who walked in the procession. That winter saw the fall of the Conservative Ministry under Lord Derby, and the fall of something much more important—at least to us, in

Miss Jones's establishment—the falling to pieces of the major's greatcoat. We had followed the progress of decay in that venerable article of clothing for some time with interest, and we had wondered what the major would do when it was worn completely out. We hoped it would hold out the winter. It did not ; it fell to pieces with the Derby Ministry.

The old man's face grew long ; he fell into depression ; no joke stirred him, no news interested him. It was obvious to all that his mind was engrossed with one absorbing question, how to provide himself with another greatcoat.

Then we residents under the roof of Miss Jones took counsel together, and discussed the possibility of providing him with one. Should we subscribe the requisite sum—that is, amongst ourselves ? We were none of us well off, but we were ready to make a sacrifice to help the old man to a new coat. As for that woman on the first floor with the teeth, we did not consult her—selfish beast ! she ate her two kidneys herself and never offered a bite to the major.

Although we would gladly have found the money, yet we felt that the plan was not feasible. The major was sensitive on the subject of his poverty, and the offer would offend his pride. We must help him some other way. Then I suggested that the major should be induced to write his reminiscences of Waterloo, and that his MS. should be sent to a magazine. Thus the money might be made by himself. He was far too humble a man to think of this expedient unprompted. We formed a deputation and waited on him, and entreated him, as a favour to ourselves, that he would put on paper his recollections of the Great Duke, and of Lord Uxbridge, of Picton, and of the battle, and then, that he would give his production to the world. He was frightened at the suggestion and demurred to it. He had never written a line that had been printed, he knew nothing of literary form, he remembered nothing of real importance. We overruled his objections; we recalled one incident and anecdote after another with which we had been favoured. We told him that we could not expect to be all our lives in Miss Jones's boarding-house, and that in our after-life we wished to possess a memorial of one whom we valued, and loved, and reverenced as a father.

The old man's eyes filled when we said this; he could not answer us; his mouth twitched, he held out his hand, and it shook as he squeezed each of ours in turn.

"Besides," said I, "I am an engrossing clerk, so shall be able to give literary character to the Recollections, and write them in a legible hand, which goes, I understand, a long way with the reader to a publisher."

Now whilst the composition of this literary venture was in progress, the weather turned bitterly cold, and the major caught a chill and coughed much. It was high time for him to provide himself with a greatcoat. He felt as though a cold hand were laid on his back between the shoulders, numbing him—in fact, the greatcoat had parted at the seam in the rear.

He overhauled the old garment, to see whether it would be possible for him to repair it himself. He tried the parted seam, but the threads would not hold, they frayed the edges. No! only a professional could, so to speak, set the greatcoat on its legs again. Then he took it to a Mr. Dawkins, a small working tailor who lived in a side lane. Mr. Dawkins sat on his table, his legs crossed, and without his shoes, his feet encased in not over-clean white stockings. With his toes he grasped the leg of a pair of trousers which he was reseating. Mr. Dawkins was a pasty-faced, small-pox-marked man, with thick black hair and a black, frowsy chin.

The major knew the tailor, and the tailor knew him. Indeed, the man did many little jobs for the gentlemen at Miss Jones's. Mr. Dawkins's eye at once recognised the customer, and then travelled down to his arm to see what hung over it for him to operate upon.

"How are you this morning, Mr. Dawkins?"

"Not at all well. Out of sorts all over. How can a man be well when he slaves all day and is worried all night by a teething baby? Squall, squall, squall! Look at my hand how it shakes. I am unnerved by that odious brat. I wish it were not against the law to drown babies. Mine would soon go over Waterloo Bridge."

"How can you, Robert?" exclaimed his wife, looking into the room.

"Go back to your work. I was not speaking to you," ordered the tailor. " I don't know what sort of work you have for me to do, major, but I tell you beforehand I can only boggle it with this shaking hand. Till the baby's teeth are cut no work worth looking at comes out of this shop. Well, major, what is it?"

"I've come to—to—just—indeed—really—with—" When the major was nervous his eloquence forsook him, he expressed himself in adverbs and prepositions, and left the imagination to supply the verbs and substantives. He stood still, stuttering, thinking he had said his say, or forgetting what his purpose was.

"Well, sir! what do you want with me?" asked Dawkins, casting a scrutinising glance at Major Cornelius, and examining every garment he wore with the eye of a critic, remorseless over defects. He looked for rent, hole, lost button, frayed sleeve, whitened elbow, worn trouser-foot, burst-out buttonhole.

"The—the—greatcoat. I—that is—it—if—with—by any means—you see it is—well nearly—just a little the worse for wear, but otherwise good—no, not new—between the shoulders—yes, I see—at the elbow also—the collar, you observe—and the lappets —the tail, I think—with a little—"

Mr. Dawkins took the greatcoat and spread it over his knees.

"It is not quite new," said the major apologetically. "It is not, indeed, at all new; but, I think, with your admirable skill it may be given another lease of life, say ten years more service. It has been an old and excellent garment, has kept me snug, and screened me from many a chill. I have become attached to the coat, and do not wish to abandon it."

Dawkins said nothing, but his face assumed a sarcastic expression the major did not like. Then he shook his head, raised the coat and held it before the window. The light revealed all its imperfections with cruel directness, it streamed through the rents, it struggled through the threadbare tracts. Then he turned the greatcoat on one side, and explored the right sleeve, and shook his head. Then he turned it over on the other side, and studied the left sleeve ; then he shook his head again. Next he turned the pockets inside out ; then he went over the collar, and broke into a short laugh. Then he examined the lining and shook the coat, and threw it contemptuously on the table at his feet.

" No good—but for the ragman."

Major Cornelius turned deadly white. The room swam round with him, the floor heaved and fell, as though it were the cabin of a transport in the Bay of Biscay. He who would have marched fearless to the mouth of a cannon, shook in his shoes before Mr. Dawkins.

" I think, Mr. Dawkins, you are mistaken. A bit of cloth put behind that angular tear, and a strip where the seam has parted, would make the old coat hold for some time longer ; and if the cloth be thin, some lining and wadding, which are inexpensive, would supply the requisite warmth. The thing is feasible if you would give your valuable time and thought to it."

"Not possible. The cloth is utterly worn out. It will not bear a thread ; look here!" he began to rip. The major uttered a cry—the only cry he had uttered since he was a baby. "In pity! Mr. Dawkins! Do not deal so roughly with my coat."

"Nothing can be done with it. Take it to the rag-shop."

"I have heard that cloth can be patched by placing a piece behind the rent, and a thin bit of gutta-percha, like gold-beater's skin, between it and the cloth of the garment, then when a hot iron is passed over the surface the gutta-percha dissolves into an adhesive substance gumming the two pieces together, and not a thread is used."

"No good. No good at all. Cloth is cloth, and this is worn to the last fibre."

"I only want it to hold out the winter. I am old. I may not live to see another year. It would be a pity to buy a new greatcoat when I may not be able to enjoy it many years. I do not care to squander money, and it would be squandering—should I not live long to wear the coat."

"No," said Dawkins shortly ; "dispose of it to the ragman. I won't have anything to do with it. You must have a new greatcoat."

"A *new* greatcoat !"

"Yes, a new one."

"Humph ! a greatcoat costs money."

"Of course. Greatcoats are not given away."

"They cost a great deal of money."

"To be sure, a great deal." On Mondays Mr

Dawkins loved to put matters in a harsh light before his customers, to stagger and throw them back into attitudes of despair before the mighty expense in which clothing would involve them. He looked complacently at the major, and drank in his misery.

"Suppose now," said Major Cornelius, nervously, "I was to—that is—but really—I doubt."

"Do you mean, what would be the cost of a new greatcoat?"

"Well—yes."

"That would depend on the quality of the cloth."

"I should not need the best and finest material, it would be unnecessary for an old man. One that would last my day would suffice. I should not wish to plunge into lavish expenditure."

"About four guineas."

"Four guineas!—Lord bless me!—did you say four guineas?"

"Not one penny less."

"Four guineas! Good heavens! Where am I— that is—"

"You must have substantial broadcloth—none of your shoddy, one quarter staple, the rest devil's dust, that goes glossy at the seams and elbows in six months. Waste of money getting that. Not fit for a gentleman. Always looks shabby."

"Mr. Dawkins," exclaimed the major, and the beads of sweat came out upon his brow, "I entreat you to apply yourself to my old coat, and see if you cannot make it last out this winter. We are now at the close of January. There are only two more months of really cold weather before us. Make the coat last over them. During the spring and summer when there is rain I will not go out. Before next winter I shall have had time to think about a new greatcoat. This comes on me so suddenly, so bewilderingly, that—that—·"

"Impossible. I don't choose to throw time and thread away."

Major Cornelius heaved a deep sigh, took the despised greatcoat, threw it over his arm, and left the tailor's shop and lane. He went along like a sleep-walker, purposeless, anywhere.

"What a predicament!" said he to himself; "I could not have believed it had I been told that the grand old coat was to serve me no more. Poor old thing! it was with me in my better days. My brother—my poor, dear, misguided brother!—how often has his hand leaned on this right sleeve. So, so! breaking down together, the old heart, the old confidence in life, the old coat, and the old head. O my brother, my brother! If I could only hear from you, or of you again, that you were living as a man of honour ought to live, and striving to redeem the past, and to repay debts—I could die happy."

As he thus walked, dreaming and despondent, he took the wrong road, and instead of coming home found himself on Vauxhall Bridge. He was nearly run over by a cab, and he ran against a policeman. He trod in a bed of mud swept to the side of the road, and splashed himself to his knees. When he found himself on the bridge, then he woke to the fact that he had strayed. Then, all at once, a cheering thought flashed upon him, and he held up his head. "To be sure!" he said, "now I remember, the young fellows often told me never to go near Dawkins on a Monday; I will go to him on Saturday, and offer him a little bottle of best brandy—that will warm the cockles of his heart, and dispose him to make the most of my old coat. It may not be quite the right thing to make use of his failing for my own ends, but it cannot be helped; I cannot possibly purchase a new greatcoat. Four guineas are—well—four guineas." Encouraged by this hope, the old man bought a bottle of excellent Cognac, put it under his greatcoat, and on Saturday revisited the tailor.

"How do you do, Mr. Dawkins? Better than on Monday?"

"Middling, major, only middling."

Then the old gentleman produced the bottle.

"Look here, Mr. Dawkins, I've brought you some real grand old Cognac. I pray you to accept it of me."

The tailor was delighted, his face lit up. He was profuse in his thanks. But the moment the crafty major approached the subject of the greatcoat, Mr. Dawkins's face fell, and he said—"No, it is of no use! You must have a new greatcoat."

"It is not really possible—?"

"Absolutely impossible. Now, look here, major. For you I will bait a point, and make the greatcoat for three-pound-ten. That is my lowest figure. Leave it to me. I will give you good cloth and good cut and good needlework. Three-pun-ten."

Major Cornelius again left the tailor's.

He had little heart to finish his Reminiscences. Finish them, however, he did, under much provocation from us. We sat in conclave over them, and suggested touches here and there ; some were accepted by general acclamation, others rejected. Robbins wanted to trim one or two of the anecdotes and give them additional point ; but the old man would allow of no improvement at the expense of truth. We greatly wanted him to corroborate or contradict the famous story of the " Up, Guards, and at them !" as some were disposed to relegate these words to the limbo of mythical *mots*, but he had been in another part of the field from Lord Wellington, and was not in a position to pass an opinion on the authenticity of the memorable order.

I, as a good scribe, wrote out a clean copy of the Recollections, and the MS. was sent to one of the magazines. It was accepted.

" I wonder what I shall receive for it ? " he said.

" I dare say four guineas," said Robbins.

" That is about the figure," said another.

Now, some thirty years ago, it was the way with certain magazines—I do not say all—to keep a MS. some three or four months, then to print it, and to pay for it perhaps three months later, so that six months elapsed between the acceptance of a short article and payment for it. Some magazines kept MS. still longer, and paid for it still more reluctantly, and these magazines in good repute. Others never paid at all. I dare say things are altered now in this

department as in many others; but such *was* the case.
Major Cornelius knew nothing of this, nor did we, all
as inexperienced as himself. We supposed that his
Reminiscences would be out in a week, and paid for
at once.

We were all so certain that, as the MS. was accepted,
it would be paid for, and so certain, also, that the
major would receive no sum less than four guineas
for it, that he ventured again to the tailor's and
ordered the greatcoat, which was promised him for
three-pound-ten.

I believe we—that is, all Miss Jones's boarders, except the old lady with the teeth—were as much interested in the greatcoat as the old man himself. We
held our breath when we heard that the coat was
ordered, we were impatient for it to be fitted, we were
consumed with eagerness to see it worn.

First the cloth had to be chosen, and the colour
decided on. Then Major Cornelius had to submit to
the ignominy of being measured. At last the day
dawned on which he was to be fitted. He went with
trembling heart to the house of Dawkins, and had to
put his arms through two holes in something which
was supposed to be the coat, but which was a mere
tabard of bits of cloth stitched together, with long
stitches of an inch each—of white cotton. Why
white cotton is always used for the preliminary stitch-
ing together, I should like to know. Mr. Dawkins
went round the major several times, with a bit of flesh-
coloured chalk between his lips, and grunted, and
raised and depressed his eyebrows, and made chalk

sweeps with the thing that looked like pink soap, especially under the arms, which tailors never, as far as my experience reaches, cut right at first, and allow for sufficiently. Then he made pink lines down the major's back. Then he caught him by the lappets and gave him a tug and jerk towards him, and finally dismissed him with a "That'll do."

At last the greatcoat arrived, brought by Mr. Dawkins himself. He brought it in the evening, when we were all at home, except Robbins, who was at the theatre. We sat round the room and saw the garment put on, expressing our delight in low murmurs and sudden ejaculations. Mr. Dawkins was proud of his performance. The major stood in the middle of the room; the table was thrust aside that all might see. Mr. Dawkins pulled the tail down with a jerk; then he buttoned the coat across the chest; then he made the major raise and depress his arms, like a cock flapping his wings. It fitted to perfection. It was faultless. The tailor drew back and looked at it, with his head on one side; then he turned his head the other way; then he walked round the major. No—nothing needed rectification. Then he looked at us all, one after another, seeking commendation. He received it. Perfection is not often encountered in life; but that coat was perfection.

"You will find the bill in the pocket, sir," said Mr. Dawkins. "After three months, five per cent."

When Mr. Dawkins was gone, then all restraint on our enthusiasm was removed; we almost danced round the major; our expressions of admiration were lavish, and, I must admit, extravagant.   The old man smiled, and bore a little banter, mixed with the congratulations, with great good humour.   His pleasant face was lighted with a smile, and a little—just a little —pride.   He was conscious in his heart, he felt in every fibre of his system, that he looked well in the new greatcoat.

"Is it warm?" asked one.

"Warm!   It sends a glow through me," he replied. "Now, my dear friends, I will confide something to you.   I am going out to dinner to-night to my old friend and fellow-soldier, Sir Archibald Busby.   The tailor has been very good; he has kept his word, and given me the greatcoat to go in.   He promised it for to-day, and, relying on his promise, I accepted the invitation.   I could not go in the old greatcoat; it was inconveniently thin, and hardly respectable."

Going to dine with General Sir Archibald Busby, K.C.B.!   We all rose in our own estimation, because we ate at the same table, and slept under the same roof, and warmed our shins at the same fire with one who was invited to dine with that distinguished soldier.   Sir Archibald Busby—a K.C.B. also!   How we would talk to our relatives and acquaintances of our friend Cornelius, who dined with Sir Archibald and Lady Busby!   We must positively see the major in his dress coat, and help him on with his greatcoat when he went forth.

It was time for him to dress, so he went upstairs. One of us expedited the universal drudge with shaving water, another took all the loose hairs out of the general clothes-brush, a third went down into the boot-hole to make sure that the old gentleman's boots were brushed up brilliant as patent leather.

He came down at last, looking very bright, and fresh, and delightful. The curl on his temple was turned with consummate art. His dress suit was without a speck. It had not been worn for several years. His collars were very erect, and white, and military-looking. We hovered about him in the passage. The old lady on the first floor came out upon the landing and glowered over the banisters, and nearly dropped her teeth out of her jaws. Miss Jones rose to the surface from downstairs ; the maid-of-all-work, with her nose blackened and polished, looked on in amazement and far-off adoration.

"What time may we expect you home, major?" asked Miss Jones.

"About twelve or half-past. I shall not be late."

"Mary Jemima shall sit up," said Miss Jones.

"Oh no! We will all sit up. We can't sleep till we have seen the major return from his dinner. Oh, Major Cornelius! what ravages you will commit this evening on the hearts of the ladies! You are perfectly irresistible. If only they could see you in the greatcoat!"

He laughed ; then three of us rushed and knocked our heads together in our eagerness to help him into the new greatcoat. When we had encased him, and buttoned him in, we made him turn round under the gaslight.

"Don't you feel tempted to kiss him, Miss Jones?" asked one of the youngsters.

"For shame! Oh, fie!" Then Miss Jones went down, down the kitchen stairs with a blush on her face; and the maid-of-all-work went off into convulsive giggles.

"Good evening, sir!" we called, as he went to the door. "We shall all sit up for you; and may you well enjoy yourself."

As he had his hand on the door the postman's rap came loud, and made the old man draw back with a start. However, he had the door open, and had faced the postman before the letter was put in the box.

"For you, sir."

"All right, thank you." He had no time to look at the letter then; he slipped it into his greatcoat pocket, and went forth.

.   .   .   .   .

We clubbed together for a bottle of British brandy we heaped up the fire with what remained of coals in the box, after Miss Jones was gone We got the "general" Jemima to supply us with hot water and tumblers. We persuaded Miss Jones to let us have a bowl full of sugar, to be charged in our bills. We sat up and discussed the major. We were so pleased that the dear old man had gone out; it would brighten his life. He would laugh and tell his stories, and recall old reminiscences with his fellow-veterans; he would associate once more with those in his own rank of life. We did not say aloud, but we felt, that he belonged to an order different from ourselves. We were jolly fellows, good fellows, no nonsense about us, and all that; but we had not his polish of mind and manner, that indescribable something which forms an invisible yet impassable barrier between the classes in life.

Twelve o'clock! He promised to be home by midnight, or shortly after, and the major was punctual. At twelve-twenty we heard his key in the door, but he seemed unable to open it. One of us went into the passage to unlatch. Two or three of us stood up and filled the doorway of the sitting-room.

"The old gentleman has taken so much port that he can't hit the keyhole. Wicked old major!" said one.

But, when the door opened, and we saw him in the glare from the hall-light, the rising joke died away on our lips.

He arrived in his dress suit, *without the greatcoat.*

"Good gracious, major! Why! what is the meaning of this? Where is the greatcoat?"

He came in, looking very white and depressed, the curl over his forehead out of twist, his collar limp, his shoulders stooping. He walked more lamely than usual. We made him come into the warm room. His hands were like ice. We forced him to take some spirit and water. We tried to rouse him. It was in vain. He looked utterly crushed.

"What is the matter, sir? What has happened?"

After a while we learned what had occurred. The evening had passed very pleasantly; never more so. When he left the drawing-room, he descended to the hall and asked for his greatcoat. It was lost. It was nowhere hanging up. It had not fallen behind a bench. It was not lying across a chair. Then the porter said he was very much afraid that some rascal, taking advantage of the door being open upon the arrival of a guest, had slipped into the hall unobserved, and had walked off with the newest and best of the greatcoats. Thus was the disappearance accounted for. It could be accounted for on no other hypothesis.

"Shall we lend you one of Sir Archibald's to go home in?" asked the servant.

"No, thank you."

So the major had walked home in his dress suit, without his new greatcoat. That was lost—lost for ever. There was not the smallest prospect of its being recovered. The poor old man was utterly cast down. Without the greatcoat he could no longer walk abroad respectably. He sat in the arm-chair, with his head down and his hands shaking. We did our best to encourage him; but what could we promise? He could not possibly raise the money for a new greatcoat. Besides, this one, now lost, was unpaid for. He would not take more than a little drop of brandy and water. He could not look before him. The future was not to be faced without a greatcoat. Presently he stood up and lit his candle; he would go to bed. He was tired; perhaps to-morrow he would be better.

We squeezed his hand, and sat speechless, listening to his foot as he went upstairs. He dragged his lame leg wearily after him.

"Poor old chap!" said I; "he seems done for completely."

Next morning we were all assembled at breakfast —that is, all but the major—when a rap came at the front door and a ring at the bell. Jemima answered. A moment after she came in with the greatcoat—yes, the identical greatcoat over her arm. Sir Archibald's valet had brought it. He had seen it, with the other, in the hall, had believed it to belong to a gentleman staying in the house, and, to avoid confusion, had removed it to the library. The mistake had only been found out when all the guests were gone, and the servant had come over with the greatcoat the first thing in the morning.

I ran upstairs, to rouse the major with the joyful news. I knocked at his door, but received no answer. I opened it and looked in. I saw the old man on his knees by his bedside. He was saying his prayers. I would not disturb him, so drew back. He was a long time over these same prayers. I looked in again. He had not stirred. Then, with a start, I saw that the bed had not been slept in, and the major was in his dress suit. I went up to him and touched him.

He was dead.

The loss of the greatcoat had been the last disappointment he could bear. The brave old heart had given up the battle, and had stopped beating.

When afterwards the greatcoat pockets were searched, there were found in them two letters. One was the bill for the coat; the other bore an American stamp. It was from his brother—a penitent letter;

he was now doing well, and he enclosed to Major Cornelius a draft for a hundred pounds. The letter had not been opened.

WANTED: A READER.

———◆———

I.

Monday, April 1.

Extract from the " Times," April 1, 188—.

"Wanted: a Reader; fluent, cultured, with good organ. Apply personally (when terms can be arranged): M. and N., 90 Red Lion Square, W.C."

Extract from the Diary of Matthew Welsford, Esq., *of* 90 *Red Lion Square.*

April 1, 188—.—I and my brother Nicolas (I say "I and Nicolas," not "Nicolas and I," because I am the elder by two years and five months) have advertised for a Reader. My throat will not allow of my reading aloud to him. I suffer from chronic bronchitis, the result of cursed inaction here in rooms in town. To a man accustomed all his life to open air, riding after the hounds, taking a five-barred gate whenever he met it, braving all weathers—it is enough to break down his constitution to be mewed up in London chambers. However, my hunting days are over for ever. I am in the sere and yellow leaf, aged sixty-seven, an old bachelor. Nicolas also is an old bachelor, failing, fast failing—he wouldn't have taken so enthusiastically to archæology till his mind is besotted, unless he were collapsing mentally. What a farce it is his setting up a simulated enthusiasm for antiquities. Why, I don't believe he can read the Greek alphabet, and his Latin is as rusty as my throat.

Ever since the death of our father, Laurence Welsford, Esq., J.P. and D.L., and squire and lord of the manor of Puddlecombe, in Somerset, have I and Nicolas been banished from the country, its fresh joys and associations and salubrious pursuits. Our elder brother, Laurence, married when he was aged forty-nine—I suppose it was right that he should—though, for the life of me, I cannot see why any man should sacrifice his independence, pleasure, elasticity, for the sake of a woman. Still, he was the elder brother, and land has its claims, and exacts of a man who owns it to marry and be the father of a son to inherit the acres after him. No doubt Laurence II. was right. I can only thank Providence I was not the eldest son. In course of time Laurence III. appeared, and then Laurence II., having done his duty to the land, died.

When Laurence II. (our brother) came to the property, I and Nicolas had to leave—that is just thirty-five years ago—and then we took chambers in town ; these same chambers we now occupy, the first floor of No. 90 Red Lion Square. Ever since then—for these thirty-five years—I have had chronic bronchitis. On the death of Laurence II. I should have liked much to have gone back to Puddlecombe, and resumed my hunting; but it was not manageable. Laurence II. behaved badly by us (me and Nicolas). Instead of constituting us guardians of and trustees for his son, Laurence III., as he ought to have done, he left the boy entirely under the control and management of his mother. It was a slight passed upon us, the boy's bachelor uncles, and it was bad for the boy, for what can a woman know of the way in which a youth should be reared? However, I forgive my brother Laurence ; let bygones be bygones. If a man will marry, he puts himself in as complete slavery as did Samson when he laid his head on the lap of Delilah. He no longer has a head of his own, a heart of his own, a will of his own. I suppose women are necessary in the world. I have sufficient belief in Providence to be sure that if they were not useful in some way they would not have been created. I believe, also, that mosquitoes, and rattlesnakes, and Terra del Fuego have their beneficent purposes, but I fail to see them.

I have no doubt that, from her own point of view, Jane—that is, the widow of Laurence II., and mother of Laurence III.—was right in letting Puddlecombe House, with the shooting, for twenty-one years. It would have been expensive to keep up the house, and she desired to be with her son whilst he went through his education. Still, it was bad taste. For twenty-one years it has debarred me from going into the country in the hunting season and having a run after the hounds. In other words, Jane confirmed my bronchitis as a chronic complaint.

I and Nicolas are fairly comfortable in our chambers. We have the first floor. Each of us has his own bedroom, and we have sitting-room and dining-room in common. When I say " in common," I mean that we have our meals together in the latter, and sit and lounge together in the former ; but as to the arrangement and ornamentation of the rooms, each exercises his own taste and stamps his own individuality on them severally. Mine is the parlour; his the dining-room. The walls of the former are adorned with hunting scenes and oil portraits of horses ; over the doors are hung my whips and spurs, and between the pictures are foxes' heads and brushes ; and the antlers of red deer rise above the paintings.

As for the dining-room—Nicolas has converted it into a library, and lined the sides with bookcases that contain the transactions of various antiquarian, and old dust, and rag, and bone, and bottle societies. I have no patience with Nicolas ! He set up to be an antiquary ! Why, there are a lot of old mounds on the down in our parish—tumuli, I believe he calls them—and he never once attempted to open them, when we were at Puddlecombe thirty-five years ago. I don't believe a word about Nicolas's weak eyes, which incapacitate him from reading, and necessitate our advertising for a reader. I believe he has donned the blue spectacles simply and solely to give himself a musty, old, archæological, palæolithic air.

Extract from the Diary of NICOLAS WELSFORD, Esq., *F.R.S., F.R.A.S., F.S.A., F.R.N.S., &c., &c.*

April 1, 188—.—The oculist has strictly forbidden my reading much, and what can be a more terrible privation to a man of letters than to be robbed of his books? Matthew and I have decided to hire a reader between us. I do hope he will not insist on *The Field* being gone through from title to colophon. I want *The Antiquary.* What a farce it is for Matthew to profess such enthusiasm about sport. Why, he has not bestridden a horse these thirty-five years, and I know what his sportsmanship was like before that. I do not believe he went half-a-dozen times out in the season. He was afraid to go out in the east wind lest he should get hoarse, and afraid to go out in a west wind lest he should get wet; and he always pretended the reason was that there would be no sport; for the scent would not lie in a frost, and would be washed away by rain. Matthew is, and always was, a humbug. He never took a hedge, much less a gate, in his life. As for the foxes' heads and brushes in his room, he bought them all in Wardour Street; I know he did. He never once deserved one or other, as he never was elsewhere in the field than last. If there be one thing I cannot abide, it is false pretence. Let a man not set himself up to be other than he is. Matthew has completely deluded himself into the conviction that he is an old weather-beaten pink. I have seen him cry over " Old John Peel "—what a , humbug he is ! He makes me quite angry.

I look back to our life at the old home with the bitterest regret. On Puddle Down are a range of barrows—five in all, if I remember right. I never thought of exploring them when I was at Puddle-combe, thirty-five years ago. Now, what chance is there of my ever being able to appear as the author of a paper in any archæological magazine? There are no mounds in London, but heaps of rubbish shot by dustmen. The great opportunity of immortalising my name is gone from me.

I don't believe a bit in Matthew's bronchitis. It is simply fancy. He has nothing else to occupy his empty mind than his own maladies. Why does he not take up some pursuit—as palæontology, anthropology, or palæography?

II.

TUESDAY, APRIL 2.

From the Diary of MATTHEW WELSFORD.

April 2.—Mrs. Sache attends to us. She lives somewhere in the areal world, below the level of the ground floor and the doorsteps, and scraper, and mat, in the region of the sewers, and gas-pipes, and water-pipes, and earthworms, into which, through round orifices in the pavement, the coals are poured. I have never been down, like Orpheus, into that nether world; unlike him, I have no desire to descend. There, however, Mrs. Sache lives and cooks. She does our rooms, lights our fires, and makes our coffee, grills our chops, devils our kidneys, and cooks our dinners. Thence she rises with a duster betimes, and also with the food; thither she descends into the dust, and goes down with the scraps to eat them in privacy. When we ring the bell, up she pops; when we wave the hand, down she drops. Oh, surely, that

areal world is the ideal region for all women ! Oh,
would that all women would efface themselves as
speedily and effectually as Mrs. Sache !

The first applicant for our readership arrived punctually at 2 P.M.—tiresomely enough, just as I, on one
side of the fire, and Nicolas, on the other, had fallen
into a nap after our lunch. We were roused out of
it, not in the best of humours.

The applicant was a tall, ill-built man, with a shock
of light hair, a pasty face, a light moustache, a frock-
coat of diagonal, very glossy at the elbows and white
at the seams. His boots were big and shapeless.
He gave his name as Mr. Niederwald.

"Will you take a chair?" I said coldly.

"You are M.," said he, looking at me, "and you,
saire, are N.," looking at Nicolas, "and I, my saires,
am ze Reader."

"You are a foreigner ?" asked Nicolas.

"Saire ! I am a Scherman, a native of Hann-over.
We did give you kings. Schorge ze First, Schorge ze
Zecond, Schorge ze Dirty, Schorge ze Forty, Wilhelm
ze Forty, and ze present Queen Victoria—all Scherman."

"But," said I, "we do not want a reader of German,
we neither of us understand the language."

"Ah, bah ! I am master of many languages. I can
read you French and Italian, and Latin and Greek,
and I know ze Hebrew alphabet."

"But," said I, hastily, for I saw that Nicolas was
pricking up, " we doubt your knowledge of the English
tongue."

"Well, now !"—he spread his chest—"you have

haired me. I know ze English speech better zan ze English themselves. I do speak her grammatically."

"Are you accustomed to horses?" I asked.

"Ze what? what you say?"

"Horses," I replied sternly. "Can you break in a hunter? Can you ride a mustang? Are you able to take a hurdle?"

"What you mean? Ride! Me—ride horses?"

"Yes."

He shook his head. "Me—me—nimmer, nimmer! Zey would kick me off and to little pieces."

"Then," said I, rising, "I am heartily sorry there has been a mutual misunderstanding. The advertisement in the *Times* was for a rider, not a reader. But, sir, if you should feel inclined for a circus—"

"Saire! I am a man of letters and learning, do you insult me?"

"Not at all. Good afternoon."

He had scarcely left the room when another applicant appeared. This was a hard-featured, elderly —well, lady she would call herself, I prefer to call her person. She made a curtsy as she entered.

"Hope I find you well, gentlemen," she said. "Well now, this is satisfactory. When I saw your adver—tisement in the *Times*, says I to myself, ' Susan, it be two old ladies, and their names are respectively Mary and Nora ;' and, gents both, I did hesitate, ·I confess it, coming to offer myself to ladies, for ladies are so mighty exacting and particular, specially when it comes to money, I always find that ladies are harder to deal with than gentlemen ; the latter are always so amiable and obliging and yielding, but as my dear ma' said to me, 'Susan, it's the way you have with 'em, no gentleman can resist you. You seem to twist 'em round your finger.' You'll excuse me saying so, Gents M. and N., it was only mother's fun, and I hope I'm taking no liberty in repeating her sportive remarks. Now I should like, if I'm not making *too* bold, to know which of you gents is M., and which is N., and also, if you'll not go for to consider me *too* forward, I should like to know whether M. stands for Maximilian, or Marmaduke, or Montague, or—"

" Madame," said I.

" I'm not married, sir," fluttered the person. " Only Miss."

" Miss," said I, " you must have misread our advertisement. We desired a *Reader*, not a *Talker*."

From the Diary of NICOLAS WELSFORD.

April 2.—It really is trying to have to think and act for two persons. My brother Matthew makes great fuss about his seniority, but when it comes to doing anything that is unpleasant, with exercise of responsibility, he leaves all to me. I must be his monkey to snatch the chestnuts from the fire for him.

We have had three applicants to-day for our vacant office of reader. The two first were very undesirable persons, a German professor and a vulgar old maid. Matthew ought to have seen their unsuitability at a glance, and discharged them, but he left that to me. I looked towards him, and coughed, and made signs, but to no purpose, I had to show them the door.

The third applicant was a man.　He was lame of a leg, dressed in a horsey costume.　He had only one boot, but that was odorous of stable.

"M. or N., sirs!" touching his forelock.

My brother and I bowed stiffly.

"I'll take a chair, sirs," said he.　"Had an accident, lost a leg, or part of one."

"You've surely mistaken your vocation," said I, "in applying for a readership."

"Not at all, sir!" touching his forehead sharply— he was jockey in all his movements.　"Do anything to earn an honest penny.　Jack of all trades, possibly master of none."　Then he burst into an explosion of laughter and spray that smelt of gin.

My blood ran cold.

"I beg your pardon," said I, "am I to understand—"

"Right you are, sir!"—with a touch of his forelock —"I'm the chap to be your reader.　I does a little ossling here and again to gents at an emporium of 'osses in Theobald's Road, and odds and ends of times I might drop in and pick up some coppers by reading."

I began to feel nervous.　My brother sat up in his chair.　He was interested in the man, as having to do remotely with sport ; so I stepped in quickly with—

"Are you a Greek scholar?"

"All I can't read is Greek to me."

"Very sorry.　We wanted the plays of Æschylus and Euripides read to us in the original tongue."

That did for our ostler reader.

III.

WEDNESDAY, APRIL 3.

The Diary of NICOLAS WELSFORD, *continued.*

April 3.—We had no more calls yesterday, and to-day none came till ten minutes to four, just as we began to suppose that we should have none for the day.

The door opened, and in came a young girl in black, with a small bonnet. Matthew and I were sitting over the fire—I, with my back to the door. I turned, and saw her standing in the middle of the room, with her large grey eyes on us.

Matthew, as usual, was of no use at all. He looked bewildered and disgusted. He hates women, or, rather, he despises them; thinks and speaks of them contemptuously. A fit of coughing came over him, and he became red in the face, almost purple.

She waited patiently till his fit was over, and then she said to me and him, " You want a reader ? "

Matthew signed towards me. " My brother has weak eyes, and cannot read to himself."

I signed towards Matthew. " My brother has a constitutional bronchitis, and cannot read aloud."

She looked at each of us in turn, and said quietly :—

" If you will indicate the book, I will read, and show you my qualification."

I looked across at Matthew, and saw him looking at me. What he meant, I cannot say. He made faces, and faces are not alphabetical characters.

She took up the *Times* that lay on the sofa, and read us the first leader.

Then I looked again at Matthew, and he looked a me.

"What hours, and how many are required?" she asked.

"Two every day is what my brother had determined on," said I; "that is, if—"

"At half-a-crown an hour," she said. "Good. Morning or afternoon?"

"My brother and I had thought that from half-past four till six-thirty would suit us best. We dine at seven."

"Good. I will be here every day at half-past four, and read till half-past six. If I come, and find you out, or indisposed, you pay the same. If I do not find myself able to come, I will telegraph."

"I think that—that—" began Matthew.

"And I—I am of opinion that—" began I.

"Yes! What?" she asked promptly, looking at one, then at the other, with her large, intelligent grey eyes.

"Merely," said I, "my brother will fix what is to be read one day, and I what is to be read the other day —that is, in the event of our—"

"Good," she said. "To-morrow shall be the first day. The elder of you, gentlemen, will fix the reading for to-morrow. Half-a-crown per hour—half-past four to half-past six. Expect me." She bowed, first to Matthew, then to me, and withdrew.

Matthew seemed throttling, as though a bandage had been put suddenly round his neck. I felt bewildered, blinded, as though a kerchief had been tied over my eyes. Matthew and I are slow people; we take long in coming to a decision, we are averse to being hurried. This young creature had come in on us—and engaged us, instead of our engaging her.

"Nick," said Matthew, "telegraph at once, and decline her services."

"Can't do it, Matt," I replied; "I know neither her name nor address."

"Very well, have five shillings ready to-morrow; pay her off, and send her packing."

IV.

THURSDAY, APRIL 4.

From the Diary of MATTHEW WELSFORD.

April 4.—Really, my brother Nicolas is insupportable. The effrontery of the man is appalling—and he an archæologist. We had arranged mutually that the Readeress was to be dismissed after her first session of two hours. Nothing of the sort was done, and we shall be infested with her again to-morrow. I gave Nicolas two half-crowns, and he folded them in an envelope, and put them in a little Japanese tray at the edge of the cheffonier near the door, before half-past four. I cannot see why it was necessary for Nicolas to be so fastidious about the table cover that day. What did it matter if one side hung down six inches lower than the other? Also, why did he arrange the books on the table, so as to radiate at the same angles from the empty flower-vase in the middle ?

All the morning he had one of the chairs turned up before the fire in the, to me, most incomprehensible position.

" What is that for ? " I asked.

" Matt," he replied, " I have a conscience. That chair has not been sat in, except very casually, for thirty-five years, and the cushion must be damp, and require airing ; and as the young lady will be here for two hours occupying it — there is no knowing—it might settle on her chest, and bring her to an early grave."

" What does that concern us ? " I asked roughly. " We shall never see her again."

" How can you—how can you, Matt ! " exclaimed Nick. " Really you require humanising."

Punctually at half-past four—no, at twenty-five minutes past four, to be exact—we heard the bell ring, and in another three minutes, Mrs. Sache opened the door and announced " Miss Smith."

" I beg pardon," said I, " I did not catch your name."

" My name is Emily Smith," she said.

She was given a chair in the middle opposite the fire, so that she could be warm, and that the light from the window might fall on her book. As my brother was on one side of the fire and I on the other, we could both hear very well whilst she read.

It was my place to fix the lecture, so I gave her that engrossing work " Stonehenge on the Horse " to read. She read well, intelligently, in a pleasant flow-

It is because the nape of the neck is so sensitive that the puggary is worn, to protect it from the burning sun. Very well, or rather, very ill—I—even I, who suffer from bronchitis, am to sit with a column of cold air impinging on my nape for two hours, that Nicolas may *glower like a ghoul* at Miss Smith! I say that, if there be one thing more than another which stirs up my gall, it is insolence shown by the strong to the weak. What is it but insolence in Nicolas to sit eating Miss Smith up, so to speak, with his eyes (screened though they be behind blue spectacles)? I do not know what rubbish he forced her to read, but I do know that for two hours he never took his eyes off her. If that is not insulting to a respectable female, pray inform me what is. I am a man of honour and conscience, and I will not allow any impertinence to be offered to a young lady of the highest character and most brilliant attainments in my apartments. I am the elder brother. I will take my seat to-morrow in my own chair, and insist on Nicolas occupying his own. Then he will see, for two entire hours, only a finely-cut dark profile against the light, the brow straight, then a delicate little dip, and then the most charming outline of a nose conceivable, a little arched at the bridge, and slightly *retroussé* at the tip. Now and then, when the head is turned, the light falls on the nostril, which is chiselled very finely. The lips are—but there, enough.

I can be satirical if I like. I said to Nicolas with a sneer: "It must be very exhausting work to Miss Smith, and I should think she would need some nourishment to support her under it." Of course I meant his insolent stare, not the reading, though that must be exhausting too. Cave men, what pretty girl can wax warm over such cold creatures as they? I went on: "To strengthen her for the task, brother Nick, had I not better order Mrs. Sache always to bring up the tea whilst she is with us?"

"Certainly, nothing more proper," he replied. He is so hard as not to feel the withering blast of my sarcasm.

VI.

SATURDAY, APRIL 6.

The Diary of MATTHEW WELSFORD, *continued.*

April 6.—I have been considering that it is hardly fair to Miss Smith to ask her to read veterinary or doggy books, so I am determined to set her this afternoon to one of Mr Surtees' sporting novels. "Jorrick's Jaunts" sounds vulgar; "Plain or Ringlets" sounds better, or "Ask Mamma." We'll have the former.

I never met with such besotted, piggish obstinacy as that of Nicolas. I asked him very politely to take his usual place this evening. I pointed to the draught through the keyhole as making the chair on the right unsuitable for me. He pouted and frowned, and said his eyes were bad as well as my throat, and he would sit beside me on the left, by bringing his chair over to that side. I showed him the absurdity of the arrangement. We could not both sit on that one side of the fire, or his head would cut off the light from Miss Smith's book. After much argument, and almost coming to high words, it was settled that we should alternate day by day. When she read my books, I would sit on the left ; when she read his books, I would go over to the right into the shade—no—into the light, that is, face the light but see only her silhouette. My brother went out this morning, which is unusual with him, and to my surprise produced some flowers he had bought in Covent Garden Market, which he put in a vase in the middle of the table. I have never known him do this before. If it had been old potsherds, or flint arrow-heads, or dolichokephalous skulls, I should not have been surprised—but lilies of the valley! Some things I have observed in Nicolas's conduct lately have made me anxious about him, not that we have lunacy in our family—Heaven forbid !

From the Diary of NICOLAS WELSFORD.

April 6.—I cannot make my brother out. I never thought he had much brains. I think I perceive tokens of softening of the brain, leading to abject imbecility. He went out this afternoon, his usual walk, as I supposed into the Park, but, instead of that, he must have gone to Covent Garden, for he returned with a narcissus in his button-hole. Never in all my life have I seen Matthew wear a flower before. If it had been a horse-chestnut, or a dog-daisy, it would have been different ; but—a narcissus!—a narcissus poeticus, too ! What is the world coming to ?

Nor is that all. I am convinced he has been to his French coiffeur and had *something* done to his hair and his moustache. Matthew is shy to-day, and stands with his back to the light to avoid my noticing him and making observations on what I see. I am positive his hair is, at least, two shades less grey than it was yesterday. There is an unwonted sprightliness in his manner that I do not like. It is unwholesome. At his age—sixty-seven—giving himself these airs! He is a great deal older than I am ; he is a man with one foot in the grave, breaking down fast.

Miss Smith came as usual, punctual to the minute. I had been down in the morning to the nether regions to see Mrs. Sache, and I had told her to be sure and bring up three cups and tea things, some nice crisp biscuits buttered, and some wafers of bread, also some cakes at half-past five. I thought that Miss Smith must need some refreshment after reading such dry nonsense as Matthew would require her to waste two hours over. My brother was, however, so far reasonable to-day as to give Emily—I mean Miss Smith—"Plain or Ringlets" to read, instead of a technical work. Emily—I mean Miss Smith—was scrupulous about the tea ; she looked at her watch, a poor little silver affair, and as she took ten minutes over her cup and bit of bread and butter, she gave us an extra ten minutes of reading after the stroke of half-past six. When she rose, she said, " Gentlemen, to-morrow is Sunday. I shall, of course, not be here till Monday." Before we could remonstrate, Miss Smith was gone.

VII.

SUNDAY, APRIL 7.

From the Diary of MATTHEW WELSFORD.

April 7, Sunday.—I detest Sundays. Insufferably dull days.

From the Diary of NICOLAS WELSFORD.

April 7, Sunday.—What a long day this is!

VIII.

MONDAY, APRIL 8.

From the Diary of NICOLAS WELSFORD.

April 8, Monday.—Matthew is an arch imposter. I don't believe in his chronic bronchitis. He has left off his flannel band round his throat. He has left off clearing his throat. He has ceased to cough.

From the Diary of MATTHEW WELSFORD.

April 8, Monday.—Nicolas is not to be trusted. I shall never believe him again. His weak eyesight is simulated. He has left off his blue spectacles.

IX.

TUESDAY, APRIL 9.

From the Diary of NICOLAS WELSFORD.

April 9.—I thought yesterday that it was possible a young lady might think her two hours heavy if devoted to the "Cave Men," so I changed the book, and gave her Milman's "Samor" to read. It is a fine poem, and opens as well as enriches the mind. "Samor" is identical with Aurelius Ambrosius, the great British hero, who was kinsman to King Arthur, and was in the slaughter of Calthacth when the flower of the British chivalry was treacherously murdered by the Saxons. The fine Welsh poem, the "Gododin," is believed to have been composed by Aneurin when prisoner in the hands of the Saxons after this dastardly piece of treachery. I have little doubt that Emily's mind has been trained to consider British history as beginning with the Saxons, and that she is so steeped in Dr. Freeman's theory that she does not believe in the permanence of the Briton in our land, nor regard British history prior to the invasion as trustworthy, nor any source of history reliable except the Anglo-Saxon—or, as Dr. Freeman presumptuously calls it—*the* Chronicle. I hope the perusal of "Samor" will kindle Emily's imagination, and make her desire to know more of the primitive Keltic and prækeltic—Ivernian, as Dr. Rhys calls them—inhabitants of our isle. I should be so happy to go through a course of prehistoric archæology with her, and the ethnology of the British Isles. I will try through "Samor" to rouse in her an interest in these matters, and then I will propose to give her every day an hour's instruction in my library, where we shall not be bothered with that old fogrum, Matthew. It would be so nice to go over the map of Ancient Britain together, and trace the limits of the Ordovices, and Iceni, and Brigantes, with our fingers and our heads together. I dare say it might be managed at half-past two, when Matthew is out for his constitutional. I am convinced she is under Freeman's baleful influence. I feel it quite a duty to disabuse her mind of this Saxo-mania.

I have eyes in my head, though they may at times be weak (they are better now), and I can see that

Emily does not like Matthew so much as me, which is only natural, as she and I are so much nearer an age.

X.

WEDNESDAY, APRIL 10.

From the Diary of MATTHEW WELSFORD.

April 10, *Wednesday.*—That tiresome, prosy old idiot Nicolas! I never can get one moment in the room with little Millie alone, and yet I have questions burning on my lips that I want to ask her, but cannot do so before that stupid Nick. There he sits in his chair opposite me, as if glued into it. What does he care for " Plain or Ringlets?" I know that the story is utterly without interest for him. Why then does he stick in the room whilst it is being read? He might as well go into his library, and take up the " Transactions" of his learned Societies and dip his nose into them. His eyes are better—I don't believe they ever were bad—so there is no excuse for his hanging about the parlour—*my* room—like a fly in November. I want to know so much about little Millie. I want to know to what part of England she belongs. I know she is a lady, her speech is so free from dialect and vulgar intonation. I should like to know a good deal about her, and I cannot get an opportunity of speaking to her privately. She would be frank with me; I have eyes in my head, and I can see she has taken a dislike to Nicolas, and leans rather to me—which, after all, is natural. My life has been spent in the open air, on horseback, "Tally-ho!" which has made me hale in body, sound in wind, and with a cheery, fresh complexion, whereas Nicolas has dwelt among Cave men, and picked among bones and dust till he has withered prematurely; and though he may be a few months my younger in years, he is immeasurably my senior in appearance and lack of vitality.

I know what I will do. I will not be baulked. I must find out all about poor little Millie, whether she is an orphan, whence she comes, how I can help her, and a thousand other things which my kind heart prompts me to learn of her. I will not be baulked by Nicolas, or any one else. If he chooses, like an old fossil, to stick in the house, I'll go out and intercept Millie as she comes tripping along the pavement of Red Lion Square ; and I'll take with me the key of the garden, and insist on her coming in to see the crocuses and daffodils there, and we will take a seat under a flowering almond, and I know her little full heart will open to me, and she will confide to me all her cares, and sorrows, and ambitions.

What fun! Nicolas will be sitting at home at No. 90 all the while, waiting, waiting, and with his sheepish eyes wide, wondering why little golden-haired, rose-cheeked Millie doesn't come to read to him.

> 'Tis a southerly wind and a cloudy sky
>   Proclaim it a hunting morning.
> To horse, my brave riders, away we fly,
>   Dull sleep from our drowsy heads scorning.
>   Tol-rol-de-rol-tiddle-de-rol.
>   Bright Phœbus the hills adorning !
>   Then hark ! hark ! forward !
>   Tol-tiddle-de——

No, I have not got it quite correct. It is thirty-five
years since I sang it at a hunting dinner. But I can't
help singing and laughing at the thought of the faces
Nicolas will make.

From the Diary of NICOLAS WELSFORD.

April 10, *Wednesday.*—Not one chance can I get of
speaking alone to Emily—my Emily. That old
hippopotamus, Matthew, blocks my way.

What a demure, self-possessed little hussy she is !

We try—Matthew and I—to interrupt the reading
occasionally for a little talk, either on the weather or
on the subject she is reading. She waits, with her
finger in the book, marking the line where she left off,
till we have done, and says nothing. When we cease,
she resumes reading. We try to draw her into conversation, but she is shy of that.

" Miss Smith," said I, " we should much like to know
your opinion on what you have been reading."

" I beg your pardon," she replied, " I am hired to
read, not to talk."

There was some difficulty at first in getting her to
lay aside her mantle or jacket, or velocipede, or whatever be the name given by ladies to the things they
put on their backs and over their arms when they go
out. Indeed, we never succeeded with the hat or
bonnet. (The thing has strings, so I suppose it is a
bonnet ; a hat, I believe has only a bit of elastic ; but
the thing is of white straw, and has a black riband
round it, and is tied down under the chin by two black
ribands that emerge from the aforenamed black,

circumambient riband, and tie under the dear dainty little chin in such a duck of a manner. Now I can understand what it is to be a bow! This is a pun, no one will see this, so I make it.)

She always brings a parasol or umbrella with her. Directly she enters the room, up leaps Matthew. I rise from my seat the moment I hear her foot on the stairs, and we run, literally run to meet her, and divest her, the one of the mantle, the other of the umbrella. She won't take off the bonnet (or hat, whichever it is), but she is obliged to let the mantle go, because we keep our rooms very hot, and the umbrella, because it never rains or snows in our parlour. Then, when we have taken these articles away, we conduct her in the most gallant manner conceivable, never seen elsewhere than on the stage and in Caldecott's pictures, to her seat, which is always aired for her by the fire all the morning. But—really—I am sometimes obliged to blush for Matthew. I have seen him hold and hug her mantilla for the whole two hours of the reading. This so shocked me—I felt ashamed at his conduct, so like that of one with softening of the brain, that next time I received the mantle; then he held and hugged the umbrella.

I am resolved to have a moment's private conversation with my poor Emily, and the only way to have it is to catch her before she comes here. To-morrow I will go out half an hour before the time she is due, and look about down Red Lion Square, or Orange Street till I see the white straw and black ribbons, when I will dart out and run and meet her. I have the key of the gardens, and I will insist on her coming into

them with me. I will go beforehand and wipe down
the green bench under the almond tree (now in flower),
as it is generally deep buried under soots. Then we
will sit there, with our backs to No. 90, and I will explain to her my plan of an hour for study together of
Keltic antiquities and ethnology.

What a joke! How puzzled that owl of a brother
of mine will be at her not appearing at the proper
moment to read "Plain or Ringlets." How he will
fume and stamp about the room, and never dream of
looking out of the window at the garden, where the
back of the white straw bonnet and the back of my
silk hat would be visible under the almond tree.

> Had I a heart for falsehood framed,
>   I ne'er could injure thee !
> For something, something, something else,
>   Which clean escapeth me !

I forget the lines ; I have not looked at verses and
repeated poetry these thirty-five years.

XI.

THURSDAY, APRIL 11.

The Diary of NICOLAS WELSFORD, *continued.*

April 11, *Thursday.*—Unaccountable fatality. I
was round the corner of Orange Street at a quarter
past four, pretending to look at the old interesting
books exhibited in Mr. Salkeld's window for sale,
but really with my eyes down the square—square it

is not, but an attenuated parallelogram. All at once, five minutes to the half hour, I saw the flash of the white straw. Away I went as fast as I could, and came breathlessly upon her, with the garden key extended in my hand, when whom should I see behind her, close upon her, but Matthew, also hot with running, and also holding out his garden key.

Emily looked surprised out of her lovely dove-like eyes, first at me, then at Matthew.

" Excuse me," I stammered, "don't ring at No. 90—here is the house-key. Mrs. Sache has rheumatism in her knees."

" Oh ! " exclaimed Matthew, "that is the garden key, Nicolas. I have hurried home to open the door with my key for Miss Smith, because Mrs. Sache has the headache, and the sound of the bell is torture to her, poor thing."

XII.

FRIDAY, APRIL 12.

Letter received by MESSRS. M. AND N. WELSFORD *on April* 12.

" April 11.

" MY DEAR UNCLES,—Expect me to drop in on you shortly. I am coming up to town on most important and pleasant business. I cannot say precisely on which day, and by what train ; but I shall venture to trespass on your wonted hospitality, and ask you to let me have a shake-down in your comfortable spare bedroom, and take pot-luck at your well-furnished table, where I shall do justice to Mrs. Sache's excellent cookery, and your not less admirable wines. My mother may detain me, but I shall come as early as she will let me, next week.

> "I remain, my dear Uncles, M. and N.,
>> "Your affectionate Nephew,
>>> "LAURENCE WELSFORD.

"To M. and N. Welsford, Esquires,
90 Red Lion Square."

From the Diary of MATTHEW WELSFORD.

April 12, *Friday.*—What a life we who live in town are called to live! We cannot call our houses our own. Just received a letter from my nephew Laurence. He is coming up to town, self-invited, to stay with us. For how long—three days, three weeks, three months —he does not say. Laurence is a fine, manly, frank fellow, and we are always glad to see him when he pays us a visit—which is entirely and solely when it suits his convenience to be in town. We see him about once in the twelvemonth for, maybe, a week or ten days. Now he is coming to London on business —legal, I presume ; and lawyers are so procrastinating in their work that there is no saying how long they may keep him dancing about them, and encumbering our rooms with his presence. What is to be done with him between half-past four and half-past six ? We cannot have him here during the Reading, and we cannot send little Millie away. I will not be deprived of my chapters of " Plain or Ringlets " for Laurence, or any other nephew. This

is one of the most aggravating *contretemps* I have endured. It will not do to have Laurence sitting here
and admiring Millie whilst she is reading to us. I'll
persuade him to go out for those two hours every
day, on the plea that we also have business, and must
not be disturbed.

How designing and serpentine in his cunning is
Nicolas. To-day he came in about four o'clock, as if
hot from a walk. " Oh, Matt," he exclaimed, " I have
just heard there is to be a meet of the Four-in-Hand
at the Marble Arch. It is to be at a quarter to five.
Jump into a hansom, and spin away. You will be in
time. I've almost run, and given myself palpatations,
to get here in time to inform you. You are so pas-
sionately addicted to that sort of thing that I knew
you would be eager, Matt, to be at the meet."

" Thank you," said I, coldly ; " I think I will *not* go
to the Marble Arch just now. I have been out, and
feel disposed to sit by the fire. My thanks to you
all the same ; but, brother Nick, as I was passing
down Holborn, I saw in Mr. Westall's window a copy
of Fergusson's ' Primitive Rude Stone Monuments,'
uncut, marked three shillings and fourpence ! Only
three-and-four for that volume so full of research, and
astounding yet well-considered theory. Run, Nick,
run with all your legs, and secure the volume. It is
certain to be snapped up. I saw several archæological-
looking men and antiquarian women prowling about
the window, snuffing at the book. Do go, Nick, you
may not have such another opportunity."

" Thank you," answered Nicolas, coldly ; " I do not
want the book. Fergusson is—rubbish ! "

Now, considering that I had taken the trouble to look at the work in question, mark its price, and observe its condition, all for Nicolas, I submit that he was rude and wanting in ordinary delicacy and gentlemanly feeling in not going to Mr. Westall's and buying the book. I would have done so if my brother had taken this trouble about me, not that I wanted the book, but to show him my appreciation of his attention.

" What a very strong smell of violets there is in the room!" I remarked. Simultaneously Nicolas said, snuffing—

" What a very strong scent of violets there is in the room ! "

" Is there ? " I said drily.

" Is there ? " he replied laconically.

Then, without another word, each took his place beside the fire. Nicolas was dissatisfied with me because I had not snapped at his bait and gone away to Marble Arch, and left him alone with Millie.

Now I could not have done that for more reasons than one. I had bought a bunch of purple violets on my walk, and intended to offer it to Millie, as a little innocent courtesy, could I only get my brother to turn his back. By each of our chairs, against the wall, on our respective sides of the fire-place, is a small folding bracket, on which we can put our glasses or books. As I took my place in the chair, I slipped my bouquet of purple violets behind a slate with memoranda I had on my bracket. Millie appeared as usual, and read to us as usual, I forget quite about what.

As she was about to leave, Nicolas, who, like a

maniac, had sat all the two hours embracing her fur-edged jacket, and stroking the fur with his disengaged right hand, as if he were coaxing a cat, started up, put his hand behind Dawkins's "Cave Men," which was on his shelf, produced a posy of white violets, and rushed tumultuously after Milly, nearly upsetting himself over a stool we had put for her feet, to invest her with her jacket, and present her with the white violets. No wonder the room had smelt insufferably, when a bunch of violets was hidden away behind a book. White violets smell five times as strongly as those that are purple.

At the same time I rose, in a dignified manner, with old-fashioned politeness, and stepping easily and lightly across the room, presented Millie, first with her umbrella, which I had been obliged to hold fast during two hours to preserve it from that lunatic Nicolas, who might have used it as a poker, and then I offered her my inoffensive bouquet of purple violets. She bowed, and combining the bunches into one, accepted them with thanks and departed.

From the Diary of NICOLAS WELSFORD.

April 12, *Friday.*—No wonder the room to-day was almost insupportable with the odour of violets. My brother had stowed away a bunch of purple violets behind his white notice slate, where the warmth of the room extracted its scent, and nearly stifled poor Emily whilst she was reading. Purple violets are unpleasantly strong, white violets have a subdued and delicate fragrance.

I intend calling in two professional men, eminent in matters of cerebral disease, to form a diagnosis of my brother's condition. To-day I could hardly contain my disgust. All the time Emily was reading, he sat holding her umbrella with both hands, and rubbing first his chin, then his lips gently to and fro upon the handle—that *she* touches. Then, when she rose to go, he went to his feet like a rocket, and got her umbrella athwart between his legs, which all but sent him sprawling on the floor ; whilst I lightly, and with the ease of a finished gentleman, handed her the mantle she wore out of doors. Then Matthew came floundering to the doorway after her, and nearly drove the umbrella into my ribs. He persisted in following her all the way down stairs, and opening the street door for her, and expanding the umbrella for her before putting it into her hands, although she assured him it was not raining. At the same time he pressed a posy of blue violets along with the stick of the umbrella into her hand.

She received it with the utmost reluctance.

XIII.

SATURDAY, APRIL 13.

The Diary of NICOLAS WELSFORD, *continued.*

April 13, *Saturday.*—What shall we do with ourselves to-morrow ? How the weeks fly ! Monday no sooner is passed, than we come to Saturday again. I had to pinch myself this morning to assure myself that I was in my senses, when I looked in the almanac and saw that to-day was Saturday. From half-past six on Saturday evening to half-past four on Monday evening makes forty-six hours, or two thousand seven hundred and sixty minutes. Two thousand seven hundred and sixty minutes! Why, it is a lifetime! I really cannot see why we should be deprived of all intellectual and moral enlightenment for two thousand seven hundred and sixty minutes, merely because of a Sunday coming in between Saturday and Monday.

When Emily was about to leave us this evening, I ventured to suggest that she should come and read to us on Sunday evening.

"Of course," I said, "we would not require you to read anything secular, such as Milman's ' Samor.'"

"Or frivolous," said Matthew, "such as ' Plain or Ringlets.'"

"But something serious," I observed.

"And edifying," spoke up Matthew.

"Such as ' Peep of Day,'" I proposed.

"Or the ' History of the Robins,'" suggested my brother.

"Gentlemen—" began Emily.

"Excuse me, Miss Smith," interrupted I, "you might have conscientious scruples against reading on the Sabbath for renumeration—"

"So come and read for lo—." A searching glance from my eyes dried up the insolent expression on Matthew's lips, for it he substituted "charity."

"Gentlemen," said Miss Smith—that is, Emily—" I am very sorry not to be able to accommodate you in this matter. Sunday is my one day that I have to devote entirely to my mother." She bowed and was gone.

XIV.

SUNDAY, APRIL 14.

From the Diary of MATTHEW WELSFORD.

April 14, *Sunday.*—Will the day never be over? A beast of a day. The French Directory was right. It made the Sunday to be one in ten, not seven.

From the Diary of NICOLAS WELSFORD.

April 14, *Sunday.*—Have lain in bed all day. What is the good of Sunday to any man? I hate it. I never could see the point of Sally in our Alley:

> " Of all the days are in the week,
> I dearly love but one day ;
> And that's the day that comes betwixt
> A Saturday and Monday."

It is opposed to all human experience. I hate it.

XV.

MONDAY, APRIL 15.

From the Diary of MATTHEW WELSFORD.

April 15, *Monday* (11 A.M.).—I had all yesterday to myself, to digest my resolutions, and I am confirmed in my intentions. I will make little Millie a present. Poor dear patient little soul! here she comes from a distance, pays sixpence for her 'bus each way—that leaves her, poor little soul, only four shillings as re-muneration for labours—on alternate days—not second to those of Hercules, in reading the tedious, pedantic lines of that prosy Milman.   I would not do it for five times the sum.   I know what an effort it is to use the voice for an hour without rest, and Millie has to read for two.   She must be exhausted and hungry at the end.   She goes home in a stuffy omnibus, and has a meagre supper of American cheese and bread and a little table beer.   Bah ! can human nature, and female beauty and sweetness, be maintained on American cheese and table beer?   She is young, and does not feel the wear and tear, does not know how much of life and elasticity and light the late Dean of St. Paul's is robbing her of by his rhodomontade about "Samor, Lord of the Bright City."

It shall not be.   I have a conscience.   I have noticed how much more worn, how much paler the little sweet-heart has become of late, and I know it is the journey —double daily, and the two hours of drudgery over that detestable poem—poem !   I see no poetry in it ; and then—American cheese, possibly canister Ram-ornie beef, and table beer as the ghastly termination. It shall not be.   In future she shall dine with us.   A cup of tea and a film of bread and butter is not sufficient to sustain nature.

I will do more.   I am determined to present her with a mark of my esteem at the brilliant manner in which she has read " Plain or Ringlets," and at the self-possession which she has shown in the face of Nicolas's effrontery.   She had always known how to keep him at a distance, without a word, merely by her reserved, lady-like, respect-commanding manner. The difficulty will be how to get her to accept the present. She is so cautious, wise, and distant. I will try what I can do in a roundabout way ; feel my ground before I take a step. If only I can get Nicolas out of the room.

I have seen a really charming bracelet in a jeweller's window, a gold serpent, with brilliants in the head and two rubies for eyes. Surely that will please her. I will go out and buy it.

Thank goodness ! No signs of Laurence yet.

From the Diary of NICOLAS WELSFORD.

April 15, *Monday* (11 A.M.).—May I never again experience such a day as yesterday. I lay in bed and ruminated. My ruminations led to one result. I am determined that this sort of thing shall not continue. We must try to put ourselves in the places of others. I did that yesterday, in spirit I followed Emily. I saw her engaged in giving lessons all day as a governess. I saw her hurry from one house to another. I felt how weary her poor little feet became, how hot and heavy her dear little head. I felt her hand, it was burning. I traced her in imagination, at mid-day to an eating-house, and saw her consume a little chop and some chips of potatoes, and sip a cup of coffee, then a butterine pat—made of Heaven knows what nastiness —and some bread, all porosity and crust. That was her dinner. On that, life and brain and nerve was to be sustained ! It shall not, it must not be ! I do not care what Matthew may say. I will insist on her staying every day and dining with us. I have a conscience, if he has not.

I will do more. My bowels of compassion are moved when I see the Golden Pet labouring for two hours through that vulgar, over-strained "Plain or Ringlets." The humour is elephantine, the jokes buffoonery, the characters defective. How she must hate the two hours over "Plain or Ringlets!" How she must sigh for the alternate days over the glowing, pure lines of "Samor"! I cannot bear to see her suffer under "Plain or Ringlets," and I cannot remunerate her too highly for the admirable way in which she renders Milman's immortal poem.

I have seen that she possesses—poor little heart!— only a common silver watch. I will go out and buy her a delicate, little, gold, lady's watch, diamond-set. It will be some token of the regard I feel for the way in which she keeps my brother at bay. Poor fellow! the softening of the brain with him has been like the removal of a balance-wheel from a watch; all his movements are capricious, there is no calculating on what he may say or do, but one lives in a constant condition of nervous tiptoe expectation of a catastrophe. If the malady would only become so pronounced as to justify me in having him sent to a private asylum for idiots, I would have him removed as speedily as possible, then—ah! well!—then—oh, then !

There will be some little difficulty, I anticipate, in getting Emily to accept my watch. She is so shy, timid, and shrinks from courtesies. I must be cautious, and beat about the bush.

What a blessing that Laurence has not come.

4.35 P.M.—I post up this evening all the events that

have taken place under the dates at which they occurred. I purchased the watch in the morning, with a gold chain, very pretty, rather costly. I hope little Emily will be pleased.

At 4.30, punctually, Emily was in our room. I flew to receive her mantle, and then—instead of depositing it anywhere in the sitting-room, with great forethought I carried it off, to secrete it elsewhere, and thus make Emily my prisoner at leisure. Without her mantle she could not go, and I would not let her have it back till after dinner.

In slipping out of the room, I did more, I ran to Mrs. Sache and told her to put an extra cover at table.

When I returned, which I did as quickly as possible, I saw that Matthew was agitated. He had been left four minutes alone with Emily. I trembled to think of what drivelling folly he might have been guilty in these four minutes, and I looked tremblingly, inquiringly at sweet Emily's sweet face. That re-assured me, it was placid as ever. Just then my planet favoured me. Matthew left the room. I looked hastily at the clock on the mantelshelf. It stood at 4.35. I had been out secreting the cloak and ordering the cover—only for four minutes. Now that Matthew was not in the room I seized my opportunity.

"Miss Smith," said I, "*do* let me persuade you to take off your bonnet."

"Thank you," she answered, "you must really excuse me."

"I want your candid opinion, Miss Smith—dear

T

Miss Smith," said I, and I produced the gold watch and chain. "What do you think of this? Is it not pretty? Is it not such as a lady would like to wear? It is a—a present I have bought for—" I hesitated; I saw her draw her lips together, "for a very dear—niece."

"It is certainly pretty," she answered. "But look at my silver watch. It belonged to my father. Though so clumsy, I would not part with it or exchange it for the best gold watch. It keeps perfect time."

At that moment I heard Matthew opening the door. I had just time to put the gold watch away before he came in. The clock stood at 4.40. He had been out of the room only four and a half minutes.

From the Diary of MATTHEW WELSFORD.

April 15, *Monday* (continued).—At 4.30 P.M., that little pearl, Millie Smith, arrived, punctual, as she always is, to the minute. I had bought the bracelet —rather expensive it was ; but still, if she likes it, what of that ?

Fortune stood me in good stead, for, no sooner had she come, than my brother Nicolas left the room. I seized occasion by the horns. I took her umbrella from her pretty, little, gloved hand.

"Miss Smith," I said, "*can* I persuade you to take off your bonnet? You will be so comfortable without."

"Thank you kindly," she said, "I am so comfortable in my bonnet that I cannot be more so without it."

"Miss Smith," I said then, with emotion in my heart, and a flutter in my voice, "my *dear* Miss Smith, may I ask you frankly to express an opinion?" I produced the bracelet. "Please to look at this. What do you think of it? Is it not very fanciful and pretty? The sparkling head of brilliants, the fiery, ruby eyes! Would not a certain young lady's arm look well with the serpent coiled round it? Would she not like to try it on? It is a present I have bought—I have bought—" I saw her draw back and look coldly at the ornament, "for—for—a very cherished—niece."

"I daresay it is nice," she answered, in even tones ; "but, when there is so much jewellery about, a lady is likely to eschew wearing anything which may be imitated in base materials. As I never go out anywhere in the evenings myself, I never wear bracelets."

Just then I heard Nicolas's steps, and I had only barely time to slip the bracelet into my pocket before he entered. I looked at the clock. The time was 4.35. I had, therefore, hardly had five minutes alone with Millie.

I took the occasion of my brother's entry to step out, carrying away her umbrella, which I purposed hiding somewhere. She could not leave without her umbrella, and I would not restore it to her till after dinner. By this innocent trick I hoped to force her to partake of our meal with us.

I called to Mrs. Sache, and told her to lay another cover at our table. Then I hurried back to the room. I was afraid of leaving Nicolas longer with Millie alone. In his state of mind there is no knowing what act of raving, roaring insanity he might be guilty of.

When I re-entered the parlour I thought he looked flurried, and I glanced with alarm at Millie, but was reassured by the unruffled sweetness of her face.

The clock hand stood at a few seconds off 4.40. I had therefore been allowed barely five minutes alone with her by that Cerberus of a brother.

At 5.30 Mrs. Sache brought up tea, and Millie interrupted her reading. At 5.35 she recommenced.

At 6.35 she put down the book, closed it, and stood up. Then I rose, and stood on the mat with my back to the fire. Nicolas also rose, and also stood on the mat, directing his back also to the fire. So we two brothers stood. We made no offer to invest our young friend with mantle and parapluie, as usual. We allowed her to look about for them in a perplexed, surprised manner, which was really very pretty and charming.

"Why—why—where are my things?" she asked.

"I have your umbrella," I said.

"I have your mantilla," said Nicolas.

I turned, and looked at my brother in surprise ; at the same moment he turned, and looked interrogatively at me.

"Oh, gentlemen! may I have them?" she asked, so prettily that my resolution almost gave way, and Nicolas took a step forward as if inclined to yield.

But I said firmly, " Miss Smith, you shall have your things all in good time. You must positively sit down again and dine with us. I hear Mrs. Sache already laying the table ; please take off your bonnet."

Then Nicolas said persuasively, " Miss Smith, you must really do us the favour of dining with us. You will find us inexorable ; unless you consent you will have to go without your things. Pray take off your bonnet."

She stood in the prettiest confusion possible, looking pleadingly from one to the other. What a head hers must be without the bonnet! Such a shape! Such hair! I was dying to see it. She shook her bonnet reproachfully and sadly.

" Thank you, gentlemen. I must go. Be kind, gentlemen, and give me my things."

" No," said I, hard at heart.

" No," said Nicolas, obdurately ; " no."

Ting! Ting! Ting! went the clock. (5.45 P.M.)

" The quarter," said I. " In another 15 minutes—"

" We dine," said Nicolas. " Now, Miss Smith."

A silence. There was something quite pathetic in the way in which the poor little head (in its bonnet) peered about, here, there, everywhere, after its mantle and umbrella.

I went to the window.

" It is raining," I said.

" Hush!" said Nicolas ; "the soup is ascending the stairs."

It was, however, not the soup. The door was thrown open, and in rushed—Laurence. Laurence III., our nephew, the last person in the world we— that is, I—wanted to see. He looked so fresh, so brutally young, so confoundedly handsome — really Nicolas seemed to shrivel up, like a Rose of Jericho, into a dry stick, in his presence.

"Why, Uncle Matt!" he exclaimed, clasping my hand, and working my arm as if I were a pump.

"Why, Uncle Nick!" he said, shaking my brother like a feather bed. "How well, how young, how jolly you all seem. And—bless my soul!—Halloa! Emily! You here? You! How, in the name of wonder, my darling? This is a delight—a threefold delight and surprise."

The ruffian caught her in his arms, lifted her off the ground, and deliberately kissed her before our naked eyes.

"Why, Uncles M. and N.," exclaimed Laurence, "I came up to town after Emily. We have been engaged since we were children. Her dead father, the rector, was my tutor; after his death, Mrs. Smith came up to town with Emily—"

"And," said she, interrupting him, "as we were left very badly off, I was obliged to do something to help out our small means. Seeing the advertisement in the *Times*, I applied, supposing the advertiser was an old lady. I was surprised, and perhaps disappointed, to find that I was to read to gentlemen; however—"

Laurence took the thread out of her mouth. "I," he said, "as you know, uncles, have not had a nest into which to put my bird, so I have had to wait till the term of the lease of Puddlecombe Hall was up. My tenants turned out at Lady Day. Now I have come to claim Emily, and I hope—we both hope— dear uncles, that you will come and visit us there this autumn. Then "—to me—" after the hunting begins, we will not let you depart till the season is over; a horse will always be at your disposal. And "—to

Nicolas—" you know there are several British barrows on Puddle Downs crying out to be opened and their contents catalogued. There you will both, I trust, learn to love your new niece Emily."

" I knew it," said I.

" I knew it," said Nicolas.

" I call little Millie to witness," said I. I drew the bracelet from my pocket. " Millie, pet, didn't I say this was for my darling niece ? " I clasped it on her wrist.

" I call dear Emily to witness," said Nicolas. He produced a gold watch, and threw the chain over her head. " Emily, my precious! didn't I say this was for a valued niece ? "

Then Mrs. Sache appeared in the door, and said in solemn tones :

" Dinner is ready."

" Lay another place," I shouted.

" Lay another place," called Nicolas.

" How many ? " asked Mrs. Sache. " I've already laid four as ordered. Mr. Matthew said 'One extra,' Mr. Nicolas said 'One extra,' and with the two masters, ain't that four ? "

" That is capital," said Laurence. " Now, Emily, dear, off with your bonnet."

And off it came.

THE END.

Cowan & Co., Limited, Printers, Perth.

WORKS BY S. BARING GOULD.

Author of "Mehalah," &c.

Old Country Life. By S. BARING GOULD. With Sixty-seven Illustrations by W. PARKINSON, F. D. BEDFORD, and F. MASEY. Large Crown 8vo, cloth super extra, top edge gilt, 10s. 6d. *Second Edition.*

"*Old Country Life*, as healthy wholesome reading, full of breezy life and movement, full of quaint stories vigorously told, will not be excelled by any book to be published throughout the year. Sound, hearty, and English to the core."—*World.*

Historic Oddities and Strange Events. By S. BARING GOULD. First Series. Demy 8vo, 10s. 6d. *Second Edition.*

"A collection of exciting and entertaining chapters. The whole volume is delightful reading."—*Times.*

"The work, besides being agreeable to read, is valuable for purposes of reference. The entire contents are stimulating and delightful."—*Notes and Queries.*

Historic Oddities and Strange Events. Second Series. By S. BARING GOULD, Author of "Mehalah," "Old Country Life," &c. Demy 8vo, 10s. 6d. [*Ready*.

"Mr. Baring Gould has a keen eye for colour and effect, and the subjects he has chosen give ample scope to his descriptive and analytic faculties. The new series of 'Historic Oddities and Strange Events' is a perfectly fascinating book Whether considered as merely popular reading or as a succession of studies in the freaks of human history, it is equally worthy of perusal, while it is marked by artistic literary colouring and happy lightness of style."—*Scottish Leader.*

Songs of the West: Traditional Ballads and Songs of the West of England, with their Traditional Melodies. Collected by S. BARING GOULD, M.A., and H. FLEETWOOD SHEPPARD, M.A. Arranged for Voice and Piano. In 4 Parts (containing 25 Songs each), 3s. each. *Part I., Fourth Edition. Part II., Second Edition. Part III. ready. Part IV. ready.*

"A rich and varied collection of humour, pathos, grace, and poetic fancy. —*Saturday Review.*

Yorkshire Oddities and Strange Events. By S. BARING GOULD. New and Cheaper Edition. Crown 8vo, 6s. [*Now ready*.

Jacquetta, and other Stories. By S. BARING GOULD. Crown 8vo, 3s. 6d.

Arminell: A Social Romance. By S. BARING GOULD. New Edition. Crown 8vo, 3s. 6d.

"To say that a book is by the author of 'Mehalah' is to imply that it contains a story cast on strong lines, containing dramatic possibilities, vivid and sympathetic descriptions of Nature, and a wealth of ingenious imagery. All these expectations are justified by 'Arminell.'"—*Speaker.*

Urith: A Story of Dartmoor. New Edition. Crown 8vo, 3s. 6d. [*Shortly*.

"A powerful and ingenious story."—*Anti-Jacobin.*

"Mr. Baring Gould has been able to create a strong interest, and to maintain it at a high pitch. Its strength and effectiveness are undeniable."—*Athenæum.*

18, *Bury Street, W.C., January,*

MESSRS. METHUEN'S
New Books and Announcements.
1891.

CONTENTS.

FICTION.

S. BARING GOULD.

URITH: A Story of Dartmoor. By S. BARING GOULD, Author of "Mehalah," "Arminell," &c.   3 vols.   [*February.*

HANNAH LYNCH.

PRINCE OF THE GLADES. By HANNAH LYNCH. 2 vols. [*February.*

W. CLARK RUSSELL.

A MARRIAGE AT SEA. By W. CLARK RUSSELL, Author of "The Wreck of the Grosvenor," &c.   2 vols.   [*February.*

W. H. POLLOCK.

FERDINAND'S CLAIM. By WALTER HERRIES POLLOCK.   Post 8vo. 1s.   [*February.*

R. PRYCE.

THE QUIET MRS. FLEMING. By RICHARD PRYCE.   Crown 8vo. 3s. 6d.   [*February.*

M. BETHAM EDWARDS.

DISARMED. By M. BETHAM EDWARDS, Author of "Kitty."   Crown 8vo.   3s. 6d.   [*February.*

W. E. NORRIS.

JACK'S FATHER. By W. E. NORRIS, Author of "Mademoiselle de Mersac."   Crown 8vo.   3s. 6d.   [*March.*

S. BARING GOULD.

TOM A' TUDLAMS. By S. BARING GOULD, Author of "Mehalah" Crown 8vo.   3s. 6d.   [*May.*

LESLIE KEITH.

A LOST ILLUSION. By LESLIE KEITH, Author of "The Chilcotes," "A Hurricane in Petticoats," &c.   3 vols.   Crown 8vo.

"Were it only a shade more cheerful it would be a perfect story."—*Manchester Examiner.*
"A really pathetic story full of human nature."—*Graphic.*

G. MANVILLE FENN.

A DOUBLE KNOT. By G. MANVILLE FENN, Author of "The Vicar's People," "Eli's Children," &c.   3 vols.   Crown 8vo.

"A clever novel. The plot is intricate and well managed. The story abounds in strong and exciting situations."—*Speaker.*

L. T. MEADE.

THE HONOURABLE MISS: A Tale of a Country Town. By L. T. MEADE, Author of "Scamp and I," "A Girl of the People," &c. 2 vols. Crown 8vo.

"Delightfully fresh and winning."—*Scotsman.*

GENERAL LITERATURE.

S. BARING GOULD.

HISTORIC ODDITIES AND STRANGE EVENTS. Second Series. By S. BARING GOULD, Author of " Mehalah," " Old Country Life," &c. Demy 8vo. 10s. 6d. *[Ready.*

"Mr. Baring Gould has a keen eye for colour and effect, and the subjects he has chosen give ample scope to his descriptive and analytic faculties. The new series of ' Historic Oddities and Strange Events ' is a perfectly fascinating book. Whether considered as merely popular reading or as a succession of studies in the freaks of human history, it is equally worthy of perusal, while it is marked by the artistic literary colouring and happy lightness of style."—*Scottish Leader.*

J. B. BURNE, M.A.

PARSON AND PEASANT: Chapters of their Natural History. By J. B. BURNE, M.A., Rector of Wasing. Crown 8vo. 5s. *[Ready.*

"' Parson and Peasant ' is a book not only to be interested in, but to learn something from —a book which may prove a help to many a clergyman, and broaden the hearts and ripen the charity of laymen."—*Derby Mercury.*

W. CLARK RUSSELL.

THE LIFE OF ADMIRAL LORD COLLINGWOOD. By W. CLARK RUSSELL, Author of " The Wreck of the Grosvenor." With Illustrations by F. BRANGWYN. 8vo. *[In February.*

P. H. DITCHFIELD, M.A.

OLD ENGLISH SPORTS AND PASTIMES. By P. H. DITCHFIELD, M.A., Author of " Our English Villages." Illustrated. Post 8vo. *[In April.*

Edited by A. CLARK, M.A.

THE COLLEGES OF OXFORD : Their History and their Traditions. By Members of the University. Edited by A. CLARK, M.A., Fellow and Tutor of Lincoln College. 8vo. *[In the Press.*

Edited by J. WELLS, M.A.

OXFORD AND OXFORD LIFE: With Chapters on the Examinations by Members of the University. Edited by J. WELLS, M.A., Fellow and Tutor of Wadham College. Crown 8vo. *[In the Press.*

S. BARING GOULD.

THE TRAGEDY OF THE CÆSARS: The Emperors of the Julian and Claudian Lines. With numerous Illustrations from Busts, Gems, Cameos, &c. By S. BARING GOULD, Author of " Mehalah," &c. *[In the Press.*

W. G. COLLINGWOOD, M.A.

JOHN RUSKIN: His Life and Work. By W. G. COLLINGWOOD, M.A., late Scholar of University College, Oxford. Crown 8vo. *[In Preparation.*

H. H. HENSON, M.A.

DISSENT IN ENGLAND: A Sketch of the History and Constitution of the Principal Nonconformist Sects. By REV. H. H. HENSON, M.A., Fellow of All Souls' College, and Rector of Barking. 8vo. *[In Preparation.*

NEW BOOKS FOR BOYS AND GIRLS.

W. CLARK RUSSELL.

MASTER ROCKAFELLAR'S VOYAGE. By W. CLARK RUSSELL, Author of "The Wreck of the Grosvenor," &c. Illustrated by GORDON BROWNE. Crown 8vo. 5s.

"Mr. Clark Russell's story of 'Master Rockafellar's Voyage' will be among the favourites of the Christmas books. There is a rattle and 'go' all through it, and its illustrations are charming in themselves, and very much above the average in the way in which they are produced. Mr. Clark Russell is thoroughly at home on sea and with boys, and he manages to relate and combine the marvellous in so plausible a manner that we are quite prepared to allow that Master Rockafellar's is no unfair example of every midshipman's first voyage. We can heartily recommend this pretty book to the notice of the parents and friends of sea-loving boys."—*Guardian.*

"In the frank and convincing narrative of Master Rockafellar there happens to be set a short story which should make the fortune of the book. 'La Mulette' is as fine a piece of story-telling as ever Mr. Russell has given us, and we heartily commend it to any boy who has the sense to distinguish between the author who has a story to tell, and the author who has to tell a story."—*Speaker.*

G. MANVILLE FENN.

SYD BELTON: or, The Boy who would not go to Sea. By G. MANVILLE FENN, Author of "In the King's Name," &c. Illustrated by GORDON BROWNE. Crown 8vo. 5s.

"Who among the young story-reading public will not rejoice at the sight of the old combination, so often proved admirable—a story by Manville Fenn, illustrated by Gordon Browne The story, too, is one of the good old sort, full of life and vigour, breeziness and fun. It begins well and goes on better, and from the time Syd joins his ship exciting incidents follow each other in such rapid and brilliant succession that nothing short of absolute compulsion would induce the reader to lay it down."—*Journal of Education.*

"The pick of the adventure books for this season. There is not a dull page in it. 'Syd Belton' is a capital book."—*Speaker.*

"From beginning to end the book is a vivid and even striking picture of sea-life."—*Spectator.*

Mrs. PARR.

DUMPS. By MRS. PARR, Author of "Adam and Eve," "Dorothy Fox," &c. Illustrated by W. PARKINSON. Crown 8vo. 3s. 6d.

"One of the prettiest stories which even this clever writer has given the world for a long time."—*World.* "A very sweet and touching story."—*Pall Mall Gazette.*

L. T. MEADE.

A GIRL OF THE PEOPLE. By L. T. MEADE, Author of "Scamp and I," &c. Illustrated by R. BARNES. Crown 8vo. 3s. 6d.

"An excellent story. Vivid portraiture of character, and broad and wholesome lessons about life."—*Spectator.* "One of Mrs. Meade's most fascinating books."—*Daily News.*

METHUEN'S NOVEL SERIES.

THREE SHILLINGS AND SIXPENCE.

MESSRS. METHUEN will issue from time to time a Series of copyright Novels, by well-known Authors, handsomely bound, at the above popular price.   The first volumes (ready) are:

F. MABEL ROBINSON.
1. THE PLAN OF CAMPAIGN.

S. BARING GOULD, Author of " Mehalah," &c.
2. JACQUETTA.

Mrs. LEITH ADAMS (Mrs. De Courcy Laffan).
3. MY LAND OF BEULAH.

G. MANVILLE FENN.
4. ELI'S CHILDREN.

S. BARING GOULD, Author of " Mehalah," &c.
5. ARMINELL : A Social Romance.

EDNA LYALL, Author of " Donovan," &c.
6. DERRICK VAUGHAN, NOVELIST. With Portrait of Author.

F. MABEL ROBINSON.
7. DISENCHANTMENT.

M. BETHAM EDWARDS.
8. DISARMED. *[Shortly.*

W. E. NORRIS.
9. JACK'S FATHER. *[Shortly.*

S. BARING GOULD.
10. TOM A' TUDLAMS. *[Shortly.*

Other Volumes will be announced in due course.

Cnglish Leaders of Religion.

Edited by A. M. M. STEDMAN, M.A.

Under the above title MESSRS. METHUEN have commenced like publication of a series of short biographies, free from party bias, of the most prominent leaders of religious life and thought in this and the last century.

Each volume will contain a succinct account and estimate of the career, the influence, and the literary position of the subject of the memoir.

The following are already arranged—

CARDINAL NEWMAN.   *R. H. Hutton.*   [*Ready*.

"Few who read this book will fail to be struck by the wonderful insight it displays into the nature of the Cardinal's genius and the spirit of his life."—WILFRID WARD, in the *Tabl.t.*

"Full of knowledge, excellent in method, and intelligent in criticism. We regard it as wholly admirable."—*Academy.*

"An estimate, careful, deliberate, full of profound reasoning and of acute insight."—*Pall Mall Gazette.*

JOHN WESLEY.   *J. H. Overton, M.A.*
                    [*In February*.

JOHN KEBLE.   *W. Lock, M.A.*

CHARLES SIMEON.   *H. C. G. Moule, M.A.*

BISHOP WILBERFORCE.   *G. W. Daniell, M.A.*

F. D. MAURICE.   *Colonel F. Maurice, R.E.*

THOMAS CHALMERS.   *Mrs. Oliphant.*

CARDINAL MANNING.   *A. W. Hutton, M.A.*

Other Volumes will be announced in due course.

SOCIAL QUESTIONS OF TO-DAY.

Edited by H. de B. GIBBINS, M.A.

Crown 8vo. 2s. 6d.

MESSRS. METHUEN beg to announce the publication of a series of volumes upon those topics of social, economic and industrial interest that are at the present moment foremost in the public mind. Each volume of the series will be written by an author who is an acknowledged authority upon the subject with which he deals, and who will treat his question in a thoroughly sympathetic but impartial manner, with special reference to the historic aspect of the subject and from the point of view of the Historical School of economics and social science. The Labour Question will be treated of in the volumes on Trades Unions and Co-operation : the Land Question will form the subject of another two volumes ; others will treat of Socialism in England, in its various phases, and of the labour problems of the Continent also. The monograph on Commerce will be of special interest at present in view of the recent development of American commercial policy. Those on Education and on Poverty will be of similar importance in view of current discussion, and the volume on Mutual Thrift will prove a valuable survey of the various agencies for that purpose already in existence among the working classes.

The following form the earlier Volumes of the Series :—

ABOUT
Feb.
1891.

1. TRADES UNIONISM—NEW AND OLD.

G. HOWELL, M.P., Author of " The Conflicts of Capital and Labour."

March.

2. POVERTY AND PAUPERISM.

Rev. L. R. PHELPS, M.A., Fellow of Oriel College, Oxford.

3. THE CO-OPERATIVE MOVEMENT OF TO-DAY.

G. J. HOLYOAKE, Author of " The History of Co-operation."

4. MUTUAL THRIFT.

Rev. J. FROME WILKINSON, M.A., Author of " The Friendly Society Movement."

UNIVERSITY EXTENSION SERIES.

Under the above title MESSRS. METHUEN have commenced the publication of a series of books on historical, literary, and economic subjects, suitable for extension students and home-reading circles. The volumes are intended to assist the lecturer and not to usurp his place. Each volume will be complete in itself, and the subjects will be treated by competent writers in a broad and philosophic spirit.

Edited by J. E. SYMES, M.A.,

Principal of University College, Nottingham.

Crown 8vo. 2s. 6d.

The following volumes are already arranged, and others will be announced shortly.

THE INDUSTRIAL HISTORY OF ENGLAND. By H. DE B. GIBBINS, M.A., late Scholar of Wadham Coll., Oxon., Cobden Prizeman. With Maps and Plans. *[Ready.*

"A compact and clear story of our industrial development. A study of this concise but luminous book cannot fail to give the reader a clear insight into the principal phenomena of our industrial history. The editor and publishers are to be congratulated on this first volume of their venture, and we shall look with expectant interest for the succeeding volumes of the series. If they maintain the same standard of excellence the series will make a permanent place for itself among the many series which appear from time to time."—*University Extension Journal.*

" A careful and lucid sketch."—*Times.*

" The writer is well-informed, and from first to last his work is profoundly interesting."—*Scots Observer.*

A HISTORY OF ENGLISH POLITICAL ECONOMY. By L. L. PRICE, M.A., Fellow of Oriel Coll., Oxon., Extension Lecturer in Political Economy. *[February.*

ENGLISH SOCIAL REFORMERS. By H. DE B. GIBBINS, M.A., late Scholar of Wadham Coll., Oxon., Cobden Prizeman.

PROBLEMS OF POVERTY : An Inquiry into the Industrial Conditions of the Poor. By J. A. HOBSON, M.A., late Scholar of Lincoln Coll., Oxon., U. E. Lecturer in Economics. *[March.*

THE FRENCH REVOLUTION. By J. E. SYMES, M.A., Principal of University Coll., Nottingham. *[In the Press.*

MESSRS. METHUEN'S NEW & RECENT BOOKS.

FICTION.

E. LYNN LINTON.

THE TRUE HISTORY OF JOSHUA DAVIDSON, Christian and Communist. By E. LYNN LINTON. Eleventh and Cheaper Edition. Post 8vo, 1*s.*

HISTORY AND POLITICS.

E. LYNN LINTON.

ABOUT IRELAND. By E. LYNN LINTON. *2nd Edition.* Cr. 8vo, bds., 1*s.*

"A brilliant and justly proportioned view of the Irish Question."—*Standard.*

T. RALEIGH, M.A.

IRISH POLITICS: An Elementary Sketch. By T. RALEIGH, M.A., Fellow of All Souls', Oxford, Author of "Elementary Politics." Fcap. 8vo, paper boards, 1*s.*; cloth, 1*s.* 6*d.*

"A very clever work."—MR. GLADSTONE.

"Unionist as he is, his little book has been publicly praised for its cleverness both by Mr. Gladstone and Mr. Morley. It does, in fact, raise most of the principal points of the Irish controversy, and puts them tersely, lucidly, and in such a way as to strike into the mind of the reader."—*The Speaker.*

"Salient facts and clear expositions in a few sentences packed with meaning. Every one who wishes to have the vital points of Irish politics at his finger's end should get this book by heart."—*Scotsman.*

F. MABEL ROBINSON.

IRISH HISTORY FOR ENGLISH READERS. By F. MABEL ROBINSON. *Fourth Edition.* Crown 8vo, boards, 1*s.*

GENERAL LITERATURE.

Edited by F. LANGBRIDGE, M.A.

BALLADS OF THE BRAVE: Poems of Chivalry, Enterprise, Courage, and Constancy, from the Earliest Times to the Present Day. Edited, with Notes, by Rev. F. LANGBRIDGE. Crown 8vo.

"A very happy conception happily carried out. These 'Ballads of the Brave' are intended to suit the real tastes of boys, and will suit the taste of the great majority. It is not an ordinary selector who could have so happily put together these characteristic samples. Other readers besides boys may learn much from them."—*Spectator.*

"The book is full of splendid things."—*World.*

Presentation Edition. Handsomely Bound, 3*s.* 6*d.* (School Edition, 2*s.* 6*d.*)

Or, in Three Parts, 1*s.* each, for School Readers.

I. TROY TO FLODDEN. II. BOSWORTH TO WATERLOO. III. CRIMÆA TO KHARTOUM.

P. H. DITCHFIELD, M.A.

OUR ENGLISH VILLAGES: Their Story and their Antiquities. By P. H. DITCHFIELD, M.A., F.R.H.S., Rector of Barkham, Berks. Post 8vo, 2*s.* 6*d.* Illustrated.

"A pleasantly written little volume, giving much interesting information concerning villages and village life."—*Pall Mall Gazette.*

"The object of the author is not so much to describe any particular village as to give a clear idea of what village life has been in England from the earliest historical times. An extremely amusing and interesting little book, which should find a place in every parochial library."—*Guardian.*

A. M. M. STEDMAN, M.A.

OXFORD: ITS LIFE AND SCHOOLS. Ed. by A. M. M. STEDMAN, M.A., assisted by members of the University. *New Edition.* Cr. 8vo, 5*s.*

"Offers a full and in most respects a satisfactory description of the country through which students must travel, and affords to parents who are desirous of calculating the expenses and rewards of University education, a mass of useful information conveniently arranged and brought down to the most recent date."—*Athenæum.*

"We can honestly say of Mr. Stedman's volume that it deserves to be read by the people for whom it is intended, the parents and guardians of Oxford students, present and to come, and by such students themselves."—*Spectator.*

Works by **S. BARING GOULD,**

Author of "Mehalah," &c.

OLD COUNTRY LIFE. By S. BARING GOULD. With Sixty-seven Illustrations by W. PARKINSON, F. D. BEDFORD, and F. MASEY. Large Crown 8vo, cloth super extra, top edge gilt, 10*s.* 6*d. Second Edition.*

"'Old Country Life,' as healthy wholesome reading, full of breezy life and movement, full of quaint stories vigorously told, will not be excelled by any book to be published throughout the year. Sound, hearty, and English to the core."—*World.*

"Mr. Baring Gould is well known as a clever and versatile author ; but he never wrote a more delightful book than the volume before us. He has described English country life with the fidelity that only comes with close acquaintance, and with an appreciation of its more attractive features not surpassed even in the pages of Washington Irving. The illustrations add very much to the charm of the book, and the artists in their drawings of old churches and manor-houses, streets, cottages, and gardens, have greatly assisted the author."
Manchester Guardian.

HISTORIC ODDITIES AND STRANGE EVENTS. By S. BARING GOULD. FIRST SERIES. Demy 8vo, 10*s.* 6*d. Second Edition.*

"A collection of exciting and entertaining chapters. The whole volume is delightful reading."—*Times.*

"The work, besides being agreeable to read, is valuable for purposes of reference. The entire contents are stimulating and delightful."—*Notes and Queries.*

HISTORIC ODDITIES AND STRANGE EVENTS. SECOND SERIES. By S. BARING GOULD, Author of "Mehalah," "Old Country Life," &c. Demy 8vo, 10*s.* 6*d.* [*Ready.*

"Mr. Baring Gould has a keen eye for colour and effect, and the subjects he has chosen give ample scope to his descriptive and analytic faculties. The new series of 'Historic Oddities and Strange Events,' is a perfectly fascinating book. Whether considered as merely popular reading or as a succession of studies in the freaks of human history, it is equally worthy of perusal, while it is marked by artistic literary colouring and happy lightness of style."—*Scottish Leader.*

SONGS OF THE WEST: Traditional Ballads and Songs of the West of England, with their Traditional Melodies. Collected by S. BARING GOULD, M.A., and H. FLEETWOOD SHEPPARD, M.A. Arranged for Voice and Piano. In 4 Parts (containing 25 Songs each), 3*s.* each. *Part I., Fourth Edition. Part II., Second Edition. Part III., ready. Part IV., in the Press.*

"A rich and varied collection of humour, pathos, grace, and poetic fancy."—*Saturday Review.*

YORKSHIRE ODDITIES AND STRANGE EVENTS. By S. BARING GOULD. New and Cheaper Edition. Crown 8vo, 6*s.*
[*Now ready.*

JACQUETTA, and other Stories. By S. BARING GOULD. Crown 8vo, 3*s.* 6*d.*

ARMINELL: A Social Romance. By S. BARING GOULD. New Edition. Crown 8vo, 3*s.* 6*d.*

"To say that a book is by the author of 'Mehalah' is to imply that it contains a story cast on strong lines, containing dramatic possibilities, vivid and sympathetic descriptions of Nature, and a wealth of ingenious imagery. All these expectations are justified by 'Arminell.'"
Speaker.

EDUCATIONAL WORKS.

METHUEN'S SCIENCE SERIES.

MESSRS. METHUEN propose to issue a Series of Science Manuals suitable for use in schools. They will be edited by Mr. R. Elliot Steel, M.A., F.C.S., Senior Natural Science Master in Bradford Grammar School, and will be published at a moderate price. The following are ready or in preparation—

THE WORLD OF SCIENCE. Including Chemistry, Heat, Light, Sound, Magnetism, Electricity, Botany, Zoology, Physiology, Astronomy, and Geology. By R. ELLIOT STEEL, M.A., F.C.S., Senior Natural Science Master in Bradford Grammar School. 147 Illustrations, Crown 8vo, 2s. 6d.

"Mr. Steel's Manual is admirable in many ways. The Book is well calculated to attract and retain the attention of the young."—*Saturday Review.*

"If Mr. Steel is to be placed second to any for this quality of lucidity, it is only to Huxley himself; and to be named in the same breath with this master of the craft of teaching is to be accredited with the clearness of style and simplicity of arrangement that belong to thorough mastery of a subject."—*Parents' Review.*

ELEMENTARY LIGHT with numerous Illustrations. Crown 8vo. [*February.*

   ,,   ELECTRICITY AND MAGNETISM.

   ,,   HEAT.

Other Volumes will be announced in due course.

R. E. STEEL, M.A.
REVISED FOR NEW SESSION.

PRACTICAL INORGANIC CHEMISTRY. For the Elementary Stage of the South Kensington Examinations in Science and Art. By R. E. STEEL, M.A., Senior Natural Science Master at Bradford Grammar School. Crown 8vo, cloth, 1s. [*Now Ready.*

R. J. MORICH.

A GERMAN PRIMER. With Exercises. By R. J. MORICH, Chief Modern Language Master at Manchester Grammar School. [*In the Press.*

H. de B. GIBBINS, M.A.

COMPANION GERMAN GRAMMAR. By H. DE B. GIBBINS, M.A., Assistant Master at Nottingham High School. Crown 8vo, 1s. 6d. [*Ready.*

E. McQUEEN GRAY.

GERMAN PASSAGES for UNSEEN TRANSLATION. By E. McQUEEN GRAY. Crown 8vo, 2s. 6d. [*Ready.*

A. W. VERRALL, M.A.

SELECTIONS FROM HORACE. With Introduction, Notes, and Vocabulary. By A. W. VERRALL, M.A., Fellow and Tutor of Trinity Coll., Cambridge. Fcap. 8vo. [*In the Press.*

SELECTIONS FROM HERODOTUS. With Introduction, Notes, and Vocabulary. By A. C. LIDDELL, M.A., Assistant Master at Nottingham High School. Fcap. 8vo. [*In the Press.*

WORKS BY A. M. M. STEDMAN, M.A.

WADHAM COLLEGE, OXON.

FIRST LATIN LESSONS. *Second Edition, Enlarged.* Crown 8vo, 2s.
[*Ready.*

FIRST LATIN READER. With Notes adapted to the Shorter Latin
Primer and Vocabulary. Crown 8vo, 1s. 6d. [*Ready.*

EASY LATIN PASSAGES FOR UNSEEN TRANSLATION. *Second
Edition, Enlarged.* Fcap. 8vo, 1s. 6d.

EASY LATIN EXERCISES ON THE SYNTAX OF THE SHORTER
AND REVISED LATIN PRIMERS. With Vocabulary. *Second
Edition.* Crown 8vo, 2s. 6d. Issued with the consent of Dr. Kennedy.

NOTANDA QUAEDAM : MISCELLANEOUS LATIN EXERCISES
ON COMMON RULES AND IDIOMS. With Vocabulary. Fcap.
8vo, 1s. 6d.

LATIN VOCABULARIES FOR REPETITION : arranged according to
Subjects. *Third Edition.* Fcap. 8vo, 1s. 6d.

FIRST GREEK LESSONS. [*In preparation.*

EASY GREEK PASSAGES FOR UNSEEN TRANSLATION.
[*In preparation.*

EASY GREEK EXERCISES ON ELEMENTARY SYNTAX.
[*In preparation.*

GREEK VOCABULARIES FOR REPETITION : arranged according to
Subjects. Fcap. 8vo, 1s. 6d.

GREEK TESTAMENT SELECTIONS. For the use of Schools. *New
Edition.* With Introduction, Notes, and Vocabulary. Fcap. 8vo, 2s. 6d.

FIRST FRENCH LESSONS. [*In the Press*

EASY FRENCH PASSAGES FOR UNSEEN TRANSLATION.
Fcap. 8vo, 1s. 6d.

EASY FRENCH EXERCISES ON ELEMENTARY SYNTAX.
With Vocabulary. Crown 8vo, 2s. 6d. [*Ready.*

FRENCH VOCABULARIES FOR REPETITION : arranged according
to Subjects. Fcap. 8vo, 1s.

See also School Examination Series, p. 15.

SCHOOL EXAMINATION SERIES.

Edited by A. M. M. STEDMAN, M.A.

Crown 8vo.   2s. 6d. each.

In use at Eton, Harrow, Winchester, Repton, Cheltenham, Sherborne, Haileybury, Merchant Taylors, Manchester, &c.

FRENCH EXAMINATION PAPERS IN MISCELLANEOUS GRAMMAR AND IDIOMS. By A. M. M. STEDMAN, M.A. *Fifth Edition.*

> A KEY, issued to Tutors and Private Students only, to be had on application to the Publishers. *Second Edition.* Cr. 8vo, 5s.

LATIN EXAMINATION PAPERS IN MISCELLANEOUS GRAMMAR AND IDIOMS. By A. M. M. STEDMAN, M.A. *Third Edition.* KEY (issued as above), 6s.

GREEK EXAMINATION PAPERS IN MISCELLANEOUS GRAMMAR AND IDIOMS. By A. M. M. STEDMAN, M.A. *Second Edition, Enlarged.* KEY (issued as above), 6s.

GERMAN EXAMINATION PAPERS IN MISCELLANEOUS GRAMMAR AND IDIOMS. By R. J. MORICH, Manchester Grammar School. *Second Edition.* KEY (issued as above), 5s.

HISTORY AND GEOGRAPHY EXAMINATION PAPERS. By C. H. SPENCE, M.A., Clifton College.

SCIENCE EXAMINATION PAPERS. By R. E. STEEL, M.A., F.C.S., Chief Natural Science Master, Bradford Grammar School. In three volumes.

> Part I.   Chemistry.
> Part II.   Physics (Sound, Light, Heat, Magnetism, Electricity).
> Part III. Biology and Geology.   [*In preparation.*

GENERAL KNOWLEDGE EXAMINATION PAPERS. By A. M. M. STEDMAN, M.A.   [KEY. *In the Press.*

EXAMINATION PAPERS IN BOOK-KEEPING, with Preliminary Exercises. Compiled and arranged by J. T. MEDHURST, F. S. Accts. and Auditors, and Lecturer at City of London College. 3s.

ENGLISH LITERATURE, Questions for Examination in. Chiefly collected from College Papers set at Cambridge. With an Introduction on the Study of English. By the Rev. W. W. SKEAT, Litt.D., LL.D., Professor of Anglo-Saxon at Cambridge University. *Third Edition, Revised.*

ARITHMETIC EXAMINATION PAPERS. By C. PENDLEBURY, M.A., Senior Mathematical Master, St. Paul's School. KEY, 5s.

TRIGONOMETRY EXAMINATION PAPERS. By F. H. WARD, M.A., Assistant Master at St. Paul's School. KEY, 5s.